Yours Truly, Thomas

"I want to live in Azure Springs with the friends and community in Rachel Fordham's *Yours Truly, Thomas*. This story is a cup of romance, a pinch of mystery, and a savory plot seasoned with memorable characters (including a wayward dog) all trying to find their way in worlds turned upside down. *Yours Truly, Thomas* is the perfect read to lift your spirits. It did mine!"

Jane Kirkpatrick, award-winning author
of *Everything She Didn't Say*

"*Yours Truly, Thomas* is a beautiful love letter of forgiveness and redemption penned into a story I couldn't put down."

Natalie Walters, author of *Living Lies*

"A deeply satisfying romance that will make you believe in the power of hope and second chances."

Jennifer Beckstrand, author of *Home on Huckleberry Hill*

"Set in the beloved world of Azure Springs, *Yours Truly, Thomas* is a charming and wistful story of a young man who pours out his regrets, hopes, and dreams in letters that will never be delivered. When Penny, an employee at the dead letter office, reads the letters, she's captivated and longs to help. What follows is a journey of love and healing, told with beautiful skill that will tug at readers' hearts, reminding us that the rewards of faith, kindness, and love are sweet indeed."

Heather B. Moore, *USA Today* bestselling author

"A tender story of finding courage to follow one's heart, letting go of past pain, and the healing power of redemption."

Donna Hatch, award-winning romance author

"Reminiscent of Grace Livingston Hill's enchanting novels filled with adorable heroines and sweet love stories, *Yours Truly, Thomas* is a pure and simple romance sure to delight readers."

Dawn Crandall, award-winning author
of The Everstone Chronicles series

"Rachel Fordham's *Yours Truly, Thomas* is a love story to cherish and make you believe in the healing power of love. This is a story to hold to your heart and reread again and again."

Regina Scott, award-winning author

"Gentle and inviting as a summer breeze, this endearing book is sure to coax smiles and happy tears from every reader. Fans of historical romance will find within its pages all they hope for in a story from beginning to end."

Amber Lynn Perry, author of the Daughters of His Kingdom series

"Faithful readers of Tracie Peterson or Karen Witemeyer will quickly be enveloped in the elegance and beauty of *Yours Truly, Thomas*. As an avid historical romance reader, I was guilty of even letting my coffee grow cold because I didn't want to put this novel down (and that is no small thing)! An endearing story with characters you'll instantly love, this is one you'll revisit time and again. An instant historical romance classic!"

Jaime Jo Wright, Christy Award-winning author of *The Curse of Misty Wayfair* and *The House on Foster Hill*

"Fresh and uplifting, Fordham's newest novel delivers a tender love story centered on a series of letters and the hopeless romantic who stumbles on them. From the dead letter office to the charming small town of Azure Springs, the heroine takes readers on her impulsive yet romantic journey to find answers for a stranger—and her own future. *Yours Truly, Thomas* weaves a unique tale of two people who had reached a dead end only to find there may be more ahead for them both."

Joanna Davidson Politano, author of *A Rumored Fortune*

"*Yours Truly, Thomas* delivers a sweet and appealing romance with a healthy dose of humor. Rachel Fordham's intriguing characters grapple with grief and guilt and becoming new people, which adds depth and heart to this warm story. Pour yourself your favorite beverage and prepare to get lost in this delightful story."

Sarah Sundin, award-winning and bestselling author of *The Sea Before Us* and *The Sky Above Us*

Yours Truly, Thomas

RACHEL FORDHAM

Revell

a division of Baker Publishing Group
Grand Rapids, Michigan

© 2019 by Rachel Fordham

Published by Revell
a division of Baker Publishing Group
PO Box 6287, Grand Rapids, MI 49516-6287
www.revellbooks.com

Printed in the United States of America

Library of Congress Cataloging-in-Publication Data
Names: Fordham, Rachel, 1984– author.
Title: Yours truly, Thomas / Rachel Fordham.
Description: Grand Rapids, MI : Revell, a division of Baker Publishing Group,
    [2019] | Includes bibliographical references and index.
Identifiers: LCCN 2018045191 | ISBN 9780800735388 (pbk. : alk. paper)
Subjects: | GSAFD: Love stories.
Classification: LCC PS3606.O747335 Y68 2019 | DDC 813/.6—dc23
LC record available at https://lccn.loc.gov/2018045191

Scripture quotations are from the King James Version of the Bible.

19   20   21   22   23   24   25   7   6   5   4   3   2   1

For Dad—
Thank you for sliding letters under my door
when I was a stubborn teenager and for so much more.

For Mom—
Who read me stories when I was little
and reads all of mine now.

A girl couldn't ask for better parents.

Love you both.

We can ignore even pleasure. But pain insists upon being attended to. God whispers to us in our pleasures, speaks in our conscience, but shouts in our pains: it is his megaphone to rouse a deaf world.

—C. S. Lewis

Prologue

After letting an involuntary squeal escape, Penny pulled the yellowed papers closer and pressed her lips to them. Then she began to devour the words.

My Darling,

I've been away only a fortnight and already I feel a deep ache for you. I dream at night of your beautiful face, and sometimes I reach out and try to touch it. The two of us were meant to never be apart.

Penny stopped reading and sighed as she rolled onto her side, careful not to bump the mahogany frame of the bed under which she lay. She closed her eyes.

In her mind's eye, she was much older than her ten years, taller, and womanly. She wore a long green dress made of silk and taffeta that matched her eyes perfectly and fit each curve like a glove. The dress swished as she walked, and when she spun around, it flowed like a perfect ocean wave.

A man approached. He was tall and handsome. "My darling," he said. Then he took her hand and kissed the back of it.

She slowly opened her eyes and stared at the flickering light of the lantern.

She'd discovered the stack of letters the day before while playing hide-and-seek with the maid's children. Since laying eyes on them, she'd thought of nothing but getting to them and reading every word again and again.

After eating dinner the next day, she'd crept away, telling her parents she was tired and wanted to sleep. Instead, she'd rushed to her parents' room, slid between the carved legs of their four-poster bed, and pushed herself underneath where she'd found the box of worn papers.

Penny cringed, knowing she'd been deceitful.

"Penny?" Her father's voice came into the room. "Penny, I know you're in here somewhere. The staff saw you enter the room. I'm afraid you've been caught."

She blew out the lantern as quickly as she could and pulled her legs in tight. Perhaps if she held her breath and closed her eyes, she'd not be found. She opened her eyes a sliver when she heard a tapping noise. The tip of her father's boot was visible beneath the bedding.

"How strange it is that my daughter is not in her room and that she was seen entering mine." Her father's foot continued to tap against the floorboard. "I wonder what she could be up to. It's not like my girl to be keeping secrets from me."

Guilt gnawed at her conscience. Her father was her dearest friend. To lose his trust would be unbearable. She pushed her toes against the floor, propelling her forward so that her head poked out from under the bed. "I'm here."

Her father lowered himself to the floor and sat beside her. He pursed his lips. His dark eyes did not look angry though. They remained the same kind, patient eyes she had known her whole life. "Are you hiding from me or something else? We haven't bandits around, have we?"

Penny pulled herself the rest of the way from under the bed. "No bandits." With her head bowed, she handed him the letters. "I took these. I'm sorry. I know I shouldn't have, but I wanted to read them so badly. I was afraid you'd say no and I'd never see what they said."

The letters looked so small in his large hands. He took a deep breath. "There are personal things in these letters. I wrote them for your mother's eyes only. You may not understand it now, but some words are meant only for a man and a wife." He paused. Then he laughed softly as he brushed at a cobweb that had entwined itself with her hair. "Seems we need to hire you to clean beneath the beds."

He flipped the letters back and forth in his hands. "I should be angry you took these."

Penny eased closer to her father. So close she could smell the sweet scent of his shaving soap and touch his suit jacket.

"But I'm not."

Relieved to not be in trouble, she let out a puff of air. "I dream about love. But what does it really mean to love someone?"

He smiled. "I love your mother." He tilted his head toward her as though he were sharing a brilliant secret. "If I finish my work early enough, I stop by the candy shop. I buy you a stick of penny candy because you like it and because you're my lucky Penny. I buy your mother maple candy. It's her favorite. When I bring it to her, I like to sneak up behind her and tell her to close her eyes. She acts surprised even though she knows I've brought her a sweet."

"That's love? Candy?" She looked at the stack of letters, wishing she could read them. Surely, they had a simpler explanation.

"Yes. That and so much more. Love's . . . well, love is candy and walks underneath a starlit sky. It's babies and . . . it's trying to make the other person's life better. It's many things."

Her father tapped the tip of her nose, which made her smile. Was that love too?

"You should believe in love. It's real. It's all around you, just in different forms. You'll see as you grow. You'll realize that not all love looks like the love I have for your mother. Don't you worry. I'll be here to teach you all about love." He stood up with the letters in hand. "I better go tell your mother that you're not lost. She worries about you."

Penny rolled her eyes. "I don't know why."

"Her worrying—that's love too."

"I'm not sure I like that kind of love. I want dancing and ball gowns and candy love." She stood and brushed the dust from the front of her dress.

"You'll look lovely in a ball gown. And there's nothing wrong with sweets every now and then, but keep your eyes open." He winked at her. "You don't want to miss the love that's perfect for you just because you're too busy searching for a fairy tale."

Penny furrowed her brows. She wasn't sure she liked the practical spin her carefree father was putting on her romantic notions. "I suppose I'll have to grow up first before I know what it's like."

"I think that's an excellent idea." He put a hand on her shoulder. "Now no more snooping around."

She agreed.

"And one more thing. Promise me that when you think you've found yourself a love match, you'll tell me all about him."

Once again, she agreed. "I'll tell you everything."

Dear Clara,

I lied. I told myself I had run westward for the promise of big sky and fertile soil. But the truth is, I just ran. I thought if Virginia were behind me, then I'd be able to leave you there. I thought if I was far enough away, then my heart would heal or at least forget. I thought I would be able to close my eyes and see something other than your face. I was wrong. You are everywhere. All around me and especially inside me. My heart hurts so deeply. If only I could go back and begin again, then perhaps there'd be a way to escape the agony.

I rode a train for a few days, then joined a group of settlers with their wagons. I suppose the idea of a wagon and horses would be amusing to you. No doubt, the very idea of it would earn me a soft giggle from you. I can almost hear the sound of it in my mind. Even to me the idea seems humorous.

I didn't make it west, at least not as far as I'd planned.

13

We had only just begun the wagon journey when my wagon tipped, leaving me with bumps and bruises. I blame the horses, but it may have been my fault. So many things are. The damage was not repairable and so the party moved on without me. I could board a train and ride it farther west, but I think I'll wait for a new wagon. Then I can see the country as I go. Perhaps the agony of the wait and the slow journey will be some sort of penance or liberation. I know not. I expect this pain I carry in my heart will follow me wherever I go. I know, though, that before I ran west, I'd never paused and looked around me so often as I did during the few days I rode the trail. I never knew how vast and wide the world is or how incredibly small I am. Alexandria had always been my everything, but there is more out there. A whole world I'd thought nothing of.

So, here I am in a strange little town that consists of a few dusty streets surrounded by endless fields. I've taken up residency in the local boardinghouse. It's a ghastly yellow building with a bright red door that always smells of baked bread and lye soap. The smell is welcoming enough, but I still feel a bit like a foreigner in someone else's land. New sights, new noises, new people. Only the unrelenting ache in my chest remains the same. That ache I carry is for you and for dreams of what might have been. This is not the life I ever wanted. I see you in the town. I see you in my mind. And each time I see you, the ache worsens. Why does it have to be this way? I've decided that living with the constant shadow of what might have been is the hardest lot to bear. Regrets are

*heavy, horribly heavy. I tried to hide from them, but they
followed me.*

> *Lost and running,*
> *Thomas*

Penny leaned her head against the back of her chair and
sighed. She pressed a hand to her own heart. It ached, just as
Thomas's did. Out of loneliness, regret, and on occasion, despair. She tilted her head toward the far wall of the dead letter
office and let her eyes roam across a matted and framed map
of the country. When her father was still alive, they'd dreamed
of travel, of adventure. His eyes had always twinkled when he
spoke of riding out of the city, away from the hustle of life.
Penny looked away. Like Thomas's dreams, they were only regrets now. Her father was gone. And, oh, how she wished he
were here. If only she could run to him and tell him her woes
and plead with him for advice. It was not to be. She was a clerk
struggling to pay bills and nothing more.

During her three years at the dead letter office, she had
learned to spot the correspondence of lovers. The letters full
of syrupy words and flowery endearments were distracting. No,
she craved the letters that captured the heart of the writer. Letters that revealed the depth of their love and strength of their
promises, that allowed her for a moment to believe there was
something more than toiling endlessly to survive. Thomas's
words rang true, and despite his sorrow, he seemed a man full
of heart. A man capable of loving someone deeply.

Penny looked again at Thomas's letter. The paper was plain
and unscented. A ripple just below the name had caught her
eye. Running her thumb over it now, she could feel where the

paper had warped. A tear perhaps. Was his heart so broken that he had wept as he wrote? What it must be like to have a man so in love that he'd shed tears for you.

Sitting with the letter in her hands was almost enough to make the rows of desks filled with hard-working clerks fade away. She closed her eyes and pictured another place, somewhere outside of DC, where there was a man whose heart was beating for another. Without a single clue about Thomas's physical appearance, she pictured him. A broken man bent over his desk, writing the desires and despair of his heart. She could almost smell the scent of sourdough bread baking, and out the window she saw golden fields of wheat. His hand painstakingly transcribing the pain he carried within.

"Look, Dinah." She leaned toward her friend and fellow clerk. "This one is from Thomas to Clara. He left her for the West, but I can tell he longs for her to join him." She pressed the letter to her heart. "Or for her to beckon him back. It's oddly romantic, isn't it? A man separated from his love."

"It's just a letter. I don't think it's overly romantic," Dinah whispered.

"No, it's more than a letter. It's this man's life. And now his life is in my hands. I have to help Clara get to him."

"You're just a clerk." Dinah rolled her eyes. The two had a long-standing friendship despite their many differences. "I don't believe the job requires matchmaking."

Penny shook her head. "I can't explain it. Some of the letters call to me and others do not." She let out a heavy sigh. Dinah's practical nature would never allow her to understand. Everything about Dinah was calculated and well thought out, from the stiff brown skirt she wore to the tight bun on her head. She certainly wasn't one to be swept away by emotions. "I feel as though their love story depends on me. If I do nothing, he could spend months, years even, waiting for his true love. Always wondering." Penny's throat tightened. "No one should have to live with regrets. I understand about life going differently than we want it to. In a small way it's as though I can feel his pain."

"You aren't supposed to care so much." Dinah shook her head. "We're allowed to open the letter so we can find clues to return them or get them to their intended recipient. Not so we can marvel over the contents. Or get teary-eyed over them. His life is not in your hands, a letter is. That's all."

Penny brought the letter closer to her face and once again admired the penmanship. "Wanting to help them is not against the rules."

Dinah set down the letter she'd been reading. "This is just a job." She motioned around the large room, with its rows of desks, walls of bins and barrels, and endless clerk resources. "It's a job. Thomas will never blame you. He doesn't even know you exist. Just put it in the disposal bin if you can't redirect it."

Penny's heart lurched at the thought. The sadness, the finality of admitting defeat and dropping a letter in *that* bin was enough to make her sick. Still, she had to do it over and over again. So many letters were just . . . dead.

Dinah smoothed her neatly twisted auburn hair. Nothing in her countenance seemed shaken. "Some letters are not meant to make it. I suppose you could say some love stories aren't meant to either. It's always been that way."

"It shouldn't be." Penny folded her arms across her chest as though her act of defiance could change the realities of romance or life.

"You shouldn't get too upset over it when it wasn't yours to worry about."

17

Penny groaned as she watched a fellow clerk walk to the disposal bin and drop a letter in. The room full of clerks went on sorting, unaffected, as if it meant nothing. Their daily toiling over the mail had to mean something.

"Here's Thomas's letter." She held it out toward Dinah. "It's neatly addressed, so I don't understand why it didn't make it."

"There's no street listed."

"The postmaster must know Clara Finley of Alexandria. Alexandria is not so big. I'd return it to Thomas, but he left no return address or last name, and he doesn't say where he's gone." She pursed her lips as she examined the letter once more. "I could possibly figure it out if I researched where wagon trains pass through, and he does mention the color of the boarding-house. But that wouldn't help me get the letter to Clara." She turned the letter over in her hands, scouring it in a vain attempt to find something she'd missed.

Dinah shrugged. "Who knows why she didn't get it. Perhaps she moved. Or married someone else."

"What if this lost letter ruins their lives?"

"If their lives are ruined because of one misplaced letter, so be it." Dinah looked over her shoulder. "We need to get back to work before Mr. Douglas comes."

"Mr. Douglas is still in his private office. He said forty percent of the letters we get make it out of here. I wish that number were higher. I think Mr. Douglas worries more about the valuables than the letters. Otherwise he'd give us more time to research the clues, like yellow boardinghouses."

"Of course he does. How else would the national treasury survive?" Dinah stifled a laugh. Both women knew that unclaimed items were auctioned off, bringing in a large profit. "Here, give me that letter and I'll drop it in the bin for you. I need to take this stack anyway." She reached out her hand. "I know you despise the disposal bin."

"I do hate it." Penny didn't give the letter up. "Mr. Douglas is forever talking about not throwing out valuables, but isn't the relationship between a man and a woman more valuable than his precious coins and trinkets?"

"Perhaps to Thomas, but not to the department." Dinah grabbed the letter from Penny, walked the short distance to the bin, and tossed it in. "If there was no information to help you forward it on, assume it wasn't meant to be. You can't waste an entire day just to return it to him. It's ridiculous. And we both know we can't risk our jobs over silly sentiments. He'll either write again or they'll go their separate ways."

Penny frowned, sighed, and then grabbed a new letter. The outside was marked "address unknown." Penny fussed over the outside label for a few minutes, hoping to discover something from it. Then she slid the thin blade of the letter opener under the seal.

"Hopefully it's not a boring one." Dinah shifted in her seat. "The last one I read was about a litter of puppies. Two pages about their colors and habits. I was sure I'd fall asleep. Who would pay to send such news?"

"I think puppies are worthy creatures to write about. I'd hardly call them dull."

Dinah laughed. "Of course you do. We all know how you feel about Honeysuckle."

"She *is* the greatest dog in the world." Penny smiled at the change in conversation.

"She may be a great dog, but her name is rather silly."

"My father let me name her. I thought it was darling. Who doesn't love honeysuckle?" Penny sat a little taller. "I think her name fits her. I still remember my father bringing me Honey and telling me she was mine. Life was so much sweeter then. I wonder sometimes if he knew he was going to die."

"How long after you got Honey did your father die?"

"A year. She's been my solace and confidant since. I'd perish from the monotony of life if it was not for her." She glanced away, the pangs of grief assaulting her. "My father often laughed when he heard me call her Honeysuckle. He liked the name."

"Are you certain he wasn't laughing at that dog's long hair?"

Penny pursed her lips. "No, we kept her hair short then."

"I'm glad you have Honeysuckle. Even if she does have an odd name." Dinah folded the letter she was holding. "What's your letter about?"

Penny smoothed the creased paper she'd been holding. "It's from a woman to her friend. Something about a banquet and a new dress."

"Postal workers, be sure your conversations are relevant." Mr. Douglas stepped out of his private office, his arms folded across his chest. An all-too-familiar frown graced his stern face.

Penny ducked her head and started reading. She had to wade through sentence after sentence of boring drivel before she found a clue. The name of the town's new library, the Tyler York Library. All she had to do was find out where that library was located and send the letter on to the town's postmaster.

If only she could have gotten Thomas's letter to Clara as easily. She frowned.

"Don't be gloomy," Dinah whispered. "I see it on your face. You're still feeling bad about the other letter."

"I wish I could have sent it on. I know you think I take this all too seriously, but I can't seem to stop caring."

"I envy you, I do. You can read an address that looks like nonsense and know exactly what it's supposed to say." Dinah reached over and patted Penny's hand. "You're good at this even if you couldn't find a way to send that one along."

Penny forced a smile. "I couldn't survive a day at this place without you. I know I ought to be endlessly thankful for the respectable work, but some days all I see are the endless piles of paper."

"You'd be fine without me now, but remember that first week? You spent most of it in tears. You'd read a letter and suddenly be brokenhearted because a stranger's dog had died or their crops had failed."

"It was the letters' fault. Some of them were so sad. Or they made me angry." She scowled, remembering the first letter she'd ever read that confessed a grievous sin. She was distraught for days worrying about someone else's transgression. "But Thomas's letter was different. It wasn't something out of my control, like a dog or the crops. If the letter were delivered, two people might get to share a future together."

"I wish it were that simple." Dinah sorted the letters on her desk. "Did you hear about LaVern Hinckley?"

"No. Tell me." Penny looked over her shoulder toward redheaded LaVern. "Her beau informed her he no longer wants to court her." Dinah folded her arms across her chest. "Like I told you, broken hearts happen. Your Thomas and Clara might have broken things off even if there was no lost letter. It's how life is."

"It's horrible. LaVern is beautiful and so sweet. I've never heard her utter a single unkind word." Penny scanned the room. "LaVern talks to Rex Beck often at work. Maybe he'll be the balm she needs."

"Rex Beck is an old retired clergyman."

Penny gasped as she turned her head this way and that, trying to get a glimpse of Rex. "No. He looks so young."

"He's at least fifty. He just has a young face. I hear he isn't very good with the letters."

"Why do they keep Rex if he isn't very good? They let women go so easily if they don't get a knack for the work."

Dinah leaned in and whispered, "Mr. Douglas believes all the money that passes through here would be too tempting to the average man. So he hires retired clergy and women." She smirked. "I guess our femininity alone is enough to vouch for our integrity. I think he keeps people like Rex around to keep everyone's consciences alive. Everyone knows, though, that it's us women who are the ones doing the work. I think Roland is the only man who earns his wages."

Both girls snickered at the truthfulness of Dinah's words.

"Even if it is a strange and thankless job, it's better than taking in washing or working in a factory," Dinah said.

Penny grinned. "So much better. But I think if I could choose, I'd do something outside. I don't know what, but wouldn't it be lovely to be outside in the sunshine? Fresh air all around you. Or maybe go to sea and feel the fresh, salty air blow against your skin. What would you pick if you could do anything?"

"I'm not the dreamer you are. I'm content enough with what I have."

"There must be something you want."

Dinah tapped her pencil against the desk. "I do think I'd like a life away from my father's apartment. I'd stay here longer every day if I could. It seems more and more he's on a rampage about something or other."

"Someday you'll have a house of your own," Penny whispered. "I know you will. And it'll be peaceful."

"Ladies." Mr. Douglas walked through the room again. "Let's keep our conversations to a minimum. There are letters to sort."

His eyes narrowed in Penny's direction. She flashed him an innocent smile, then bent over the letter in her hands and set to work. When his back was turned, she whispered, "Someday you'll be free of Mr. Douglas and your father."

Dinah squeezed Penny's hand. "And you'll be at peace with your mother. And someday I hope you find a man who makes your heart flutter and writes you heart-wrenching love letters."

———

"Penelope? Is that you? You're late." Penny's mother, Florence, greeted her when she stepped into the small rented apartment.

"I was at the library," Penny said.

"Every night you work late despite my telling you to hurry home." Florence's face puckered in disgust. "You're twenty-two. I read in the paper about one of your peers from your younger years. She's marrying the Rockmoore man. You remember him, don't you? You ought to be thinking about marriage and your future. If you aren't careful, the years will race by and you'll die an old maid." She smoothed one of her perfect curls. "You're *always* so busy. I wonder sometimes if a respectable marriage is even important to you."

"I'm sorry I'm late," Penny said through gritted teeth. "I wonder sometimes if you have any idea why I do what I do. You do realize that I can't marry the Rockmoore or Vanstofferson men even if they asked. I'm not part of that world any longer." Penny closed the door behind her. "I work so we can survive. Then, after all that, I walk home, often in the dark."

Florence patted her daughter's cheek. "You really shouldn't make that long walk alone."

Penny fought the urge to push her hand away. "I'd take Honey if I could, but there isn't anywhere for her to be all day. I'm already indebted to the Wilsons for letting her spend the days with their children."

"I wish you could take that dog. It's always underfoot."

"They bring her back in the evening. You only have to step over her for a half hour or so before I'm home."

"It seems longer than that." With contempt written across her face, Florence looked toward the sleeping Honeysuckle. "Enough about that dog. You should have a chaperone or companion when you are out walking. It's appalling the way you walk all over the city."

It was so like her mother to speak of their life now as though it was something Penny had handpicked for herself. "I walk alone because there is no one for me to walk with. I go so we can have this place to live and food to eat. I didn't ask for this life. I've only tried to adapt to what we've been given. I thought someday you'd accept it." She could hold the bitterness back no longer. Just looking at her mother with her coiffed hair and disgruntled frown was more than she could handle. "You sit around all day wishing we still had money. I miss those days too. Don't you think I'd rather be doing something else?" Her voice rose as the emotion and turmoil within her grew. "Father is dead. Our old life is gone and has been for years. You can't pretend you're still the belle of the ball by curling and pinning your hair."

"I don't—"

"That world shut us out. Even if they took us back, I don't know if I'd fit there. The truth is, I don't know where I fit. I feel restless working every day, but . . . well, what difference does it make? The dead letter office is my future. This apartment is yours. This is our lives now. We're two forgettable people living our days out."

"You may have lost sight of who you are, but I *am* important," Florence said, standing tall. "I am the wife of Calvin Ercanbeck. And you are his daughter. You ought to act like it."

"You're right." Penny took a deep, calming breath, then forced her words to come slowly. "I am his daughter and that is why I get up and walk alone to the dead letter office every single day. He'd be proud of me for facing this hard lot. I wish you could be too."

Before her mother could utter another word, Penny stepped away and crossed the floor toward her dog.

"Honey!" Penny called to the dog she'd raised from a pup. "Come here, girl. Come say hello to me."

Honey leaned back on her long hind legs, stretched, and yawned. Penny sat down and stroked Honey's long, dark curly locks.

"You'll be covered in hair," Florence said.

Penny shook her head. Honey had lived in their house for six years and still her mother knew so little. "She doesn't shed much. If there's any hair on me, I'll brush it off later. Right now I'm going to tell Honeysuckle about my day." With her back to her mother, she grabbed the giant animal's big, floppy ears and scratched them. Honey put her head on Penny's shoulder and finally Penny felt as though she was being welcomed home. "It's so good to see you," she said in the sing-song voice she used so often with her furry friend. Honey licked her hand, then pushed her nose against it. "You want more love, don't you?"

"I've already eaten." Florence's voice interrupted Penny's

moment. "I'm going to go unpin my hair and get ready for bed."
Florence walked over to Penny and kissed her cheek. It wasn't
the warm, motherly kiss Penny craved. It was a stiff, customary
gesture. "Good night, dear."

"Good night, Mother," Penny answered, then returned her
attention to Honey. "I know you want to hear how I spent my
day. Don't you, girl?" Honey scooted closer. "Well, I read so
many letters that I thought my head would explode. But I did
have a favorite letter. It was from a man named Thomas to his
true love."

Penny picked up a wire brush and began running it over the
dog's long hair. The man Penny's father had gotten Honey
from vowed the puppy was a poodle, and there were some re-
semblances to a poodle, but Honey's hair was longer than the
average poodle's and she was taller and broader.

"I wonder if I were to have a true love, would someone get
a lost letter to me? Or would it be tossed out? I hate to think
I'm playing a role in someone's heartache." Honey cocked her
head at the sound of Penny's voice, but aside from her friendly
eyes, she offered no reply. Penny leaned her head back. "What
if Thomas's life is altered all because his letter came to me and
not to Clara?"

The dog licked Penny's hand, earning her a grin. "You understand, don't you? You know that the letters matter. And you're
right—they *do* matter. Each one was mailed for a reason." She
kissed the beloved dog's furry head. "I sometimes feel like you
are the only one who understands me." She lowered her voice to
a whisper. "Mother thinks I'm foolish. She's always telling me
that I've forgotten myself. I wonder if she even realizes where
we'd be living if I hadn't gotten this job. Even Dinah thinks I
take it all too seriously."

Penny's throat felt tight as a dull melancholy crept over her. "Father would understand. If he were here, he'd talk to Mother the way he used to. He'd say the right thing and suddenly she'd understand me. Mother would smile and be happy again. If he were still here, he'd sit by me and listen to my troubles. He wouldn't think I was foolish for clinging to hopes of something more. There's so much I was never able to ask him." A tear crept down her cheek. "Do you think the world will ever feel right again?"

Penny buried her face in Honey's soft, thick fur. "I think if I didn't have you, I'd feel completely destitute. The monotony of this life alone would be more than I could bear."

Honey shifted her body, curling into Penny even more.

"Someday we'll find our place in the world. We will, won't we?"

AZURE SPRINGS, IOWA

Thomas looked around the little store. Without planning to, he nodded his head in approval. This store was small, but the walls were lined with shelves that reached to the ceiling and tables with displays were placed around the room. Goods covered nearly every inch of the space. He put his thumbs through his belt loops and stood marveling for a moment. Pots and pans, flour, penny candy, stacks of paper—the store had everything. He had never pictured the West being so well equipped.

"Can I help you find something?" A pudgy man behind the store counter set down the sack he was carrying.

"I'm looking for something to pass the time." Thomas leaned against the counter. He had used his minor injuries as an excuse to keep to his room, but he couldn't take the solitude any longer. He needed a distraction. Something. Anything to pull him from the darkness that filled his mind. He cleared his throat. "I need something to keep me busy while I wait. I'll be leaving soon as I can find a wagon train to join up with."

"Books, Bibles?" The man started grabbing books from the shelf behind him and setting them in front of Thomas. "We've a few things on hand. If you don't see something you're interested in, I can get most anything here in a matter of days. We have a railroad that comes right through town. Come to think of it, you could probably take it west. We aren't the end of the line." He scratched his head. "Aren't those railroads something?"

"I plan to go to a territory with no trains. The real frontier. I'll bide my time here." Thomas rubbed the back of his neck. He didn't know what books he wanted. At least a dozen books were on the counter in front of him now and the man was going back for more. Thomas stopped him. "I'll take these books. Whatever you got there on the counter, I'll take them. I'll read most anything. What you got there will do." He hadn't meant for his voice to sound so gruff. He paused. "Just tell me what I owe you."

The man raised a brow. "If you're sure—"

"I'm certain. I'm not particular."

"Very well. I'll wrap them up for you so they're easier to carry. Or if you'd like, I can deliver them."

"I can manage." Thomas knew his still-healing scrapes and bruises weren't too pretty to look at, but they didn't hinder his ability to carry his own load. When the man finished tying string around the books, he pushed the bundle toward Thomas. "Thank you."

"Glad to do it. Name's Abraham Howell, and I consider it my privilege to help out. I'm guessing you're Thomas Conner. Margaret was in a few days ago and told us she had a gentleman holed up in one of her rooms." Abraham spoke slowly as he worked. "Sitting around waiting can be a miserable sentence to bear."

"I won't argue with you on that." He had been struggling with the weight of his past ever since he'd left Alexandria, but now sitting around was worse.

"If you don't mind me asking, what happened?"

"I was in a wagon accident just outside of here. We were a small group headed to Montana. They all went on without me. I plan to make my way out there as soon as another group passes through." He ran a hand over the scratches on his forearms. "I'm hoping a couple weeks is all, and then I'll be on my way. I don't think I can sit around watching the clock hands much longer than that."

"Well, Azure Springs is happy to have you." Abraham straightened the jars on the counter. "Real happy."

"The town is happy to have me?" Thomas asked. "I'm just a stranger passing through."

"I suppose the town itself can't say too much. But I've been here a long time. I've seen it grow and change. And no matter what's come or gone, it's always been a good place. Even for a man passing through. It's a real good place."

Thomas's gaze wandered. "I'll trust your word. I don't think I'll be here long enough to know for myself."

"Well, whether you're running to something or from something, we're glad you at least passed through." Abraham reached in his pocket for a handkerchief and blew his nose. "I know they may sound like a bunch of hollow words, but Azure Springs is our home. And we do enjoy company."

Thomas wiped at the beads of sweat that were forming on his forehead. "I suppose I'm running from something. Though I like to think I'm running to something." He swallowed. "Hard to say exactly. I guess it doesn't make much of a difference since I'm not going anywhere until I get a new wagon and team." He laid a few bills on the counter. "Will that cover the cost?"

"This'll more than cover it. Let me get you some change."

Abraham picked up the money. "These books will keep you busy for a while, but if you ever need more than them to pass the time, I'd gladly help you find some work. I'm not sure what your skills are, but if you're willing to work we can find you something. You might even be able to save a few dollars to put toward your western dream."

"I won't be here long enough to find work." Thomas stuck his hand in his pocket. His fingers brushed against a thick stack of bills.

Abraham reached under the counter for a little box. He began counting out coins. "Jonas Reed is putting up a new barn this Saturday. Anyone who's willing is welcome."

"A barn?" Hadn't he just told the man he wasn't looking for work?

"It's sort of a tradition around here. Whenever a man puts up a new barn, his neighbors come and help. We make a big to-do about it."

"No one is paid?"

"Not a soul." Abraham patted his round stomach. "Unless you count food as pay. There's always plenty of that. It's more of a neighborly gesture. I suppose with you living at Margaret's place, that makes you a neighbor too."

The bell above the door rang. Thomas turned his head toward the sound and in walked a woman wearing a simple dress and a long braid in her yellow hair. A basket hung over her arm swayed easily as she walked.

"You must be Thomas." she said when their eyes met. A friendly smile played across her face.

"Yep. Let me guess, Margaret told you." He'd never get used to these small-town ways.

Her head bobbed up and down. "She's a friend of mine. I'm

Em Reynolds. Welcome to Azure Springs. Caleb and I have been meaning to stop in and meet you." She blushed. "I'm sorry. I'm getting ahead of myself. Caleb's my husband. It's always exciting when someone new comes to town."

He nearly balked. He hadn't expected a welcome. "Thank you. I'm not really new. I'm just passing through. I'm headed west."

"There was a time when I thought I was simply passing through. Now this place is home." She ran her hand over her swollen belly, the size testifying to the life she was carrying within. "It's nice to meet you." She stepped behind the counter and stood beside Abraham. "I was in town to see Abigail and the girls, but I couldn't leave without saying hello."

"I'm glad you did." Abraham's eyes softened when he spoke to Em. Thomas watched the exchange with open curiosity. "Let me get Thomas here his change. I got busy talking and have kept him waiting. Then I want to hear how you are. And if Caleb is happy."

Thomas pulled his gaze away and looked at the nearest display. A table covered in cups and saucers busied his eyes, but his ears continued to listen.

"He's very happy. It's been a month since he turned in his badge. But it's been a wonderful month. He's so at ease working the land. I thought he was happy when he was sheriff, but now he's forever smiling. It's like he can breathe easier."

"Of course he's happy. He has a happy wife and a baby on the way. And he gets to walk the land he loves every day. It's the life he was meant for."

Thomas turned away. He was pricked by the words. *"It's the life he was meant for."* What about himself? Was there a life he was meant for? Surely, if there was, he had lost the chance to ever have it. Once again he wished there was a way to go back. But he could not.

"Fifty cents. I'm sorry it took so long." Abraham's voice brought Thomas around. He took the coins and shoved them in his pocket.

"Thank you."

"Let me know if I can get you anything else. And think about coming on Saturday."

Thomas picked up the bundle of books and lodged it under his arm. "I'll come. I've nothing better to do."

"Saved this for you." Dinah waved a wrinkled letter in the air. "It's another one from Thomas to Clara. I know you felt bad about throwing his letter in the disposal bin all those days ago, so I told all the women and a few of the men to watch for anything from him." She held out the letter. "Rex overheard and made some nasty remark about being selective and not putting in a good day's work."

"Why does he care?" Penny took the letter from Dinah.

"I told him it was none of his concern." Dinah pointed toward the bags the letters arrived in. "We've marked the bag this one came in, so now we know where to watch for them. They're coming in with the letters from the south of us."

Penny stared at the letter in her hands. "I've been wondering for days what had become of Thomas and Clara. Two letters! He must be writing them before he even waits for a reply." Penny ran her finger across the front of the letter. "Don't you think he has the finest penmanship? I think he's educated. He must be."

"His lettering is most certainly *not* the reason his correspondence isn't getting to her." Dinah reached into a bin and pulled out a large, thick envelope. She squeezed it between her fingers. "You enjoy your brokenhearted lovers. I bet this one has real treasure in it."

Penny watched with curiosity as her friend tore into the bulky package. Before Penny could even see what was inside, Dinah flailed her arms and threw the package on the floor.

"Ugh! Get it away from me!" Dinah shook her hands in disgust.

Penny shrieked simply because Dinah had. Only when she realized nothing was moving did she stop. By then a small crowd had gathered.

Pamela and Grace Stewart stood at the front of the group. Pamela, the older of the two sisters, leaned forward and cautiously lifted back the torn front of the envelope. "What is it?"

"It's a snake! A horrid, awful snake," Dinah said, practically shouting.

Using a writing stick, Pamela pushed back the paper even farther. "It isn't a snake. It's not moving."

All the women leaned in for a closer look. Dinah finally relaxed. "Well, it's the skin of a snake." She brushed her hands against her skirts and straightened her shoulders. "It could have been alive, and then my outburst would have been justified."

The Stewart sisters giggled together as they so often did. Dinah glared.

Penny let out the breath she'd been holding, then she too laughed. She couldn't help it. So many dull letters passed through the office—this, at least, was exciting.

"Who would send a snake skin?" Penny asked. "It's such a strange thing to send in the mail."

Dinah reached for the letter. "Billy says here he wanted his uncle Charles to see how big rattlers can get. He's been watching for a skin for a long time. This one is in excellent shape. And even though it's not the biggest he's ever seen, he knew his uncle would appreciate it."

Penny nodded. "I suppose that's a good reason. We should be grateful he chose to send a skin and not a live snake." Laughter filled the room. "I think this is the first skin that has passed through here. Aside from the one on the back of that live snake in that package Priscilla opened last year."

The crowd of clerks laughed again, then slowly returned to their own piles of mail. Several mumbled about it being "just a skin," while others continued to laugh at Dinah's reaction or reminisce about strange findings.

"Don't touch it," Dinah said with her nose turned up. "It's horrid."

"It's dead. It can't hurt you." Penny picked up the skin. "I've never felt anything like it. I bet Billy is an adventuresome child. Do you think he had to wander to some faraway fields day after day to find this?"

"Maybe you ought to be the one to find Uncle Charles. I wish I hadn't opened it." Dinah folded her arms across her chest.

"Roland would like it. You could give it to him." Penny set down the snake skin and scooped up the letter from Thomas. "I'm going to look for clues about Thomas and Clara. I must have missed something before. I'm going to help Thomas get his happily ever after."

Dinah picked up the thin snake skin between two fingers and held it away from her body as though it were something dangerous. "You and your happily ever afters."

Penny smiled at her friend. "Roland might think you're after your own happily ever after. You know how he loves the unusual finds. If there's a way to that man's heart, it's through snake skins and other oddities." Roland's beady eyes would light up behind his spectacles whenever something outrageous landed in his hands. "He'll probably swoon like the Stewart girls do when they read a romantic letter."

"And like you do. You're as eager for love as the rest of them." Dinah grimaced as she carried the snake skin toward Roland's desk. "I'm certainly not after Roland's heart, but I don't mind seeing him smile. After all, he saved us from that live snake once, remember? This"—she held the snake skin a little higher—"and every other disgusting thing I happen to open will be gifted to him."

Penny laughed softly as she moved to the opposite corner of the office to a few open seats near a window. "I'll be reading."

"And swooning," Dinah said to her back.

Although Penny had heard Dinah's remark, she sat down and didn't acknowledge it. But she certainly recognized the truth of the statement. Her heart did beat wildly when she thought of love. Even someone else's.

Dear Clara,

Penny paused and looked again at the perfect penmanship. She swallowed hard at the thought of a man writing so neatly and precisely to her. Oh, to have a man write to her . . . Someday she hoped to open a letter and have it read, *Dear Penny.*

She brushed the thought away. Dwelling on what was not to be only lowered her spirits. Instead, she delved into Thomas's letter.

There are times when my room at the boardinghouse feels like a prison. I feel trapped, as though I can't get out.

My heart races and my temperature rises. I always think of you then. I think of you and wonder what it must have been like. But thinking that only makes it harder to breathe.

When it becomes unbearable, I step out away from the yellow boardinghouse. I leave with no real purpose or motive. I just know I have to get away. I've wandered up and down the streets. I know them, but they are still not my streets. This is not my home. I am a lost man even though I know the name of each building I pass.

This isn't my town, but I wonder if it ever could be or if it could have been if the past had been different and I was simply a man looking for a fresh start. In all the time I lived in Alexandria, I never felt half as welcomed as I do here. I tell everyone I meet that I am simply passing through and they still embrace me with warmth. They offer to let me join them on their farms or to sit by them for dinner. It's comforting and strange and confusing.

I spent a day on a farm working side by side with farmers, merchants, and railway men. Together we hammered board after board. Our individual efforts offered on behalf of an old farmer amounted to a barn. I've never before witnessed such a generous act, much less participated in one. My work amounted to nothing financially and yet it was the most rewarding work I've ever done. I wonder if I'd been to an event such as this when I was a boy if I'd have grown into a different man. I believe I would have been a better man. I find myself wondering if I could have been.

They know nothing of my past. Perhaps if they did they would not be so amiable. I wonder if they would welcome me even if they knew why I set out west. Would they still want me working beside them? Would they ever build me such a barn? I'm not sure I'm brave enough to ask.

I spend a great deal of my time wondering and wishing. Praying that somehow I could find a way to truly apologize for the past and let it go. Repentance, retribution. Set it right. I can almost hear the pastor preaching his words of redemption. I never thought much about those words until now. And here I sit, yearning for a way to right my wrongs, yet I find there is nothing I can do. If there were, I would do it. I would do anything. If only you were here beside me, I would tell you how my heart hurts. It wants to be healed, to beat in the type of man who uses his tools to help another. It wants to wander these wheat-covered fields and marvel at their beauty. It wants to laugh and smile and discover what it means to live a purposeful life, but it cannot. Or maybe it can or could. I don't know. There is so much I don't know.

With a penitent heart,
Thomas

Penny looked out the window to the right of her. The melancholy of the letter matched the listless gray bricks of the building next door. Twice she read it, hoping to discover a reference that would help her find Clara or at least tell her where Thomas was. He needed Clara. Not just to ease his broken heart or for a happily ever after but because his pain was so deep.

"How is the lovesick Tom?" Dinah asked as she walked up

beside her. Penny's head jerked up. "Has he given up on his forever love?"

"He yearns for his Clara. Something must have happened between the two of them, but he's sorry about it. I can tell he is." Penny folded the letter and tucked it into her pocket. "There are no clues. He says in the letter that she lives in Alexandria, just as it says in the address. But it's marked undeliverable again. I don't understand. The two were obviously very much in love, at least I believe they were. She's somewhere and doesn't know how he needs her. Or how sorry he is." She stood and began pacing, her well-worn boots clicking against the old wood floor. "What if she's sick? Living with some distant relative so she can have better care? Or perhaps she's suffering from financial trouble. She's been evicted while waiting for him to come and sweep her off her feet."

Dinah's eyes danced. "Or perhaps she's been eaten by a giant sea monster. I think you ought to give up your job here and take up writing dime novels. You have a knack for drama."

"You think I'm jesting, but something truly tragic could have happened." Penny pivoted away from her friend. "You may not care, but I do. He's hurting and I could help him if only I could find Clara."

Dinah laughed. "How do you plan to do that?"

"There's nothing comical about it." Penny folded her arms across her chest. "I really do want to help them."

Dinah stepped closer. "Calm down, Penny. Your determination is admirable. No doubt the department wishes everyone cared like you do. Most of us have become numb to the letters we read. The words mean nothing to us unless they contain clues. We no longer care about the stories or the people.

Thomas is lucky his letter fell into your hands. Perhaps it wasn't an accident."

Penny felt her temper defuse. "Dinah, you care too. I know you do."

"Not like you do. I want to do my job well. I care about that." She shrugged. "I feel good when I can send a letter on its way, but I watch your face when you put a letter in the disposal bin. You look defeated. Every part of you shows how disappointed you are. I don't feel that way. I toss it in and go on to the next letter. I don't think of it again." Dinah brushed her hands together. "You haven't forgotten that each letter was written by a real person."

Penny wrapped her fingers around the letter in her pocket. She knew Thomas had written his letters for a reason. He was real. And so was his pain. She wasn't supposed to take anything from the office, but she couldn't dump it into the bin. Not this letter. Not Thomas's letter.

Changing the subject, Penny asked, "Have you seen all Roland's entries in the blind reading book? He had another one come back yesterday."

She'd been introduced to the little handmade book when she first began working at the office. Some envelopes were so poorly addressed that no one believed they'd ever be redirected. When a clerk managed to find the intended destination, they often mailed return postage asking if they could keep the envelope as a souvenir of their detective work.

"I heard." Dinah sighed. "Everyone was talking about it."

Penny glanced over her shoulder toward the little red book. "I thought having two or three additions in the book was an accomplishment. I think Roland has ten times that many. The man can rehome letters that have nothing legible on them."

"I don't have entries yet."

Penny looked at the letter nearest her. It was a simple mismatch in city and state. "This is an easy one. It won't make the book either. I don't know if the book matters as much as I thought it did. It's what's in the letters, the lives behind them, that matters."

*A*loud thumping roused Thomas from a fitful nap.

"Dinner's in ten minutes. I'm not about to let a man miss a meal on my watch. I'll bring it up or you can come to the dining hall." Margaret Anders hollered through Thomas's bedroom door. The unusual woman, with her wild curls and no-nonsense ways, ran the boardinghouse like a tight ship, as well as the boarders. "You in there?" She didn't wait for him to answer. "Of course you are. You spend far too much time inside. Well, you did get out for the barn raising. That sunlight did you good. I saw it in your countenance when you came back. Come out and get another taste of it."

He groaned as he rolled over. "I think I'll take dinner in my room."

"A man can hole himself up for only so long. I think a change of scenery would do you good. Besides, the company in my dining hall is always the best. People travel for miles to eat my meals. Consider yourself lucky you only have to walk the stairs."

He sat up and the old bed creaked beneath his weight. "I'm not about to believe that lie. I know what kind of company attends your dinners. Remember, I've been eating in your hall for days on end now." He rested his elbows on his knees. "The food is good, I admit that, but the company is in need of some serious reformation."

"It'll be worse without you. How dare you leave me to the devices of those unruly men."

"So, you agree! The crowd's not as polished as you'd like."

"I admit it." She let out a boisterous laugh from the other side of the door and Thomas smiled despite himself. "I'll see you downstairs in ten minutes. Otherwise, it's the switch for you."

Thomas wasn't sure why she'd even asked where he wanted to eat his meal. There was no use arguing with that woman. He could stand to comply for another week or so before he headed out west again. With any luck, a wagon train would be passing through soon. He'd load up his new wagon and join them. That'd been his plan. It was what he'd clung to when he could find nothing else to reach for. But now a wave of apprehension hit him whenever he thought about setting out again.

He pulled himself to his feet. Back in Alexandria, he would've dressed for dinner. His hair would've been greased, and his pants creased, and a tie would've been knotted perfectly at his neck. Thomas looked down at himself now. His shirt was wrinkled and half unbuttoned. With clumsy hands, he threaded the buttons through the holes. He couldn't do much to smooth the wrinkles or tame his thick, unkempt hair, which had not been trimmed since weeks before he had left Alexandria.

A terse chuckle escaped. Where was the man who wore three-piece suits? Where was the man who never left home unless his face was shaved? He fingered his long beard. He was hardly the same man. It had been weeks, or was it months, since he'd taken a razor to his face.

Who are you? he asked himself, only to shake his head in utter confusion. Someday perhaps he'd have an answer.

A little mirror hung above the washbasin. He splashed his face with the cool water. Then he ran his hands through his hair, trying to force the obstinate strands down.

He paused and stared at his own reflection. A tightness existed in his features that aged him beyond his twenty-seven years. His brown eyes met the ones in the mirror. They were the same walnut color they'd always been, but they were not the same eyes. The eyes that stared back at him were not the bold, confident ones he'd seen so often before. They were pained, confused. His neglected face—all of it echoed the ache in his soul. Before him was a hurting man. The world, or at least all of Azure Springs, must see it. Was that why everyone had been kind? Because they pitied him?

For years he'd been admitted into the finest social circles in Alexandria. Not merely admitted but sought out. In the elegant ballrooms, beautiful women had surrounded him. What would they think of him now? Would they pity him too? Or merely move on to someone they deemed worthy? Victims of the misguided society he had once ruled as king, they'd likely see nothing of any worth when their eyes roamed over him.

The man looking at him was broken.

He pulled his eyes away from the mirror. Even a broken man knows adding pain to pain serves no use. He wasn't about to cross Margaret. With two minutes to spare, he slid onto a bench in the dining hall. He sat in the corner as far from anyone as possible.

She stepped near him and gave him a knowing look. "I was

RACHEL FORDHAM

about to come up those stairs with a switch and scare you on down here."

"I thought I'd save you a trip. After all, I'm supposed to be the guest with manners."

"How considerate of you. Maybe next time I'll insist you clean up before you come down and see if you'd oblige me then." She looked him over. "Sure wouldn't hurt you."

"I tried." He ran his hands through his hair again.

She picked up a large bowl and started scooping potatoes onto plates. "We've a barber. He moved into the building on the corner. Imagine Azure Springs having a real barber."

"It's just hair."

Margaret moved to his side. "True. But your outward appearance can at times shout to the world what it is you've got going on inside. And right now, I see a man who doesn't care." She scrunched up her nose. "Or perhaps you do but don't want anyone to know it. Is that what you want us all to think—that you're a man past caring?"

He didn't know how to respond, so he didn't. Instead, he focused on the mound of potatoes on his plate. The hills and valleys mimicked the mountain ranges he'd hoped to put between himself and his past.

She bent near him and added another scoop. "You ought to care. Not because of how everyone sees you but because you're here and you owe it to yourself. You're young yet. It's too soon for you to give up on this life. It's too soon for any of us. Even me and I'm much older than you." She nudged his shoulder. "You need more days of barn building under your belt."

"You act like you know my story. But you don't." He set down the fork he'd been holding and turned toward her. "I've

45

got burdens I'm going to be carrying my whole life. And you think something like my hair matters or that a few more days of hammering nails will fix it? All that hammering did was cover my hands with blisters. You don't know a thing." Hurt and anger boiled through his veins. His pain was so real that it tore at him.

"You're right, I don't. I can tell you where a barber is and to get down for dinner. I can introduce you to fine folks and point the way to the church. I can beg you to let go of your troubles and reach out to someone. But I can't fix it at all." Margaret's voice was just above a whisper. She spoke for his ears only. "But locking yourself up in your room day after day, that's what cowards do. Living in a cave pretending none of this exists won't get you anywhere. Going for a ten-minute walk once a day is not living. That's just dying slowly."

She moved on then, serving the men at the other tables. It didn't take long before the benches filled and the ruckus of the dining hall crowd drowned out the turmoil within him. He shoveled bite after bite of Margaret's roast and potatoes into his mouth without hardly tasting it. All the while he listened to strangers talk.

A fair-haired man boasted about his fields. Another about his horse. Then a man with a thick mustache and wide girth set his drink down on the table and stood. He belched like a man who had lost his senses to the bottle. No apologies were offered. Thomas wondered if this man too carried a burden. Was there some tragic tale that had led him to darkness? A shiver raced through him. Was he destined to become like this pathetic man? Never had his future seemed so bleak.

"You got your fields and your horses." The man pounded his chest. His voice was raspy and deep. "I ain't got either. But last night I went to the saloon and picked out the best-looking gal, a pretty thing with swaying hips and—"

"Enough!" Margaret banged a spoon against the back of a pan. "There will be no talk like that in my dining hall."

The man staggered toward her. Then he spit, only just missing Margaret. "I can speak any way I want. I ain't 'bout to let some crazy woman tell me what I can and can't say. You just jealous no one's looking at you."

"In my hall, you *will* do as I say. And this crazy lady says she's heard enough." Margaret, her shoulders square, took a step toward him and stared him down.

He let out another belch, but this time he purposely blew the foul air in Margaret's direction. Then he laughed in her face. "Don't like me talking about pretty girls and the things—"

Thud.

Thomas's fist connected with the man's jaw. How he'd gotten from the bench to the man, he could not recall. Rage and anger filled him. Long suppressed feelings erupted in that one blow.

"Get out of here." Thomas's voice was a low, coarse whisper. The normally noisy hall was silent, so silent that Thomas's voice boomed like thunder. "You heard Margaret. Your filth is not welcome here."

Thomas grabbed the man by the collar, pulled him to his feet, and dragged him out the door. "Women, all of them, matter. They deserve to be treated well." He pulled the man closer so they were face-to-face. "They matter, you disgusting pig." Then, with a great deal of force, he shoved the man into the dusty street.

With his hands still fisted, he turned and saw Margaret stepping out of the boardinghouse. "I'm sorry," he said. "I'm sorry."

She locked eyes with him, her gaze so intense that he dared not break it. "That man's had a run of bad luck." She put a hand on Thomas's arm, her touch cooling the rage inside him. "He's not the only one though. We all suffer. We all hurt. But we don't all have to be like him."

He broke her gaze then. The words were meant for him and he knew it. But he wasn't ready to hear them.

Her voice kept coming. There was no escaping it. "He stopped living for the good. He's been nothing but trouble for years now. It's a vicious trap he's been swallowed by. He won't let it go. He won't change. But it doesn't have to be that way."

It doesn't have to be that way. It doesn't have to be that way. Like church bells, the words rang within him over and over again. He felt dizzy and shook his head to clear it.

Margaret patted his arm. "Thank you for stopping him. For defending me and for defending all women. We don't need his poison. We need honorable men like you."

"I'm not honorable." With his knees shaking, he stepped away from her. "I'm not."

"I've watched you." Her voice followed him as he walked away. "You're better than you believe. Your true colors shined through the gloom when you were building that barn. And now, tonight, I've seen it again."

"You're wrong about me."

"No," she said as he turned the corner. "One day you'll see it too. You're just a man still finding his way. But I believe you'll find it. You are good."

"Mother. Honeysuckle," Penny called as she walked through the door.

"You know I don't appreciate you using my name in the same sentence as that dog's."

"Sorry, Mother. Where is Honey?" Penny asked.

"Billy asked if he could keep her longer today. He has a cousin staying with him. A terribly dirty little cousin who apparently likes dogs. I didn't think you'd mind. Besides, it meant less time I had to watch the animal. That dog is not meant to live in a space this small. You know that as well as I do. You should have found her a different home when we moved to this despicable apartment, or just set her free."

"If I could give her a bigger place, I would. But I'm not giving her up. I've told you that at least a thousand times. You can't tell me you've forgotten how much Father enjoyed Honey." Penny set her empty lunch tin on the table. "Let's not quarrel over Honey. How was your day?"

Florence's normally stoic face brightened. "I've news! Sit. I'll tell you."

"What is it?" Penny sat quickly and leaned toward her mother. "Has something happened?"

"I've a letter. It came just this afternoon from my brother Clyde. You remember your uncle, don't you?"

"I do. I remember him scowling at me and the way his forehead became creased with so many lines. I remember him telling me what to do and me never being able to do it well enough for him. I haven't missed him." She felt a strange twinge of fear rush through her. "It's been such a long time. What is his letter about?"

Florence smiled. "Yes, that's him. Poor man inherited our father's features—and his temper."

"What did he say? I didn't think you'd heard from any of your family in a very long time."

"I haven't." Florence rubbed her forearm as she spoke. "They wrote me off in a sense when your father's business collapsed and the money was gone. Everyone was so angry about it. I've missed them though."

Penny's chest tightened. Despite their many differences, Penny did not like knowing her mother had suffered. "Of course you have. They never should have rejected you. Even if they did lose a little money in investments."

"It's in the past now. Uncle Clyde is going to save us from this horrid life." Florence reached behind her and retrieved the letter. "He says here his wife, Beatrice, has died from pneumonia and his house is far too quiet. He wants us to move there. He's getting old and wants me to help him manage his estate."

"Move there? With Uncle Clyde?"

"Beatrice was the one most ashamed of our ruin. She never liked your father much and practically despised him after his death. She tolerated us those first years, but when the investments failed and the money was gone, she became angry and bitter." Florence hugged the letter to her chest. "It doesn't matter now. We can have our lives back. This is our new start. It's what we've been waiting for."

Their lives back . . . but not Father. Not their house. Not even their money. Penny had dreamed of the freedom she'd had before, but moving in with Uncle Clyde did not feel like a ticket to freedom.

Penny straightened in her chair. She stared forward but saw nothing. "When?"

"Soon. He says he needs to ready the house, but he'd like to move us by summer, perhaps sooner." Florence stood. Her wrinkled hands worked to smooth her skirts. "Aren't you happy?"

"I . . . I'm surprised. I need to think about it." Penny stood and put a hand on her mother's shoulder. "I am happy for you. I know these years have been hard. I've wished for something different for a long time. I never expected . . . this."

"This is a good thing. With your dark hair and fair skin and"—Florence patted Penny's cheek—"those green eyes, you could still catch a worthy suitor. It's not too late. We'll buy you the perfect dress and maybe a lesson or two in decorum, and you'll be able to secure a husband. All you'll have to do is let go of the bad habits you've acquired and remember who you were born to be. Philadelphia is far enough away that we can truly leave all of this. No one will know we were so destitute. Uncle Clyde will line up the right man."

Penny put a hand on her dark hair. It was dark like her father's. She loved her hair because it reminded her of him, not because she could woo a man. She had long dreamed of love, but this talk of securing a husband did not awaken anything in her heart.

"I don't want to trick a man. I'm not sure I want to dress up and pretend I'm someone I'm not. I do have dreams, but I'm not sure they are the same as yours. I'll think about it all." She swallowed, unsure of what to say. Her mother was smiling. She was happy and Penny didn't want to take that away. "I better go check on Honey. Last time Billy took her out, he let her get ahold of Mrs. Lewbrinksy's laundry and she's been glaring at me ever since."

*W*ho's the lady with the frown?" Thomas motioned toward a woman standing outside the mercantile.

"That's Eliza Danbury. She's the store owner's daughter." Hugh's eyes lingered on the woman. "Town beauty, or at least she was." Hugh had a far-off look on his face. Surely, he was remembering long-ago days in Azure Springs that Thomas would never fully understand.

"She married Jeb a few months back and hasn't been the same since. I guess marriage doesn't suit everyone. At least not marriage to Jeb." Hugh shook his head. "It's not right. You should have seen her before. She was always laughing and smiling. She was different then."

Thomas leaned back against the hitching post. "Seems you know everyone."

"Can't help it in a place like this. Won't be long until we all know about you too." Hugh scratched his forearm. "You got a girl?"

"Nope." Thomas untied his horse and threw the reins over the mare's head. His horses had been injured so badly in the accident that he'd had to let them go. This new mare he'd bought was a shaggy, ill-mannered beast. "I came out here alone."

"What's that look for?" Hugh prodded him with his finger. Though Hugh was equal to Thomas in age, his persistent smile gave him almost a boyish look. "You do got a girl, don't ya? She coming later?"

Thomas, already regretting this foolish outing, swung his body into the saddle. He didn't want to talk about women or the past. For the two days he'd been working on Hugh's land, he'd done all he could to avoid personal questions. And now Hugh had asked him to ride to the old Dawson place with him. Even though Thomas had insisted he wasn't interested in staying in Iowa, his new friend had somehow coaxed him into seeing what was for sale. But no piece of land was worth dredging up the past for.

"Come on. Tell me about her." Hugh pulled himself up into his saddle. He wore the same grin he'd been wearing since Thomas had first met him at the dining hall.

"I don't think you'll let up, will you?" Thomas rubbed his chest. "Back in Alexandria, there was a girl who changed my life. It's a long story and not a very enjoyable one."

Hugh scoffed. "Why not bring her along? Is she too much of a city gal to handle the West? Any girl who doesn't love all this"—he motioned toward the vast green landscape—"may not be right for you. Who am I to say though? Maybe she would take to Azure Springs. It's not nearly as primitive as Montana."

"It's not like that. It's complicated." Thomas dug his heels harder into the horse's side in a vain attempt to control the stubborn animal. "I've worked on your land for two days and it's obvious no woman lives there. I hardly think you're in a position to lecture me on matrimony. Besides, the bachelor life isn't so bad."

"I may be a bachelor too, but I'd change that if I could."

Thomas raised a brow.

Hugh slowed his horse. "You can't marry a girl who's already married. That's my story. I was too slow to speak up, too slow to even try. And until I find another gal who keeps me up at night thinking of her, I'll just keep busy digging rocks out of my soil. It's not a life I'd recommend. No one should be lonely if they can avoid it."

Thomas rode in silence. Regrets seemed to be a universal burden. Hugh at least had found a way to smile beneath their weight.

Hugh looked over his shoulder in the direction of the town. "Look around. We've got women here. Your chances are better here than farther west. Maybe there's an Azure Springs woman who could fill whatever void you have. Smile occasionally. I'm sure we could find you someone to make your house a home and keep you warm at night. You keep going and settle in Montana, you might die a single man."

"I'll keep that in mind. Though I doubt it will be enough to entice me to stay."

"You haven't been here during an Iowa winter. I hear Montana's worse. Having someone beside you might hold more appeal when the snow starts falling." Hugh laughed at his own joke. "It's your life. If you want to risk frostbite, I can't stop you."

"Better show me this homestead. As it is, I won't be around long enough to court a girl. I can't stay at the boardinghouse forever. I've already been there too long. Margaret's forever threatening to use the switch on me. I think she really might one of these days. I'm itching to be on my way."

"Follow me." Hugh clicked his tongue as he led his horse farther down the path. "You're going to love this spread. You won't find a place like it anywhere in this whole world. Besides, in Montana you'll end up with some plot of land that doesn't even have a fence post in it. Your smooth city hands might not be up for that challenge. The Dawsons left this place with the soil already turned. You want to learn farming, start here."

Thomas rubbed his hands together. There was truth in what Hugh said. He could run to the West and trade in his city duds for loose farm clothes, but he wasn't prepared for the reality of such a life. His two days at Hugh's and the day at the barn had taught him that much. Every muscle in his body ached, his hands were blistered, and at times he was certain his eyes would close while he worked because he was so tired. Never had he been so physically exhausted.

"I'm free to go or come as I please. That's the luxury of being unattached. I can settle here and move on later if it pleases me." Thomas patted his mare's neck, only to have her balk at his touch. "Blasted animal. I can't seem to win her over."

"Maybe she's longing for you to settle down. Put her in her own stall and she might treat you better."

Thomas groaned. "You're as bad as Margaret. She hassles me about seeing the barber and when to eat. The stall at the stable is fine. This horse just doesn't like me."

Hugh smiled. The man was always smiling. All Thomas's life, he'd surrounded himself with conniving businessmen who smiled only when it served to further their success. Their every move motivated by some potential personal gain. Thomas sensed none of that in Hugh. It was unsettling. So unsettling that at times he found his own scowl loosening in the good man's company.

Over one small rise and then another they rode. Seas of

blowing grassland on either side rippled in unison at the will of the breeze. There was a beauty to it. He'd been slow to notice any beauty since his life had taken a turn. No, the truth was, he'd never been good at appreciating real beauty. But he saw it here, in the fresh, open air. He saw it in the dancing grasses and droplets of color made by the spring flowers. He saw it in the rare and unusual friendships he was making. For a moment, life held a bit of promise. As quickly as his ability to see beauty came, it vanished. Replaced once again by pangs of remorse. A cloud of guilt so dark it blocked the newly risen sun. The colors faded, leaving only shadows. Whatever beauty he had found was pushed aside, lost to the darkness.

"I don't need to see the homestead." Thomas pulled on the reins, directing his horse away from the path. "I'll take it. I'll give it a go. If I take to it, I'll stay. If not, I'll continue west."

"You'll buy it? You haven't even seen the place." Hugh rode up beside him. "You'll give up your Montana dream without ever seeing the land you're purchasing?"

"I know it seems irrational, and maybe it is, but I need a place of my own. I'm not going to stay with Margaret forever. And as much as I like working for you, I'm a man who likes a bit of control. My wagon's done, but I don't know when a group will be heading west. This land and house you speak of seem as good as any. I'm a man wandering. Why not stop here?" He looked at his hands. The leather reins rested in them. "Besides, you're right. My hands are soft. I can toughen them up here as well as I could out there."

"You're a strange man," Hugh said. "I don't understand. You're willing to work for next to nothing digging holes for fence posts. Even when you have the funds to buy one of the nicest spreads in Azure Springs—"

"I needed to get away from the boardinghouse. I couldn't stay locked up in there all day, every day. Working for you was never about the pay." He shrugged. "I don't blame you for finding me odd."

"I'm not belittling your work. I'm grateful for it. I just don't understand you." Hugh smiled again. "I'll tell you my whole story, every detail if you want. I'd listen to yours too."

"Someday . . . perhaps." Thomas wanted to end it there, but then he thought of Hugh's patient teaching. Each new chore had required Hugh to stop his own work and come teach Thomas. There'd never been any malice in his looks or his words. Thomas had never had a friend like him. The least he could do was offer some sort of an explanation.

"See that tree there?" Thomas pointed to a stubby tree scarred by an old prairie fire. "I feel like that tree. Battered by the elements. Look at it. It's not much of a tree. Sometimes I don't feel like much of a man. I have a whole past behind me that I'd just as soon forget if I could, but the scars won't go away. I don't know how to go about finding a future. I don't know which way to grow or whether to keep growing at all."

Hugh wiped the sweat from his brow with the sleeve of his shirt. "That tree survived a fire that devoured all its neighbors. It survived, and if you look at the base of it you'll see saplings. Whether or not it has scars, it's doing something. If you're that tree, then there's a reason you're here. That tree fought for its life. Fight for yours. Fight for it at the old Dawson place." Hugh started back toward town.

Thomas took a deep breath. His lungs filled with the sweet scent of grass. "I will."

"I got a day's work ahead of me. I'll see you soon. When the deed's signed, I'll come help you with your land."

Thomas said a quick farewell, then slid off the back of his horse and watched Hugh ride toward town. The breeze blew across the open grasses and rustled the leaves of the mangled tree. Thomas walked to it. Kneeling on the ground, he inspected the small saplings at the tree's base. Their leaves were fresh and green. Unscathed by the storms and hardships of the land.

Thomas reached for the grass nearest the little trees and pulled. Repeatedly he pulled handfuls of grass from around the saplings—handful after handful. The hot sun beat against his back, but he did not slow. Hunched over, he continued on until each sapling had a circle of space around it.

"Fight," he whispered to them. And to himself.

Penny flipped the end of her braid back and forth while she read through a stack of letters. Nothing interesting had grabbed her attention the entire morning. In fact, she had found nothing exciting for days. And she needed a distraction. Something to pull her away from her own worries.

The next letter began like so many others—with someone addressing their mother. At least half the letters she went through were to mothers. When she was younger, before her father died, she dreamed of being a parent herself. And if that dream had come true, perhaps she'd have gotten a letter addressed to her with the words *Dear Mother* on it.

> *Dear Mother,*
>
> *I couldn't sleep last night. I lay in bed missing you and missing Father. I can't believe he is really gone. I suppose it is the curse of youth to believe life can go on as it always*

has. But I never imagined a world without Father. Despite his quiet ways, I always knew I could turn to him when I was weak. He was so strong. So good. I know he'd know what to tell me. I know if he were only here, he'd be able to comfort me.

"Penny. Penny," Dinah whispered. "You're crying."

Penny wiped her face. She hadn't noticed the tears. Her mind had been too busy thinking of her own father, who also had been good and strong and wise.

"Dinah, do you ever worry we will spend the rest of our lives reading other people's mail? I'm so often swept up in someone else's love letter or my heart soars as I read of a new baby, but it's never my baby or my love story." Penny could almost hear her father telling her to make time for the simple joy of love and family. "I've been here so long. And if I go to Uncle Clyde's, I think my chance for true love and adventure will be lost to decorum and presentation. I get older every day, and always it's money or work that decides what I do. And soon it will be Uncle Clyde. I wonder if anyone will ever write me a love letter. Will I ever have a say in my fate?"

Dinah's eyes grew soft. "I think any job has mundane days. No life is all adventure. Not here or with Uncle Clyde."

"I know. It's just . . . I want something of my own." She glanced down at the paper in her hands. "When I was little, my father used to put me up on his shoulders and we'd walk through the city parks together. Once he pointed toward the government buildings and told me this land was a land of freedom. That we owed it to our forefathers to make good lives for ourselves."

"Your father did that, did he not? He lived a good life."

"My father was a hardworking man. He made his fortune and invested. Doubling, tripling it over time. He was brilliant. You know the rest—how two years after his death, his financial advisor cheated us and we lost it all. But that's not what I was getting at. I no longer care about all we lost." Penny took a deep breath. "My father wanted me to do things worth writing home about. Big things, little things. All of it. He wanted me to find joy and purpose." She threw her hands to her sides, nearly dropping the letter she held. "He laughed. No one laughs like he did. And I hardly laugh anymore." Penny's voice became more intense. "I remember watching him. His eyes were always so alive. They were full of love. Even my mother was calm and happy when he was around. Everything was simpler and happier then. My mother used to smile. And it wasn't forced—it was real. Their love was perfect, and now . . . Sometimes I feel I've lost both my parents, my dreams, and my hopes."

Dinah didn't tear into the letter she held in her hands. She waited.

"I can't explain it. I wonder if there will ever be a chance for me to truly take after my father and go see something new. I wish I could ask him what I ought to do with my life."

"You've told me so much of your father and his wisdom. Surely, when the time is right, you'll know how to follow his lead."

Penny reached over and grasped her friend's hand. "Until then, I suppose I'll continue reading this endless stack of correspondence. I'll try with all of my might to keep from throttling my mother when she talks of how joyous it will be to dress me up and put me on display. And I'll try not to lose faith."

A raspy, wet noise drew the girls' attention. Roland stood

over them. He pushed up his spectacles with his forefinger and cleared his throat again.

"I heard you were collecting letters from Thomas. I know which bin to look in. Here." Roland took a handkerchief from his pocket and blew his nose, then he dropped three letters onto her lap, turned, and shuffled away.

Such an odd man.

"Thank you," Penny called to his back before fanning the letters in Dinah's direction. "These two are from a different Thomas. I can tell by the penmanship. But this one is Clara's Thomas. He's a determined man."

"You're smiling." Dinah nudged her shoulder. "Remind me to thank good ol' Tom for brightening your day."

"They're only letters." Penny ran her finger over the perfect script. "I'm not sure why I enjoy them so much."

"Better scurry off to your corner"—Dinah shooed her away—"and savor it."

"My corner?"

Dinah pointed to the chair near the window. "You always read the letters you are most excited about right over there, away from all of us."

Penny felt a little sheepish knowing her habit was so predictable. "I suppose I do."

Once she settled into the tall-backed chair, she took a deep breath and began.

Dear Clara,

I'm buying a bit of land with a house on it. Strange, is it not? Me in a small home surrounded by green fields. I haven't seen it yet. To be honest, I do not care where I live. This place seems as good as any. I wanted to put more space between myself and the past, but I believe now that your face will haunt me anywhere I go. I've tried to accept that my future will forever be shadowed by the past. I am alive, though, and so I must put a roof over my head.

I have decided I will not allow the past to corrupt me. I saw the other night what happens when a man lets his pain lead him. I will live out my days bearing my burdens, but I will not allow myself to become a burden. I'll not be a nuisance to my neighbors. I've made those commitments and I'll honor them. That much I can do.

There is a goodness here that both frightens and entices me. I wonder sometimes if I deserve even glimpses of happiness or if that is unfair of me to dabble in. For someone who once lived life in such a calculating way, I'm surprising even myself with the life I'm leading now. Am I an imposter? It's a question I've yet to answer.

I'll move out to my land, the old Dawson place, in a matter of weeks when the money is transferred and the deed is signed. When I live there on my own land, I hope to be able to say with surety who I am. Someday I want to rise with the sun and know I am not fooling anyone but am the man I woke up to be.

Until then, I've a landlady who bangs on my door if I go too long without leaving my room. I've become a day laborer, making abysmal wages, just to keep her from threatening me with the switch. I jest. She is a good woman and has been my champion in many ways. And the labor I offer to my new friend is good for my body and soul. I do look forward to the ownership and accountability that comes from working one's own spot in the world.

I will miss the dining hall and the finely cooked meals. I don't imagine I'll be eating very well once I leave here. And I certainly doubt I'll have the same kind of adventures around my own table as I've had in the crowded dining hall. Believe it or not, I hit a man the other night.

Penny stopped reading. Her mouth hung open. She had to reread the line to make sure she'd seen it right. She had never imagined her Thomas was capable of striking another man. There must be some explanation. She read on.

I hadn't planned to. I heard the foul direction his words were going in and anger overpowered me. I believe the man received several months' worth of my pent-up frustration in that blow. All my anger in one solid swing. I've had battles in my day. Battles of wills and of words. Striking a man was a first. I walked away feeling weak. I looked at my own hand and wondered what I'd become.

I thought perhaps I'd be an outcast after my angry display, but the good people of this town seemed to find amusement in it. Admiration even. Little do they know I acted outside of my control. I should have tried harder to convince them that I'm not as noble as they believe. But part of me wants to believe I could be what they see in me. A defender of goodness rather than a man who is simply looking for a target to throw his anger at. With that blow, I like to believe my anger left me. I've turned a corner.

Restless and searching,
Thomas

"Does he fare better than before?" Dinah asked as she walked up to the corner where Penny sat.

Penny jumped to her feet. "I'm going to Alexandria tomorrow to find Clara. I have to. There's a man out there trying to make a life for himself, and I can't help but believe his life will be more fulfilling if he can share it with the woman he loves. Besides, he's not the man he was when he left. I feel his goodness, but something in his past causes him to doubt it. It's holding him back." With each word, the passion she felt crept into her voice. "He has a life ahead of him, but he's afraid to seize it. Will you come with me and help me find her?"

"Yes." Dinah's voice was low, but her eyes were bright. "I'd love to go with you. If I can convince my parents to let me."

Penny squeezed Dinah's hand. "It's for work. We will be putting a letter in Clara's hand. Besides, you're entitled to a life of your own. We both are. We have to seize it while we can. And Clara should get to choose too."

"Your father would be proud," Dinah whispered. "You can't tell me that uniting two lost and heartbroken souls is not something worth writing home about. It's an adventure, a small one, but an adventure all the same."

"I think he'd still chide me for not being married. But he'd be proud that I believe in others. He always had time for a stranger." Penny folded the letter back up. "He also believed in love. I only wish my father—"

"No matter your father. Mr. Douglas is coming. Put that one in your pocket and tear this one open." She handed her an unopened letter. "Quick."

"A re you ready?" Penny asked the moment Dinah opened the door.

"Yes. Let's hurry before my mother doubts my story. She's having trouble believing I have to work today." Dinah pulled her arm through her coat.

"Of course she doesn't believe you. She thinks you're sneaking off with Lucas." A child poked her head out from behind Dinah's hip.

"Hush, Brigette." Dinah's voice was sharp as she glared at her little sister.

"I wasn't going to tell her about you kissing him."

Penny nearly laughed aloud when she saw Dinah's face. Her lips were firmly pressed together in a straight line, her brows one solid line of rage, and her cheeks flushed. "Enough!" snapped Dinah.

"Come on, Dinah. We can talk on the way." Penny pulled Dinah away from the apartment.

"Dinah! Slow down." Penny gasped when they'd walked three blocks as though they were fleeing a fire.

"What is it?"

"Tell me about Lucas," Penny said. "We are supposed to be

enjoying our day together and I think I'd very much like hearing about the man who has your face turning so pink. And I have to know about this kiss. Tell me everything."

Dinah slowed her steps but not much. "I should have known Brigette would not keep it a secret. She's a horrible little pest."

"She's so young. I doubt she meant anything by it. Besides, I may never have heard about Lucas if she hadn't spoken up."

"I didn't tell you because of all your romantic notions. You're always talking about true love and broken hearts. It doesn't seem fair for me to have someone when you want a love story of your own. I didn't want to hurt you."

"Your happiness could never hurt me." Penny said the words and listened to her heart, wondering if it would ache in envy, but it did not. She sensed only the same familiar desire to be cared for that she always harbored. But at the same time, she felt her heart leap with joy for her friend. "Is it love, then? Tell me all of it. I'll be happy for you, I will."

"Are you upset I didn't tell you?" Dinah finally met her eyes. Penny expected to see them shining with delight, happiness. Something. Instead, they were the same calm, practical eyes Penny saw every day.

Penny managed to shake her head.

"I should have told you. I did want to. I am sorry I kept it from you, but . . . well, I hope you aren't angry."

"I'll be upset if you don't tell me the whole story right now! Every detail." Penny smiled at her friend, hoping to encourage her. "But I could never be upset with you. I've prayed so often for you. And now you're telling me you've a beau!"

Dinah shook her head. "It's a simple story. I met him walking to work. He made some comment about the leaves being so green and then every day we talked a bit more. It's not a very exciting courtship."

Penny sighed. What Dinah had said was true—it was not a thrilling story, but it was still sweet. "What happened then?"

"We walked and talked every day for a few weeks. He works as a clerk in the legislative building."

"What's he like? Is he tall? Short? What do you talk about?" Penny couldn't hold back her questions. "I want to hear it all."

"Well, he's a little taller than I am. He's twenty-five and has been living with his family. He's eager to get out on his own." Dinah blushed. "I don't know what to say. He's friendly and kind. We both believe in hard work. Some mornings we walk in silence. Other mornings we talk about the letters, the weather, or his job. I've told him how hard it is at home. And he's told me about his own family."

Penny raised her eyebrow. "Is that all?"

"For a long time that was all we did. Then he asked me to dine with him and I agreed. I had to sneak away, but it was worth it. He took me to a real restaurant."

"That's exciting! Was that the night Brigette saw you kissing?"

Dinah rolled her eyes and groaned. "She's always spying on people and forever getting into trouble. I had to bribe her to keep her from telling everyone. It wasn't nearly as passionate as she made it seem. Just a kiss on the cheek, but it was my first kiss." They stopped just outside the stables. Dinah put a hand on Penny's arm. "Don't tell anyone. I don't know what will come of it all."

"I have no one to tell. But is it love?"

"I hardly know. I admit it's different from what I had expected, but it's not so bad. I want a man I can rely on and trust. A man who will get me out of that crowded apartment before

I'm too old to ever leave. I hear my mother telling everyone I may never get married. She's not very quiet about it." Dinah wrung her hands together. "It's humiliating."

"I understand overbearing mothers. But I don't want to marry simply because it solves one problem but adds new ones. I want something more. I want love. I want a man who would stop by the candy shop just for me. Someone who would adore me." Penny scrunched her nose as the smell of the stables wafted through the air. "I thought you did too."

"I'm not sure I have time to wait for butterflies in the pit of my stomach. He's a good man. I know that. When he goes into his building for work, I sometimes watch and he opens the door for others. Honestly, I gave up on love years ago and now I've Lucas."

"I'd rather never marry than marry for any reason but love." Penny studied her friend's calm eyes. They showed so little emotion. Where was the feeling, the joy? "What does your heart do when you're with him?"

"It beats like it always does. He's a fine man and he's kind. I could do much worse."

"Don't you want something more? Someone you cannot imagine living without? My father said when he met my mother, he knew his life would never be the same."

"I think I *could* feel that way about Lucas. I believe with time we could build a life together." Dinah sighed. "The truth is, I still live with my parents. I'm not building anything right now. I've been giving them my entire paycheck for years. I share a bed with an eight-year-old who changes positions every half hour and a four-year-old who still wets the bed. I think with Lucas I'll get to experience something outside my father's home. You talk of adventure. This may be mine."

Penny felt her shoulders slump. "Does he know this? That you feel this way?"

"He knows I care for him." Dinah looked out at the vast city before them. "We don't all get to be Thomas and Clara."

Penny swallowed hard. She'd always known some women and men married strategically. Their unions were merely means to specific goals. Could those marriages grow with time? Suddenly, she felt very naïve and unsure of every belief about love that she held on to so tightly. If only she could ask her father the many questions that swirled inside her.

"I do hope you find happiness and love." Penny took Dinah's hand and grasped it tightly. "I care about your happiness. I didn't mean to upset you. Marriage, courtship—they're just different from what I'd dreamed of. Maybe I need to grow up and stop dreaming. I shouldn't doubt you."

"I doubt myself often enough. Love is much more complicated than I'd expected. I believe, well, I hope it can grow with time and work and kindness." She reached out and grasped Penny's hand.

Penny swallowed. "I hope you're right. Today, let's hope Thomas and Clara's love is perfect . . . and simple."

———

Thomas pulled his hat from his head and wiped his brow. He longed for the evening hours, when the sun would set and fill the sky with oranges and reds. Then, if today were like the others, he knew he'd lean his tired body against the side of the house and watch the day draw to a close. In those moments when the sunlight was giving way to darkness, he felt peaceful. Just knowing the sun would leave and then rise again gave him a bit of comfort.

One week was all he'd spent at the old Dawson place. Each of those seven nights he'd stopped what he was doing and marveled at the setting sun. He liked putting his tools aside when the day was done, knowing he had put in a full day's work. Tight and strained muscles proclaimed that he was still alive.

Alive and working.

Little things done over and over again were his life now. Today, for the first time, he had passed through his garden and seen tiny green shoots breaking through the soil. His plants had begun making an appearance. His hours of work had already started bearing fruit. Thomas had knelt in the dark soil and touched the tiny shoots with his large, recently callused hands.

Six of the seven days he had spent in complete solitude. It had been just Thomas and his land. Well, not *just* his land. Birds had visited in the morning and deer in the evening. This morning, though, after he'd greeted his sprouting seeds, a man had stopped by.

"I been riding by this place for months, just looking at the empty house with its fences and barn. It's pretty quiet this far out of town." The stranger swung his leg over the side of his horse and walked toward Thomas. He walked with a confident swagger, his hands loose at his sides. The man was large and muscular, with dark, leathery skin. Thomas had learned to spot a man with a motive and this man had one. What it was he'd not known right away.

"Jeb Danbury," he said as he stuck out his hand. "I live with my wife, Eliza, on the big spread next to you."

"Thomas Conner. I was headed west and fate landed me here. No wife, just me." Thomas shook the man's hand. "It's good to meet a neighbor."

Jeb let out a low chuckle. "Call it fate if you want. I think it was good ol' Hugh." The man's laugh was hardly a friendly one. Thomas sensed something more than humor behind it. Something about the sound of his voice and the narrowness of his eyes made his skin crawl. "Hugh's always been jealous of what I got. He couldn't stand the idea of me getting this place. His place ain't nothing but rocks. Since we were boys, I've known he couldn't handle me always succeeding where he failed. I think he'd love nothing more than to wring my neck."

"Fate or Hugh, it doesn't matter, seeing as I live here now," Thomas said, using the calmest voice he could muster, which wasn't nearly as calm as he'd have liked it to be. "I've been wondering who else lived out this way."

"Not many folks. I own most of the land around you. I'd like to own this piece too. You done much farming before?" Jeb's eyes scanned the property, slowly roaming over the crooked rows and then the untouched fields to his left. A mocking sneer formed on his face. "You aren't making much progress. That soil was already turned and it's nothing but weeds now."

Angry heat rose to Thomas's face. How dare this man set foot on his soil only to spit on it with his words.

"I'm learning to farm as I go." Thomas rubbed his tired forearms in a vain attempt to cool his rage. "I hope to grow faster with time." His jaw clenched.

Jeb gnawed on the tobacco in his mouth, then spit. "Well, when you can't get the land to produce what you want and your cupboards are empty, I'll take this place from you. I was a harvest away from buying up this land and adding it to my own. Everyone in town knows this place should be mine."

"*I plan to make this business mine.*" Thomas put a hand on the post next to him, steadying his swaying body. He could hear his own voice from the past. The voice of who he'd been—a

71

man who got what he wanted. He looked up and met Jeb's
eyes. He realized he knew Jeb's kind. He knew about wanting
more. About never being satisfied. Deep down they were both
shrewd businessmen, or at least that's what Thomas had been.
Men who cared more about their own wallets than anything
or anyone else.

"I'll keep that in mind." Thomas's voice was low and tense.
"But I aim to make a go of it here."

Jeb reached for his horse's reins. "It's a tough land. Some
years the weather cooperates, others it don't. Then you get a
good year and find out the prices are bad. Sometimes it feels
like you can't win. Only the right breed of man can succeed. I
don't think you're the right breed."

Thomas ran a hand over his chin. "You've managed."

"Farming's in my blood. Besides, I got men working for me.
We're working all the land I've got and it won't be long 'til we're
working more. I own equipment no one else in the county has."
Jeb spit, then wiped his mouth with the back of his hand. "I
never lose. Not at farming or anything else. I'd like this piece
too. Remember that. I have a history of getting what I want."

There wasn't much use arguing. The set of Jeb's jaw, the squint
of his eyes. Thomas knew the man had no plans of backing down.

Jeb was the husband of the beautiful strawberry blonde he'd
seen in town, the one Hugh had said had changed for the worse
after she took her vows. She was married to this self-promoting,
pompous man. Thomas's knuckles were white at his sides—this
situation wasn't right.

"You're married to Abraham's daughter?" Thomas asked
through gritted teeth. "She another thing you won?"

Jeb spit again. "Call it what you will. She was the prettiest
girl in town and now she's mine."

"I hope it's a happy union." Thomas's voice rang with sarcasm. "Marriage is a long sentence otherwise. Or so I'm told."

"It is what it is. Look, I didn't stop by to talk about women." He swung himself back into his saddle. "I just wanted you to know we're neighbors."

"I'm glad to know who's nearby."

The man smirked before leading away his horse. "Welcome to Azure Springs."

rop us off here," Penny said to the driver. "We'd like to get out at the post office."

"Very well," the man said. He pulled back the reins, stopping the horses.

"You ready?" Dinah asked as they got out of the carriage and headed toward the post office.

"Yes! I've been thinking of Thomas and Clara for weeks now. Don't you feel as though we're doing something important?" Penny straightened her collar and smoothed her pleated skirt. "I feel as though I've been standing at a crossroads, and somehow delivering this letter changes everything."

"I should've known you would see this little adventure as a pivotal moment in your life." Dinah stepped closer to the large post office. "Crossroads or not, it's an exciting diversion."

"I think somehow it will prove to be pivotal. Today, I'm deciding to go and do something. I decided it on my own. Desperation did not dictate my choice. That's something." She took a deep breath. "And now I'm going to go into that post office and ask the postmaster why this letter didn't make it. And then I just know he'll point me in the right direction."

The post office was large and narrow. Through the glass

windows, Penny could see rows and rows of what looked like little boxes stacked on top of one another.

"Isn't it funny that we handle letters every day, but I rarely go to the post office? I wish I had a reason to." Penny put a hand on the door. "Wouldn't it be lovely to have someone of my own to write to? I think I'd like getting mail. Waiting for it and then finally holding it in my hands. Can you imagine?" She pushed the door open without waiting for a response. A little bell above the door announced their entry with a chime. "Did you hear that? I love the sound of bells." She breathed deeply. "It even smells good in here, like paper and cinnamon."

Dinah didn't say anything, but Penny could hear her laughing softly.

An older man with spectacles approached the counter. He wore a dingy white shirt with a black vest that he pulled on the sides of as he stepped closer. "Can I help you?"

"We need to locate Clara Finley. We know she lives in Alexandria." Penny put the letter on the counter. "See here? There's no street listed. Have you any information on her?"

"Where'd you get that?" His relaxed features became tense. "I sent that on to the dead letter office. You shouldn't have that." He reached out his hand, palm up.

Penny stepped back, bumping into Dinah, who steadied her.

"We work there," Dinah said in her usual composed way, "in the dead letter office. It's our job to research and return letters. We've seen so many come through for Clara Finley that we thought we'd come here and try to figure out why they aren't being delivered. It's an unconventional approach, but I assure you our motives are pure."

The man pulled back his hand and slapped it on the counter. "They aren't wanted. That's why them letters didn't make it."

He put a finger in the air and pointed toward the door. "They won't do any good being delivered. Go on. Take that letter and leave. Do with it whatever it is you do with letters that have no homes. Burn it, tear it to pieces, but don't bring it back here."

With a racing heart, Penny started to leave. Over her shoulder, she asked, "Why aren't they wanted?"

"They don't need no reminders." The man spit out each word slowly but with venom. "Go on. The letters went to the dead letter office for a reason. Let them die."

"But—"

"Come on," Dinah whispered under her breath. "Don't stir up trouble. It's not worth it."

Shaking and near tears, Penny allowed Dinah to lead her away. This time the chime of the bell above the door held no appeal as they walked out of the post office.

"I don't understand. Thomas is heartbroken. I thought it was my job to tell Clara so she could go to him or at the very least write to him." Penny shook her head. "I believed doing so was important."

"It's early yet. Let's ask someone if they know the Finleys." Dinah's features were expressionless. Her down-to-business sensibilities had kicked in. At times Dinah's demeanor was exasperating and at other times, like the present, Penny was utterly grateful for her friend's level head.

"All right," Penny managed to say despite her still-churning innards.

"Getting upset will not help us find her. You're so good at looking for clues and putting pieces together. That's what we have to do now. We'll find another way."

"Very well. I'll ask someone." She glanced up and down the street. "Ummm . . . who should I ask?"

76

Dinah grabbed her hand and pulled her toward the large mercantile. "Let's step into this store and ask someone. Honestly, there are days when I wonder how you have such high return rates at the office."

"There it is. Over there," Dinah said as she pointed toward a three-story mansion. After being directed to the correct street by the men in the mercantile, they'd had to stop and ask three other strangers before they found someone who could tell them exactly which house was the Finleys'.

"Was your home like this one when you had money?" Dinah asked as they walked.

"The style was different. Mine had columns and balconies. This one, with its iron railings and steep roofs, is very different. But I'd say the size is about the same. There are days when I hardly believe I lived in a home so large." Penny could almost feel the deep sorrow and shame she had felt when she walked away from her childhood home for the last time. She'd loved her home. More than that, though, the solemn faces of the onlookers had wounded her. Penny cleared her throat, trying to make the knot that was stuck in it go away. "Now twenty of my apartments could fit inside my old home."

"Try to remember what it was like being the daughter of a wealthy man. I have a feeling these people are like the people you sashayed with in your early years. I've no experience with the front doors of these houses." Dinah's pace had slowed. "The only way my people ever got inside was through the back door so they could sweep the floors and do the wash."

Penny felt her heart race again. She wasn't like these people, not now. Dinah was like a sister, not a servant, to her. "We're here to deliver a letter. That's all. They won't care a thing about how much money we've got in the jars under our beds."

"You're the one who believes Thomas is aching for his sweet Clara. You get to knock." Dinah slowed her pace even more, making it practically impossible for Penny to do anything but lead the way or stand there gaping like a fool.

"I'm going to knock on the door, hand them the letter, and go," she said as she stepped closer and closer to the front door. Two steps more and she was to it, the brass knocker, with its ornate flourishes, mere inches from her hand.

"Be brave," Dinah cheered her on from a few paces back. "Just knock. Don't overthink it."

I am brave. Penny raised and dropped the knocker. A few moments dragged slowly on before she heard footsteps on the other side of the door.

"Can I help you?" a woman in a simple servant's uniform asked after opening the door.

"We're looking for Clara Finley." Penny's voice was steady. "We need to speak to her. It's important. We were told she lives here."

"Clara?" The woman shook her head.

"Do you know her?"

"I . . . I can't." She leaned closer and whispered, "I can't help you."

"Perhaps you can tell us where we can find her. How can we reach her?"

"Why are you looking for her?" The woman glanced over her shoulder. "What are you doing here?"

"We've a letter for her from a man named Thomas." Penny felt her resolve weakening. She took a step back. *Maybe this is all a mistake.* "We wanted to help. He seems heartbroken. We thought Clara needed to know."

"No one wants the letter," the woman said. "Take it away from here. It'll only cause trouble. Clara can't read it now and no one else wants it."

"What do you mean?" Penny's voice quavered. "Why can't she read it?"

"Clara . . . She's dead. The whole family is grieving. Oscar, her father, more than anyone. You can't come in here. Go."

Penny, struggling to make sense of what she'd just heard, stared at the woman. "Dead?"

"Yes. There was a fire—I can't . . ." She glanced over her shoulder again. "It's not wise for me to talk about it. Just take your letter and go."

"Is someone there?" a voice called from inside.

"These women are at the wrong house. They're leaving now." Then softly she said, "Go. And don't come back. It won't do any good."

ead. How could it be?

"I wanted to help him." Penny wiped at her eyes. "I wanted to ease his pain."

Dinah put a hand on her arm. "I may not have your romantic side, but I too thought we'd be able to put that letter in her hand. I'm very sorry it didn't go as you'd dreamed. I wish you could have given Thomas his happy ending."

"I'm only sorry for Thomas and Clara, not myself." Penny pulled the letter from her pocket. "I didn't want this one to die. I wonder if he lived near here too. Can you imagine? The two of them probably strolled these perfect streets. Just look around us. It's like a fairy tale. The trees, the homes. I picture Thomas and Clara as a handsome couple. Young and in love. And now they'll never be together again."

"You've read his letters. You know they quarreled. Perhaps you've imagined it better than it truly was. He could have been a bad man, or old and after a young thing with a fortune."

"I suppose we'll never know now." She looked back once more at the Finley home. "I don't think Thomas is a bad man. It's strange though. Why would someone with all this head west?"

"Open land. A fresh start," Dinah said. "Maybe he liked new places like your father did. Or perhaps he wasn't from this part of town. He could have been someone who worked in her home. Or perhaps their parents didn't approve of their relationship, so he left. It could be he was trying to do the right thing and found it was harder than he thought it'd be."

"A difference in financial standing is not enough to justify ending a loving union." None of this was right. The story didn't add up, but she could think of no way to unravel it. "I don't think that was it at all. I think it was something different. I just don't know what." She swallowed, trying to fight the lump in her throat. "It doesn't matter now anyway. Clara can never go to him." The weight of her own words pressed against her. Her chest pounded beneath the pressure as she looked away. "Poor Thomas. This loss will be such a blow to him."

Dinah put a hand behind Penny's elbow. "We better head back now."

Penny didn't want to. She wanted to keep her feet planted on Alexandria soil until she had made peace with it all. Then perhaps she could close the book on Thomas and Clara. But the mystery would stay just that—a mystery. "I'm sorry you came all this way and we didn't even deliver the letter."

"Don't be. It was a lovely idea."

—

Penny sat up in her bed and lit a candle. "Honey, are you awake?"

Honey's hairy face poked above the side of the bed. Her dark eyes glistened in the candlelight. Penny moved toward her and scratched her ears. Her fingers combed through the dog's long fur.

"She's dead," Penny whispered. A tear trickled down her face, landing on her nightdress. "Clara's dead, Dinah has a beau she doesn't know if she loves, and soon I'll be Uncle Clyde's prisoner. Nothing is right."

A soft whimper came from Honey. Penny cooed at her. "Don't you be sad too. One of us has to be brave. Somehow it'll be right again, won't it? Father told me if I leapt when I felt compelled to leap, my feet would land on solid ground." She kissed Honey's head. "But how does one know where to leap or how to leap? I'd go anywhere, if I only knew where."

Dear, sweet Honeysuckle did not answer, so Penny sent her questions heavenward, pleading silently for some sort of divine intervention. There had to be a solution. Softly, she whispered her heart's desires, her woes, and her heartaches.

For several minutes, she mulled the situation over. But when no immediate answers came, she crossed the floor, sat at her rickety desk, and composed a letter to Thomas. Someone had to tell him about Clara's death. And though it tore her heart to do so, she knew he deserved to know the truth.

Dear Thomas,

Providence has placed your letters to Clara into my hands. I work in the dead letter office in Washington, DC. It's a crowded office full of boxes, bins, and letters. I'd paint you a beautiful picture of it with my words, but in truth, it's a rather dull building. A large room lined with desks and overcrowded with lost mail. Sometimes the oddest and most bizarre things come through the mail, but normally we receive letters. Thousands and thousands of letters pass through our hands. Yours fell into mine.

When I read your words, I made it my mission to place

them in Clara's hands. I wanted her to know you ached for her. I wanted it so badly that I went all the way to Alexandria. I stood on her doorstep, only to learn a tragic accident had taken your Clara's life. I do not wish to be the bearer of such news. I only write it now because I know you yearn for her and life has lost many of its charms without her beside you. I hope knowing she will neither write nor come to you will at least allow you to gently close that door and perhaps someday open another. I hope with time you will carve a new path for your life and have a bright future.

I too have suffered loss. Not the loss of a beau, as I've never had one to lose, but the loss of a parent. I know the emptiness when you awake and realize the one you wish to see is not anywhere within reach. I know the feeling of wanting to be near someone you hold dear and not being able to. I ache for my father in that way. The hurt is real. The anguish is deep. I am sorry for your pain.

I hope your new home is a place where joy can find its way back into your life. My father firmly believed that if we are here on this earth, then we still have work to do. He believed we have a purpose even when we cannot see it. He was full of wisdom, and though at times I've struggled to heed his words, I do believe them. You ought to as well. Before my father passed, I promised him I'd go on with my life and find joy and purpose. I want those things and I hope you do too. I hope you find not only the work you are here to accomplish but also the joy you are here to experience.

Know someone out there is praying for you.

Your friend in loss

Penny almost wrote her name but stopped herself. She knew the rules at the dead letter office. Already she'd broken one of them by taking a letter outside the building. Writing Thomas about the contents of his letters was another offense. He couldn't know she was the one who had written him. She folded the letter and tucked it away. Somehow she would track down Thomas's address and mail it to him.

My exquisite Julianna,

*I miss the sweet smell of your hair. I long for the touch
of your lips. You are like the first flower of spring, radiant
and vibrant. My eyes want to drink you in. The love I have
for you seeps from me. It oozes and gushes all for you.*

Penny rolled her eyes.

"Why did Roland save me this one? I only wanted him to save
ones from Thomas. Although I doubt there will ever be another
from him. I plan to mail my letter as soon as I can figure out
where the old Dawson place is. Once he knows about Clara,
he'll have no reason to write." Penny shook the letter she was
holding. "I don't want this one."

Dinah leaned away from her desk. "You've always wanted
the love letters. I'm sure Roland thought you'd like that one.
The prose is . . . descriptive."

"This may as well be a letter from a debt collector. It's equally
appealing to me." Penny sank back in her chair.

"You've always found them entertaining."

"I suppose Thomas's letters have ruined all others for me.
I know I must tell him about Clara, but it does make me a

bit blue knowing I'll likely never read his words again." She tapped her fingers on the desk. "I liked having something to look forward to."

"You mean, besides moving in with Uncle Clyde."

"You're horrible. You know I'm dreading it."

Dinah leaned closer. "Perhaps a few more letters from Thomas will come through before he receives yours. He seems to write often."

"I hope so. I keep hoping his new farm will be a fresh start for him. I'd love to read a letter that is optimistic before they stop altogether. Otherwise, I'll always wonder what happened to him." Penny let out a terse laugh. "I'm not sure why I care so much."

"If he doesn't write, that could be a good sign too. Maybe he's begun courting someone new. Or lost himself to his farming."

"Or it could mean he is not well and is so distraught he doesn't know how to go on." Penny groaned. "I want to know so badly."

"You said he sounded more hopeful in his last letter and he's settling down." Dinah fanned the letters she was holding in the air. "I have to get back to this stack of mail. I have one with one thousand dollars in it. That's my largest sum yet. It's bound for a college I've never even heard of. I think it'll be a day of querying for me. And you have to get the illustrious Julianna her letter."

"Exquisite."

Dinah laughed. "Pardon me. Exquisite Julianna. How did he close the letter?"

"'My heart and soul belong to no other. Yours both day and night, Percy.'" Penny laughed. "I bet Percy uses too much wax on his mustache and always has food stuck in his teeth."

"Perhaps Julianna likes mustache wax." Dinah giggled.

"If that is the case, I better get his letter to her."

Once she had sent Percy's letter to Julianna, Penny stole away to the resources room and found a map of the routes west.

"Need help?" Roland stood beside her. "I have to look at the maps too."

"I'm trying to find a town on the routes in farm country out west. I don't know too much, only that the man lives on a piece of land formerly owned by a Dawson family." Penny pushed her hair out of her face. "I also know it's far enough west that wagon trains pass through, though not frequently."

"You looking for where that Thomas fellow lives?"

"I need to get a letter to him." Penny shuffled her feet back and forth on the tile floor. "It's important."

"What else do you know?"

"That's all." Penny scrunched up her face in thought. "Actually, it's not. I do know the town has a yellow boardinghouse and a man named Abraham owns the town's store. But there are no registries that list the color of buildings."

He tipped his head and grunted. "Maybe someday there will be a registry for paint colors. If it's a small town, there won't be many stores. You could look up registered businesses. If you find an Abraham who owns a store and a boardinghouse listed, you might have found the right place. I suppose then you could contact the land office and see if there was a recent sale of property by a Dawson." Roland pushed up his spectacles. Then he reached around her. "Excuse me. I need a map of South Carolina."

Penny stepped aside. "Roland, you're a genius. I'm going to find him now!"

"It wasn't so hard." He leaned in close to his map and studied the fine print. "It's our job."

"I'm very grateful," she said and then began her research of registered businesses near railroad lines. Three hours and two telegrams later, Penny finally pointed to a dot on the map and practically shouted, "Azure Springs, Iowa!"

———

Penny pushed open the door to the apartment. "Honey. Mother."

"Penelope," a deep voice came in response.

Penny jerked her head toward the sound. "Uncle Clyde?" His wrinkled face looked older and sterner than when she had last seen him. "I . . . I didn't know you were coming."

"Stop gaping." He turned to her mother. "You were right, Florence, she'll need to work on her conduct. Even her posture could use improvement." Uncle Clyde faced her again and his scrutinizing eyes roamed over her. "I was here on business and thought I'd see for myself the deplorable conditions of your life." He picked up a chipped teacup and turned it around in his hand. "I can't move you and your belongings today. But in a week, perhaps two, I'll send a driver. You will need to be ready then. I know it's sudden."

"A week?" she managed to say. Penny looked past her scowling uncle to her mother. "I can't—"

"It'll be lovely. Clyde's going to have dresses made for us. No one will know we lived in rags." Florence looked near tears. "All this will be nothing more than a distant memory. We're saved. We're so grateful. Aren't we, Penny?"

She managed a small smile.

"I've spoken to a dress shop. Pick out something fashionable. Once you're settled." He took a step closer. "Get rid of all these clothes before you come. You'll have no need of them. Once you're settled in with me, we'll complete your wardrobe."

"It's very kind of you." She blinked quickly, her hands moving to her waist. Nothing she owned was fashionable, but she'd worked hard to clothe and provide for herself and her mother. Was she to pretend these years of toil and self-preservation didn't matter? Was this to be her life—always putting on a facade? Acting the part of the wealthy niece? "I have my job here—"

"Give them your notice. You needn't work any longer. I'd prefer you don't mention it. No one need know."

"What am I to tell them?" She felt the frustration rising up within her. "Are you ashamed that I worked or are you ashamed that you did nothing to help us all those years?"

"Enough. Watch your tongue, girl."

"She didn't mean it. It's all just so sudden." Florence put a hand on Penny's arm.

Uncle Clyde let out a big breath of air. "You'll be ready when the driver comes. You'll dress and behave like a proper lady. I've already made arrangements for Horace Stedman to meet you. He's eager to find a second wife."

"Horace?" Penny's head began to spin. Honey stepped beside her and nudged Penny with her head. "Who is he?"

"It doesn't matter!" Florence stepped near her brother. "Clyde, if you've made the arrangements, she'll be delighted. She's just tired from working so hard. I'm sure once she's settled and rested, she'll be more agreeable. I'll talk to her. We'll put this part of her to rest."

Clyde patted his sister's hand. "I'll let you manage her. It'll be good having you in Philadelphia." Then he spoke to Penny. "I'm leaving now. Be ready when the driver comes."

Penny said nothing. She only watched as he grabbed his hat and walked out the door.

"Oh, Penny." Florence crossed the floor to her. "Only a few days and we can leave this wretched place. And you don't have to ever go back to the letters." She clasped her hands together. "And a suitor. I never thought we'd be so blessed."

Penny bit her lip. She wasn't ready for this. Not for any of it. "Mother? What if I don't want to dine with Horace or pretend I never worked for a living? What if I don't care about my posture? Or putting this part of me to rest? I like that I know how to work. I'm proud that I can speak my mind. Uncle Clyde's house is . . . it's not a place I want to live. I've dreamed of something more."

Florence pursed her lips. "Don't let your foolish ideals keep you from seizing this gift. Your Uncle Clyde is saving us. The least you can do is don a pretty dress and let the men court you."

Penny fought the hot tears that tried to escape. "But Mother . . . I'll never be my own person living like that."

"Nonsense!" Florence snapped. "You'll be important again. You're too impulsive. You need a man beside you. Uncle Clyde, with his connections, will help you find the right sort."

Penny winced. *Impulsive.* Perhaps her mother was right. But wasn't it up to Penny to behave as she wished? Honey whined beside her. "I'm going to take Honey outside. She needs to go out and I need to think."

"Don't be a selfish child. The world's being handed to you. Think about that while you walk your ridiculous dog." Florence stomped away from her.

"She's not ridiculous," Penny muttered under her breath as she went to the door and stepped from the small apartment out into the evening light.

The pair did not go far—just to the side of the building, where she sat. Penny slouched with her back against the wall and through the gap in the buildings looked up at the darkening sky. A plume of smoke from a nearby factory blurred her view, making it impossible to know the color the sky truly was.

"I wonder what the sky looks like in Azure Springs. Do you think Thomas can see more of it than we can?"

Honey tilted her head but didn't make a sound. The dark mop of hair on her head fell from side to side.

"Do you remember Father?" Penny ran her fingers through the dog's hair. "He used to take life in his own hands and mold it into what he wanted." She tried to picture her father's face. His dark hair and square chin. His dimpled smile. "What would he do? Would he tell me to be impulsive? Submit to Mother and Clyde? Marry Horace?"

Honey opened her mouth wide and yawned.

"I don't know what he'd do either." Penny leaned down and kissed the dog's nose. Then they sat in restless silence.

When she finally crept back into the darkened apartment, she penned the pain she felt.

Dear Thomas,

I am hurting tonight. I find I am trapped in a world I don't belong in. I am not who I once was, yet I don't know who I am to become. I feel like a wanderer with no idea of where to go. I don't know why, but I believe if you were here you would understand. You left Alexandria and went west. You made a big, bold decision. Were you brave or were you afraid and running? I don't think I am brave, but I do feel like running.

Penny stopped writing. In despair, she crumpled up the paper and threw it on the ground. But then something happened. Her heart started beating faster. It pounded in her chest. The fog she'd felt since hearing Uncle Clyde's plans for her dissipated.

"Honey, what if we ran away from all this? Just for a while. We could take all the money I've been saving and go see something new. We'd come back, of course, but . . . we could see something else first." Honey scratched at her ear with her hind leg, then settled into a sleeping heap.

"We could go somewhere different than this stifling city." She stood and paced in silence, wondering where she could go. Her whole life was here, but the world was bigger than DC.

"We could go to Azure Springs. We could see Thomas and the old Dawson place. We could smell the wheat and see the yellow boardinghouse. Father always loved leaving the city behind. Perhaps, away from the chaos of life here, I could think more clearly. I was saving for the unexpected, but I won't need it at Clyde's. And if I came back to work, I could save up again." She stepped toward the dog. "Am I a fool to consider it?"

Honey leapt up and barked and jumped excitedly. "You feel it, don't you?" She knelt down and put her arms around her large, furry friend. "We have to do something. Why not this?"

When Honey continued to bark and prance in a circle, she shushed her. "Not so loud. Soon, though, we'll be away from the city and you can yap and bark all you wish. And I'll look up at the sky and see stars."

*I*s your mother upset?" Dinah asked as they walked together.

"She's not speaking to me," Penny said. "I don't know what to do about it. When I told her I was going to go to Azure Springs so I could have some time to figure out what was next for me, she yelled and accused me again of not caring."

"I'm sure you'll be glad to be free of her."

Penny shook her head. "No. She's my mother. If I had my way, we'd be making plans together. I hate leaving her like this, but when I kneel beside my bed each night, I feel nothing but peace about going. I wish she could understand. Leaving would be easier if I knew I had her blessing."

"I'll miss you." Dinah looped her arm through Penny's. "You've been a good daughter to her and you're not leaving her with nothing. She chose to go to Clyde's and you've made a choice too. There's no shame in that."

"If she never forgives me and refuses to let me join her at Uncle Clyde's when I return, I'll go back to work. Mr. Douglas promised me my job back if I choose to take it. I was surprised when he conceded. I think it helped that Roland was in the same room. He interjected a comment about my high return rates."

"I'm glad you've a plan."

Penny laughed. This was hardly a plan. "My mother called me impulsive, and I suppose she's right, but I'm not so flighty that I'd go without having options for myself when I return."

"If you do end up working again, I'm not sure I'll be there."

"What do you mean?" Penny asked.

"I'm going to marry Lucas—that is the leap I'm going to take. We only just decided. We're going to marry in secret."

Penny pressed her lips together while she fought to form the right words. "If you're convinced it's the right course for you, then I'm happy for you. Will you write me?"

"I'll tell you everything." Dinah and Penny embraced again as tears streamed down both their faces. When they parted, Dinah pulled something from her pocket. "I've something for you. Roland found more letters from Thomas. One is addressed to the clerk who wrote him. Roland read it and decided you must have been the one who wrote Thomas. The other is to Clara and must have been written before your letter to him had arrived. Perhaps they are God's way of saying it's right to go."

Penny took the letters slowly, almost reverently. "Thank you." She pressed them to her chest. "It wasn't an accident that his letters found me. I need a place away from all this where I can decide my future. I believe Azure Springs is the right place to leap to. In time, I hope I understand why."

"I know it is," Dinah said, wiping the tears from her face. "But I'll miss you desperately."

⁓

"Goodbye, Mother." Penny looked out the train window toward the spot where her mother should have been. Only an empty platform met her eyes. "I love you," she whispered.

94

When the train left and she could no longer see the familiar station, she settled into her seat and fought off the tears that kept trying to escape. Rather than despair over her lonely departure, she began to read.

Dear Clara,

I've settled into the old Dawson home. It's two stories, with a big front porch that looks toward the gentle hills that are my land. It's more room than I need and quieter than anywhere I've ever lived, but in many ways it feels more like a home than I've ever known. I spend most every hour of the day working in the dirt. I stop often and breathe the fresh air, filling my lungs with it and gaining strength and life from it. This is all very different from my life before. Part of me feels like I'm pretending and another part of me feels like I'm finally beginning to find myself. Do you think it is possible for a man my age to finally understand himself? Can a grown man turn and go down a different road, or is it too late?

I've a neighbor who tells me when I fail, he will buy the old Dawson place. The smile on his face does not fool me. I know he's fueled by greed. Little does he know if he'd just sat back and waited, the deed would have likely been on the market again. But his words awakened in me that old desire to conquer whatever stands in my way. Only this time, I'm determined to use that desire for good. I hope to at least. And farming this land is a good pursuit. I know it. This work is different from anything I've ever done, but the seeds are growing.

I only wish ambition alone was enough to fix all my problems. Perhaps my stubbornness creates my trials. The only thing I truly know is the sun sets and rises day after day. And though there is a pattern, it is not the same day. When the sun rises, it is a new day and there is no going back. I cannot undo what happened in Alexandria. I cannot reverse the path of the sun. I cannot go back.

When the sun sets and I can no longer plow my fields, I find the errors of my past creeping into my mind again. I've tried to quiet the voice by reading. I've read all the books Abraham at the store sold me. I've read many of them twice. I now know them so well they do not distract me the way I need them to, so I've opened my Bible. I grew up listening to verses. But now, as a man reading it not out of subjection but out of free will, I find there is more to it than I had believed. Perhaps I'll find my peace yet, as I hope you've found yours.

> *Forgive me if you can,*
> *Thomas*

After she had read the letter twice, the train finally lurched forward. Her stomach lurched with it. She tried to forget about all she was leaving behind and where she was going. She also tried not to worry about Honey in the cargo car.

In her hands she held the first letter she'd ever received. So often she'd imagined tearing open a seal and devouring words written just for her. She turned the letter over in her hand. The seal had been torn by Roland, and it was not personally addressed to her, but still, it was written by Thomas and intended for her.

> *To my friend at the dead letter office,*
> *I confess I never knew what became of letters that were*

lost. I suppose I thought they simply disappeared. Since they do not, I am glad they found their way to your hands. My heart feels alive knowing you'd go to look for Clara, someone who is a stranger to you. Your sacrifice is a testament of goodness, and one I will not soon forget. I am sorry she was not there for you to find and deliver the letters to. You've no idea how sorry I am. So many things sadden my heart. I take solace in the prayers you've offered on my behalf, though I fear the grief will never fully leave me. I've never had someone pray for me before. I thank you for that gift. You spoke of the loss of your father. I could feel your pain and I wish I could ease it. He sounds like he was a man of wisdom. I believe he was right that we must keep seeking purpose and joy. I can attest to the difficulty of doing so. But both purpose and joy are out there. We must seize them when and where we can. There is so much we cannot control. So many mistakes, so much pain. But we can keep living. I've vowed to try.

Azure Springs is quickly becoming my home. I am finding myself here in this strange little town that feels like a haven for the lost and weary. Don't worry yourself over me. I am moving forward one step at a time.

> *With warm regards,*
> *Thomas Conner*

Penny tipped her head back against the soft seat and closed her eyes. He had written to her. He had stepped away from his farm and all the demands on his time and written to her. The train bumped along the rickety track, and as it went, the only world she had known shrank until it was far behind her.

*H*ugh took a long, slow drink from the ladle. "It's gonna be a warm summer. I can feel it in the air."

"I've never minded the heat before. In fact, I was always glad when it didn't rain. I have a feeling I'll see this summer differently from all the rest." Thomas pulled another bucket of water up from the well. "I'm beginning to see a great many things differently." A hawk sailed across the sky. Thomas's eyes followed it as it flew over his property and toward the neighboring land. "You know much about Jeb Danbury?"

"Of course I do. I've known him since we were boys." Hugh put down the ladle. "Jeb was the boy in school who could earn good marks without doing an ounce of work. He has a way of getting whatever he wants without earning it. His parents died and left him the biggest farm in the county. Once he got that, he went and got the girl we'd all been dreaming about since we were children. Someday things'll catch up to him. A man can't frequent the saloon as often as he does and not have something fall apart in his world."

Thomas felt a sinking sensation in the pit of his stomach. He too had excelled in school. When he was a boy, his teachers and parents often called him "naturally talented" and "brilliant." Being labeled as such had been both a blessing and a curse. The constant praise during his childhood had only made him want more of it as he grew up and became an adult. He'd acquired his father's shipping company, but even that hadn't been enough. He'd forced it to grow—bigger than necessary—at the expense of his neighbors, his friends. And then there had been Clara.

He shook his head. "I think Jeb wants my farm."

"I could've told you that." Hugh slapped Thomas's shoulder. "We were all hoping a good man would buy it. Jeb was so puffed up walking around town telling us all how he was going to buy up every farm that failed until he owned all of Azure Springs. Too much power in the hands of Jeb Danbury wouldn't be good for any of us."

"Most days I see him ride by. He slows as he passes. There's something wicked about the way he looks at the place." Thomas picked up his spade. "I don't know a thing about farming, but I know this. I'm not going down without a fight."

"Looks like you've got a little fire back in you."

"I've never been good at losing. The truth is, I'm not so different from Jeb, or at least the old me wasn't so different. I know all about wanting more." Thomas rolled the spade handle back and forth in his hand. "I aim to work hard. I think that might be my one trait worth keeping. But the greed from before— I'm done with that. I want to be satisfied with what I have." Thomas looked out at his fields of waving grasses. "I figure if I want something different, I have to go about it differently."

"Something different?" Hugh said.

Thomas paused a few moments before answering. "I'm not sure what exactly. Once, when I was in the store, Abraham's twin daughters ran in. One of them had fallen in the street and had tears in her eyes. She didn't see me standing in the corner. She saw her father and only him. She ran into his arms and I watched as her sorrow left her just from being near him. And one time I saw Margaret take leftover food to the man who had lost his house because of debts. He's living in a tent at the edge of town. She didn't have to go. I've never seen acts like those before. I lived in a world apart from such thoughtful gestures. I don't fully understand it, but I think I'd like to fill my life with a bit more of it, whatever *it* is. Kindness, purpose."

"I'd say you're a different man than Jeb. He don't care a thing about how people look at him. Not even his wife. He's no good for her." Hugh's voice was tense. "Anyway, you ever gonna tell us why you left? What really brought you west?"

"The appetite I had back then grew too big. It was consuming everything around me. I was dying too, though I didn't know it. I had to get away. I tried to run as far as I could and ended up here. You know the rest."

"Nothing wrong with a fresh start."

"I suppose that's what this is. It's hard to start over, though, when the past is still there. Even putting all these miles between myself and what I left behind hasn't set it right, not completely. Sometimes it feels like I could have a future here. Other times I feel like a man hiding out. Waiting for something. I don't know what. Just biding my time."

"At least you're keeping busy." Hugh reached into his saddlebag and brought out his lunch. "I meant to ask, what was in that letter I brought out to you a couple weeks back? Was it from your girl?"

Thomas thought back. It had been well over a week now since that letter had come. Thomas had been surprised when Hugh handed it to him. And then that night when he had opened it with shaking hands and read the words of a stranger, his heart had been touched.

"It wasn't from who you're thinking of. It was just someone concerned for me." He looked down at the brown earth. "I don't actually know who it was from."

"Hmm."

"I was surprised by it." Thomas had read the letter and then immediately written back. He wished the sender had included her name and address so he could have written her directly. As it was, he'd had to send his return letter to the office of dead letters in hopes it would get to the proper hands.

"Always nice getting mail." Hugh took a bite of his biscuit.

"I don't have much experience with receiving friendly correspondence, but I think you're right."

When Hugh left, Thomas retrieved the letter from his bedroom and reread it for no other reason than that the ink on the paper eased his loneliness.

> . . . I hope your new home is a place where joy can find its way back into your life. My father firmly believed that if we are here on this earth, then we still have work to do. He believed we have a purpose even when we cannot see it. He was full of wisdom, and though at times I've struggled to heed his words, I do believe them. You ought to as well. Before my father passed, I promised him I'd go on with my life and find joy and purpose. I want those things and I hope you do too. I hope you find not only the work you are here to accomplish but also the joy you are here to experience.
>
> Know someone out there is praying for you.
>
> Your friend in loss

Who was this good person who was praying for him? Who was this selfless, caring woman? All he could do was hope his return letter had made it and she knew how grateful he was. No. That wasn't all he could do. He could wake up each morning and offer the same goodness to others he'd been offered in this letter and by the strange new friends he'd met in Azure Springs.

*A*braham waved from the store. "You needing anything? I'm about to wire an order. It's
going to be quite the shipment."

The proprietor's twin daughters stood beside him. They
leaned into each other and giggled. They did an awful lot of
that whenever they saw Thomas. He wasn't sure if he should
be flattered or if he had food on his face he didn't know about.

Taking his hat from his head, he bowed in their direction,
which sent them into another fit of giggles. Their laughter was
infectious and he found himself smiling in return. "Ladies."

"Mr. Conner, we heard you bought a house and are fixing it
all up because you got a lady coming," one of the curly haired
twins said, her head bobbing up and down as she spoke. "I bet
she's beautiful. Does she have dark hair, or is it light like the
wheat? Oh, I can hardly wait to meet her. I bet she's from the
big city and has fine manners and wears ball gowns when she
goes about town."

"Mae." Abraham's normally slow, easy voice was stern.
"Enough. Those are not things for you to ask."

"I'm sorry, Papa." Mae's cheeks flushed red. "I was only

hoping to hear what she looked like. I'm sorry I wasn't more polite."

Thomas knew Abraham wasn't like his own father, but he couldn't help remembering the many times he'd been rebuked in public. The way his father had spoken and belittled him had been more painful than any physical beating.

"Well, Mae," Thomas said, "if a girl shows up in town for me, you'll be the first to know."

Mae's face brightened. "And Milly?" she asked, pointing to her sister. "Can we tell her too? She's as eager to meet her as I am."

"Of course. I'll be sure the Howell twins are part of the welcoming party."

"We love parties. We could use the social hall and decorate it." Mae grabbed her sister's hand. "It'd be so much fun. We could get the Ladies' Aid Society to bake and the schoolchildren could decorate."

Thomas rubbed his callused hands together. "Let's not get ahead of ourselves. I'm sure things like decorations can be decided on later."

"Girls." Abraham got their attention. "Best run along."

"We have to go help Mama," Milly said. "But we're both looking forward to meeting your girl when she comes. Goodbye, Mr. Conner."

"Good day to you both," he said before turning his attention to their father. "I hope they aren't disappointed when no one shows up for me."

"I think rumors are going 'round because of all the letters you send. This town loves a good story. Anything to keep life interesting." Abraham opened his order forms. "What can I get you?"

Thomas glanced around the store. "I know my kitchen is running low, but I don't need to order anything. Your store is always well stocked. I could use a book on animal husbandry. Don't tell anyone I'm ordering that though."

Abraham nodded. "I haven't told anyone about the farming books or the cooking books. I respect a man's secrets."

"I appreciate it." He patted his stomach. "I really ought to make more time for those cooking books. At the rate I'm going, I'll never get fat off the land."

Abraham let out a jolly laugh. "It's not the land that makes you fat. It's a wife who knows how to cook and always makes a bit too much. That's my Abigail. She's a fine hand in the kitchen."

"We better hope your daughters are right and there's a lady headed my way." Thomas picked up a can of peaches. "Otherwise, I'm likely to die out there and require only a narrow grave. Farming is hard enough, but working on nothing but poorly made biscuits and beans makes it twice as hard. It's all more work than I'd imagined."

"Most things worth doing are. Jeb says you're late getting your seed in." Abraham flipped through a catalog, then pointed. "Here's a book on animals. I should have it here in a couple weeks at the most." He looked up then. "If you're needing help, let us know. John Polson was in the other day. He said his fields are in. He might be able to come help for a day or so. There are others too. Some of the young men are hiring out. If you have a little money to invest now, a good harvest will make it all worth it in the end."

"Hugh has come over a few days, even though I've told him he doesn't need to. His land needs him."

"I've seen his place. That soil is the worst in the county.

Knowing Hugh, he'll make something out of it. That man's got spirit and heart."

"That he does. You hear of someone needing a few days' work, send them out to my place." Thomas gathered up his few supplies. "I know I missed the last social. Hugh tried to talk me into going, but the truth is, I was too worn out to make my way into town. Hugh said another is coming up." He looked at the floor and rubbed the back of his neck. "I wasn't planning to go, but that might be a time I could make some arrangements for help. If I don't get all my seed in soon, it'll be too late. From what I've read, I might already be too late. I'd like to avoid a smug look from Jeb if I can." Thomas's head jerked up. "I'm sorry. I shouldn't have said that."

"No need to apologize. I wish I could make excuses for Jeb, but I think you're probably right. I keep hoping he'll change his ways. I'm not one to give up on a man, but he's not likely to change before the harvest." Abraham's eyes took on a solemn, faraway look. "He's certainly not the man he could be. I wish he were."

Thomas could only imagine that this doting father was thinking of his oldest daughter . . . the one saddled with Jeb. And then Thomas thought of Clara's father and regrets crept in once again.

"I'm sorry," Abraham said when he spoke again. "Friday night's the town social. You'll want to be there. Everyone comes. All the young men from the whole area will be there, so I'm sure you'll be able to secure some labor. Besides, the women always fix a fine meal." Abraham wrote down a few notes while he spoke. "I've been hearing a whole lot of whispering about the man who bought the old Dawson place. I'd say at least the womenfolk are anxious to know you better. The social would be a good way to quiet their wagging tongues."

Thomas grumbled. "I'm not sure I need a bunch of women-folk after me. I'll see if I can pull myself away from my fields, but it's the food and the laborers I'll be after. I'm only now learning to live this kind of life. I can't bring someone else into it."

Penny's body lurched in the seat as the train came to a stop. Using the back of her hand, she wiped at the corners of her mouth and hoped she was able to erase any evidence of the nap she'd taken.

"Azure Springs. Azure Springs." The conductor walked up and down the aisle announcing the destination.

Grasping the seal of the window, she leaned toward it. Then with a combination of apprehension and eagerness, she peered out. A dull brown platform with a single ticket booth met her eyes. Her heart raced. She was here. This was it. What now?

"This is Azure Springs. Isn't it your stop?" the conductor asked as he stopped beside her.

Penny nodded. But she didn't rise. Suddenly, she doubted what she'd been so certain of.

"You have family here?"

She shook her head.

Why am I here? She couldn't seem to remember. Telling the man she had traveled here on a whim hardly seemed an adequate reply.

"The train won't be stopped here long. It's just unloading and loading." He leaned against one of the seats, arms folded across his chest. "Do you need some help? Are you waiting because your bag is heavy?"

"No. It's not that. I'm quite capable." She wrapped her fingers around the handle of her carpetbag. "I'm just nervous."

"You meeting someone?" His eyes wandered up and down her body. She squirmed under his gaze. "You aren't one of them mail-order brides, are you? We had a few of those a month or so back who were headed even farther west. They weren't too pretty, but they were nervous too." He continued to study her. "I'd say you're too easy on the eyes to be some stranger's bride. Naw, it can't be that. You don't look like someone who would have to traipse across the country just to land yourself a man."

She rose then. "I'm taking some time away . . . for myself. That's all." None of this had anything to do with a man. Of course it didn't. Did it?

The man's eyebrows came together. "Some time for yourself? In Azure Springs? It's not much of a destination city."

She forced a smile, knowing she was going to have to think of a better explanation—and soon. It wouldn't do to have everyone in town look at her the way this man was.

Pushing past him, she made for the door. "Thank you for telling me what stop it was."

"My pleasure. Enjoy your *time*."

He might as well have been laughing. His words, his tone, the sparkle in his eyes. He thought she was foolish. She straightened her shoulders and faced the door, reminding herself that what he or anyone else thought wasn't important. But what had she been thinking? How did she end up here? She stepped from the train with a knot in the middle of her stomach.

She clutched the handle of her bag and searched for someone to ask directions. "Can you tell me where I can find a boarding-house?" she asked the man in the single ticket booth.

He set down the stack of papers he was holding. "Hello, miss. Welcome to Azure Springs."

"Thank you."

"Nice thing about Azure Springs is there isn't much to it. Directions are easy to give. Go on down Main Street and look for the only bright yeller building there is. That's Margaret's place. We also got us a hotel. But if you aim to stay for a while, I'd suggest Margaret's. She's a mighty fine cook, and if I were picking a place to stay, food would be what I'd be after." He wiped a handkerchief across his bald head. "Besides, Pete over at the hotel isn't much of a gentleman and nearly everyone who stays there ends up going to Margaret's dining hall for dinner anyway."

"You are a fountain of knowledge." Before she could step away, his voice started up again.

"I'm sure she's got rooms open. I know Thomas Conner moved out, and I think the Rushmores fixed up their place and are gone too. 'Course, you don't know none of them. Or maybe you do. It ain't none of my business what you're doing in these parts." He drummed his fingers on his desk. "What are you doing in these parts?"

"No, I don't know them. I'm just . . . I'm here to, um . . ." Her roaming eyes stopped on the pencil behind the man's ear. "I'm here to write." She felt beads of sweat creeping down her forehead as she stumbled over the rest of her story. "I needed to get away and work on my novel. I thought I'd find a quaint little town to enjoy some peace and quiet in while I wrote. Azure Springs sounded like the perfect place. Don't you think *azure* is a lovely word? Sky blue. People ought to use it more, don't you think?" She paused and looked around. Yellows and greens, brown. Those were the colors of the little town. "Though I haven't seen anything azure here yet. Aside from the sky. I'm sorry, I'm rambling." She tried to calm her racing heart. "And, well, I wanted to make sure I could accurately describe a small town. I'm from the big city, so, well, I have little experience with country living." She was out of breath, so she stopped talking and waited. Would he call her bluff?

"Miss," a voice called from behind her, "we've unloaded your dog. Do you want us to bring her to you?"

"Oh, yes."

The man in the ticket booth leaned forward and looked toward the train. "Well, ain't that something. We get all sorts through here. Mostly just passing through on their way west. It's mighty fine to have someone come to our town because they want to. And look at that dog. I ain't never seen an animal so hairy as that one."

Penny straightened a little. "She's due for a trimming, but I assure you she's very tame."

"I meant no offense."

"None taken. I forget she's so unusual. To me she's simply the most beautiful dog in the world."

A strange noise escaped from the ticket man. Penny wasn't sure if it was a laugh or a grunt. She didn't spend much time trying to decipher it and instead bent down and put her arms around Honey.

"So, you picked us off the map?" The ticket man whistled low. "Imagine that. We'll have to ask Abraham at the store to order in some of your books. Everyone will be wanting a copy. I can't wait to tell my wife. She's always reading something. She's educated." He looked ready to burst with pride when he spoke of her. "Four whole years of schooling. I got three myself. Together that makes seven years."

"Oh," Penny said, trying to hide her surprise. "I too love to read. I'm sure we'll have a lot in common."

The man looked past her. "Sorry, miss. Someone else is waiting."

"Of course." She moved to the side. "I'm sorry to take up so much of your time. Thank you for the directions."

He smiled a big, toothy smile. "What is your name? I'll be wanting to tell the missus."

"Penelope Ercanbeck."

"Welcome to town, Miss Penelope Ercanbeck. Welcome to Azure Springs."

"Thank you, sir." She led Honey down the street and into the town she'd imagined so often in recent weeks. "Come on, girl. It may not look like much, but it's not DC. We're free. Let's have an adventure."

*P*enny spotted the boardinghouse easily enough. The yellow building was brighter and more vibrant than she ever could have imagined. It stood out among the other dull brown buildings. The door was red and rich and welcoming.

She quickened her pace but stopped when she heard, "Are you new here?"

Turning, she saw two girls approaching. They were identical. Each round-cheeked with curls framing her face. "Yes. I only just arrived."

The two girls leaned in toward each other. Penny could pick up only a few of their whispered words. "You ask." "No." "I think it's her."

Penny cleared her throat. Both girls looked up at her. One took a little step toward her and asked, "Have you come to see Thomas? Are you the girl he's sweet on?"

Penny balked. No words came.

The one on the right had asked the question, but they both looked equally anxious for her reply. When she remained silent, one of them spoke. "You must be surprising him. We saw him not long ago and he didn't tell us you'd be here yet."

"He would have told us otherwise." The girl on the left clasped her hands together. "I knew you'd come. I wish we'd known. We would have decorated and had a whole welcoming party waiting for you."

Who were these girls? And was it *her* Thomas they were referring to? It was all so puzzling.

"I've come to write . . . a novel," she said. "I'm glad to be here, but I don't know what you're referring to."

Their bright expressions dimmed a little. The girl on the left spoke up. "I was sure you were Thomas's girl. We knew his girl would be beautiful, and you are. He writes letters to a woman who lives far away." She frowned. "He told us he'd tell us if she ever came here."

The other girl reached over and dug her fingers into Honey's long coat. "Your dog is the oddest-looking dog I've ever seen."

"Don't say that. It's not polite," the other sister said while glaring in her twin's direction.

"It's all right. Let me introduce you to Honeysuckle." Penny told the dog to sit. "This is my dearest friend, Honey. That's what I call her for short. I've had her since she was a puppy. We thought she was an ordinary poodle, but once her hair started growing we knew otherwise. I even have it cut, but it just keeps growing back. Sometimes I sit beside her and put little braids in it. My mother always insists I take them out before anyone sees her."

"I think she'd look nice with braids," one of the girls said.

"Someday perhaps you can sit and braid her hair." Penny patted the dog's head. "You've met Honey. Will you tell me your names?"

"I'm Mae Howell," said the more assertive sister on the right, "and that's Milly. What's your name?"

"Penelope Ercanbeck, but everyone calls me Penny." She kept her eyes on the dog. "Tell me about Thomas. Is he a friend?"

"He's a handsome newcomer to our town. He's living on a farm now, so we don't see him much. He's all alone at the old Dawson place. I don't think I'd like living alone. I think he'll be happier when his lady gets here."

"He's expecting a visitor?" Penny kept her voice level.

"I think so."

"We aren't certain," Milly said with a bit of a bashful look on her face.

Mae took over again. "Papa says we are presumptuous and shouldn't spread rumors about things we know nothing about. But I don't think it's a rumor. I've seen him go to the post office from my window. I know he's mailing letters. Even Georgiana from school said he mails letters to a woman, so it's not a rumor. Her pa's the postman. He's not supposed to talk about the mail, but he does anyway and then she tells us." Mae turned to Milly and asked, "Do you remember her name?"

"I think it was Catherine or Cora. Something like that," Milly answered. "I hope she comes soon."

Penny smiled down at them. "You certainly are observant. Do you watch everyone so closely?"

"We live in that house over there." The girl pointed toward a perfectly groomed two-story house. "Papa owns the store. Between us watching from our windows and spending time at the store, we usually know what's happening. But not much ever happens in Azure Springs. Except when Em came, but that was a long time ago. I can't wait to tell the girls from school about you and Honey. They'll be jealous we saw you first."

"I'm not sure I'm much to talk about. But I'm flattered." She felt more at home knowing these two little locals. Their eager,

114

welcoming ways were infectious. Even in a primitive place such as this it seemed that children were still much the same—full of sunshine and excitement. "What errand am I keeping you from?"

"We were on our way to the store. Mama wants us to tell Papa she needs brown sugar, wheat, and something else." Mae turned to Milly. "What else were we supposed to tell him?"

"Ink. She wants to write to Grandma Howell about Eliza." Milly sighed. "I wish she had married someone else. We never see her now. I thought since Jeb was so handsome she'd be happy, but she just frowns and tells us to mind our own business."

Penny couldn't follow the conversation. She didn't know who Eliza and Jeb were. And she certainly didn't understand the rush to write Grandma Howell. "You best run along and deliver your message. I'd hate to keep you from it."

"Mama gets worried if we take too long. I'll tell her we've an author in town and that's what kept us." The girls started away from her. "You will have to come and eat with us sometime. Mama's a great cook and loves visitors. It was lovely meeting you, even if you aren't Thomas's girl. If his girl never comes, maybe he'd court you."

"It was lovely meeting you too," Penny said. Honey barked. "I look forward to meeting Thomas."

The girls waved as they frolicked away.

Penny laughed to herself as she watched their brown curls bouncing behind them. When they disappeared into the general store, she again turned and faced the yellow building. Yellow was an expensive paint color. She'd learned that from an especially dull letter from a painter to his father. If she hadn't read Thomas's letters, she'd have been completely stunned to see such a building in this tiny town. But it was real and she was here.

Penny knocked, and then mere seconds later the door flew open. There before her stood a tall woman in a bright blue dress trimmed in yellow. Her brown hair was curly and wild, but her face was soft and full of life.

"Well, aren't you a pretty thing?" The woman stood with her hands on her hips. "I'm Margaret Anders. Tell me why you're standing on my doorstep."

Penny stood gaping, her feet planted firmly like the roots of a tree.

The woman winked and Penny felt the blood pulsing in her limbs once again. Margaret reached out and grasped Penny's hand, pulling her and Honey inside. "My, my, look at this dog." She moved her gaze to Penny. "And you—such dark hair and green eyes. My goodness. Let me guess, you're here to meet someone?"

"No."

"Even if you're not, I've a whole list of fine folks for you to meet. Don't you always feel more settled in a place when you know a few friendly faces? Makes you feel less like a stranger."

"Yes. I suppose. I've met the Howell twins so far and the ticket man. They've all been very welcoming. I haven't traveled much. I'm new at being . . . new," she said lamely as she pulled on Honey's leash, urging the dog closer to her side.

"That's a good start. Those twins are mighty well connected for being only nine. Stick by them and you'll know the whole town before the week's through. How long you here for? You are here to rent a room, aren't you? And the dog, will it be staying?"

"I'm staying, if you've a room. My dog too, if you don't mind. I should have had her hair trimmed before coming. She's a good dog even if she doesn't look it."

"She'll draw some attention, that's for sure. If you'll keep an eye on her, then she can stay. Tell me, though, are you planning to be here a good long while?"

Penny struggled to find an answer. "I'm not completely sure. Two or three weeks. Less . . . more. It's hard to say."

"That's fine by me. Two or three weeks is long enough. I'll have time to introduce you to everyone, and who knows, maybe we can even convince you to stay." Margaret smirked as though she had a secret. "The men in this town are going to be thrilled to have you here. There's a social Friday night. That'll give you two days to recover from your journey before you stay up way too late dancing. I'll get anything washed and pressed you need. I'm hardly a lady's maid, but I can help you with your hair too if you wish. It'll be good fun getting you ready." Margaret reached a finger up and twisted it around one of her wild curls and winked. "I do my own every day."

"Oh. It's very . . . nice."

Margaret filled the air with a deep, rolling laugh. "It's wild. Don't you worry though. I take more time on other people's. I gave up on my curls long ago. They are what some people like to call disobedient. I've been called a good many things. Between my hair and the color of this house, everyone seems to think I've lost a few of the screws in my upstairs."

"That's not very kind."

"I don't mind. I don't really want to blend in with the town. That'd be a bit dull. Tell me, are you the type who wants to dress and act exactly how you're told to? If you are, that's fine. Best to know now, though, so I can watch what I say around you."

Penny shook her head. "I don't know. To be honest, I don't know where I fit in this world."

Margaret pulled her farther into the house. "I think you

and I will get on just fine. I've never known exactly where I fit either. It's a wonderful way to be. Only one who matters is the Lord, and he has a way of getting you where you need to go if you're willing to listen."

If only it were so simple. "Sometimes not knowing is not an option. One cannot simply meander through life never making a decision." ·

"I suppose decisions are part of life, but while you're here, there'll be no worrying about fitting in." Margaret shrugged. "Come to the social and you'll see. We all dine and dance together."

"I'm not sure I should be going to the town social. I'd feel like an intruder. I'm only here temporarily."

"Nonsense. Of course you should come. Everyone will love having a new partner to dance with. We're mighty close to even numbers, but often the men still outnumber the ladies, which works out fine for me. Besides, I don't cook that night. Even I need a night away from the kitchen. The way I see it, you'll have to come." She nudged Penny with her elbow. "We've got a few eligible men. You aren't married, are you?"

Penny pointed to herself. "Me? No."

"Good! Things have been a little slow around here lately. I could use a little fun in my life again." She put a finger to her chin. "Maybe a little matchmaking will liven things up."

Penny wrinkled her brow. "No. I'm not—"

"Don't you worry. I won't let just anyone have you. I only make good matches." She patted Penny's arm. "You can trust me."

"I suppose I should thank you." She giggled despite herself. "I'm not willing to marry just anyone. But I didn't come looking for a match. In fact, I left a scheming mother and uncle back home."

"Most people who find a good match find one when they are not looking. They tend to sneak up on you. Although, I've known of a match or two that were made by clever friends." She motioned toward the stairs. "Come along. Bring your dog too and I'll show you around. Don't worry too much about my teasing ways. I'm just having a bit of fun." She began climbing the stairs. "I had a man staying here while he waited for a wagon. He was determined to go as far west as possible. But in the end, he bought up land here. He's a mighty fine fellow. I simply delighted in teasing the poor man."

"How do you know he's a fine fellow?"

Margaret turned and gave her a quizzical look. For a moment Penny feared she had given herself away.

"I'm a good judge of people," Margaret said as she continued up the stairs. "And with Thomas, I could just tell. That's his name, Thomas Conner. Room's been open since."

Penny followed in silence, but within she quivered with excitement just knowing she was going to walk where *he* had walked. And then there she was in the little room. She wasn't sure what she'd expected to find. Truly, it was an ordinary room. It contained a bed with a brightly colored quilt, a washbasin, and a little desk. Her eyes paused at the desk. He'd written to Clara from that very spot. Absently, she walked to it. She touched the smooth wood and looked out the window and admired the same view he must have gazed upon.

"Will this suit you?"

"It's perfect."

"You let me know if you need anything. I take care of meals and board, but I've also been known to offer a good listening ear. Sometimes I think that's why the good Lord's left me here. I get the pleasure of feeding a houseful every night and listening to the life stories of the friends who stay under this roof."

"I'd like to sit and talk with you." Penny didn't turn from the window. "I would very much love to be considered one of your friends."

"When you're ready, come and we'll share a cup of tea, or better yet, a thick slice of buttered bread. And then we'll really get to know each other. For now, you just get settled."

When Penny turned around, Margaret was gone.

———

By her second morning in Azure Springs, Penny found herself already wondering how she ought to fill her time. The idea of being aimless and free had seemed more appealing prior to her arrival. She found herself longing for something engaging to do, a plan to work toward, something. Anything.

"What do you think Father would do?" Penny asked Honey as they walked down the street for the fourth time. "I think he'd tell me to enjoy myself. Or to have an adventure. But how does one go about that?"

A few blocks from the boardinghouse was the edge of town. Penny took the leash off Honey and let her run and play while she sat with paper in hand and attempted to write a rousing letter about her travels.

Dear Dinah,

I'm here in Azure Springs. It's a charming enough little town. I've walked the main street and the side streets many times. I'm grateful for Honey beside me. She draws attention, though, with her long hair. Everyone stops and asks about her and then they ask about me. I should see if the town's barber would cut her matted coat. That would fill an afternoon and allow me to blend in at least somewhat better. Plus, her ridiculously long hair carries along with it dirt and grass. And if she decides she must jump into a creek, then she is nothing but the filthiest creature to ever walk this earth. Luckily, Margaret has a giant washtub set up behind her house, but I've seen her jaw set firmly when Honey's tracked mud into her boardinghouse. I must break Honey of her newfound love of mud and water. I fear my beloved four-footed friend may become a bit of a menace.

I believe I have wasted enough of my page space on Honey. I must tell you about two charming twin girls I met when I had just arrived in town. They stopped me before I'd even reached the boardinghouse and peppered me with questions. They were certain I was Thomas Conner's lady. Can you imagine that? I wonder, though, if he does have a lady. What if he is one of those wicked men who has a woman in several different places? Since arriving, I've had far too much time to think, and lately I've been creating the most absurd ideas about the man. I picture him old one moment and the next he's a terrible drunk. What I hope, though, is that he is neither old nor drunk. I try to remind myself that I did not come to this town only to meet Thomas Conner. I came because I needed a place to think and this place was good enough. But I'm anxious to get a look at him. I wonder if we've passed each other on the street and I've just not known it was him.

Oh dear. Honey just ran off to who-knows-where in pursuit of a bird. Mother always said Honey was not meant to be kept in small places, but here may be a bit too large.

I shall go traipsing after the disobedient animal in a moment. First, I must tell you of the atrocious tale I've told. Upon arrival, I was practically interrogated about my reasons for coming to this quaint little town and somehow my wagging tongue declared I was here to write a book. I am now known throughout town as an aspiring author. I could write about my exciting life as a reader of other people's mail and the consequences of forgetting that all that mail was not intended for me. Do you think such a book would sell?

Write me when you can. I'm at the boardinghouse. There's only one. I desperately want to know if you are married. And if you are, I want to know what it is like to make vows with a man.

> *Wishing I had my friend*
> *beside me,*
> *Penny*

She folded the letter and slid it in her pocket. Then she stood, lifted her skirts a few inches, and went stomping through the golden field, yelling for Honey.

"You looking for that hairy dog?" a large man with a scruffy beard asked from atop his horse. "I've never seen a dog like that before. You know, there's no law against trimming a dog's hair."

"When I become acquainted with the barber, I'll see if he can oblige." Penny put a hand above her eyes to block the sun and pointed. "She went that way chasing a bird. I'm afraid she's not used to so much freedom. And I'm not used to keeping this close a watch on her."

The man slid off the horse's back. "I'll help you. I saw her as I rode toward town. She wasn't too far away."

"Thank you. I'm sure you're busy." She stopped worrying about her dog for a brief moment and looked at this helpful stranger. He was handsome in an unkempt way. For a moment she wondered if he could be Thomas. But Thomas wasn't a rugged man. He was a city man. A bark a fair distance away pulled her attention back toward her present predicament.

The man approached her, leading his horse behind him. "It'll be faster on horseback."

She looked at his impressive gray mare. "All right."

Then, before she could speak again, he reached for her waist, and the next thing she knew, she was up on top of the horse and sitting in the saddle. Only a moment later he was behind her. She sat up straight and stiff. "I must warn you, though, this horse has a mind of her own."

She braced herself. "I used to ride. I'll manage."

His arm came around her waist. She felt the air leave her lungs. It had been a very long time since she'd been so close to a man. The last time had been . . . years ago when she used to attend dances.

"Tell me where you're from while we ride." His breath warmed the back of her neck and a chill raced through her. "If you wish to, that is."

Did she hear a quaver in his voice? Was he uncomfortable too?

"I'm from DC, but my mother just moved north of there to Philadelphia to live with her brother, so I suppose that is my home now. Or most likely will be shortly." She paused, trying to relax enough so that she could breathe. "I have some decisions to make."

"You're from DC?"

"Yes."

"Hmm."

She looked over her shoulder to see his face so she could understand what he meant by that. "Do you know someone from there?" Then she laughed. "I suppose that's a silly question. Azure Springs is so far from there."

"It is far." He pointed then. "Oh, look." She felt him shake with laughter. "Isn't that your fur ball?"

Honey was rolling on her back in the mud. She barked when they got closer. It was her excited, happy bark, the one Penny normally loved to hear. This time it only made her want to tan Honey's hide.

"Honey!" Penny shouted. "Get over here."

The man stopped his horse and helped her slide down from the saddle. "Do you need help?"

"No. I've a leash. I'll walk her back and see if Margaret will let me clean her with the wash water again." Penny groaned. "This will be her second bath of the day."

"Margaret has a sense of humor. I think she'll forgive you."

"Do you know her well?" Penny asked while trying to step as carefully as possible into the mud. With one hand she held up her skirts and with the other she reached for her filthy dog. "Stay," she said to Honey as she approached. "Stay there. I'm coming."

"I lived at Margaret's for several weeks before I bought the old Dawson—"

"What?" Penny turned quickly—too quickly—and lost her footing, slipping into the mud and landing on her backside. Honey ran to her, barking and yapping. She planted her front paws on Penny's chest, pushing her flat on her back in the mud.

124

For a moment, Penny did not move. With her eyes squeezed tightly shut, she simply lay there, refusing to face the embarrassment. If she waited long enough, maybe he would go away and she could meet him some other time, in some other way.

When the ridiculousness of the situation dawned on her, she opened her eyes a crack, only to find him standing above her with his hand out. "Help up?"

"What's your name?" Penny asked from her bed of mud. "Who are you?"

"Name's Thomas Conner."

She pulled a muddy hand up from the ground and placed it in his outstretched one. "Penelope Ercanbeck," she said while watching the mud drip from their hands. She pushed her hair out of her face with her other hand, then pulled herself to standing. This man, this was her Thomas. She put a muddy hand to her heart and pressed against it. Gawking at him in mud-soaked clothes would do no good. It would only add to her humiliation. "I best get back. It appears my dog isn't the only one who needs bathing." She tried to stand tall and proud, but everything in her wanted to collapse into a pile of mush and shame.

"Do you want me to walk you back?" He looked as though he was fighting to keep a straight face.

"No. I've already taken up too much of your time." She wiped her hands on her dress, but there was no getting rid of the mud. "I do appreciate you helping me."

She yanked on Honey's leash, urging her toward the boardinghouse. Then, with as much dignity as she could muster, Penny raced away from Thomas, all the while knowing that now she had one more shocking tale to write to Dinah about. How would she phrase it?

I met a handsome man while I sat bathing in the mud, only to learn the man was the Thomas Conner I have dreamed so many nights of meeting.

Or perhaps something more specific and honest would be appropriate.

I have officially humiliated myself. If I had ever been foolish enough to imagine that Thomas Conner could think me charming, I have dashed that dream to pieces. I now know Thomas Conner will never see me as anything but a clumsy girl.

I've walked the streets but haven't noticed the post office," Penny said when she came down the stairs of the boardinghouse, her hair braided but still damp from being scrubbed, and walked into the kitchen.

"We do have one. It's not its own building though. It's the other half of the land office." Margaret pointed down the street. "It's that way. The sign for it is very small. No doubt that's why you missed it."

"Thank you."

"I'm glad you've someone to write to." Margaret stirred a giant pot of soup.

"It's a friend. We used to work together. She will enjoy hearing about Honey's mischief."

"Have you any family to write to?"

Penny knew from a previous conversation that Margaret was a mother. She'd told her about a daughter named Scarlett who was married and living several towns away. "Did you ever feel like you and your daughter were very different?"

"Of course I did. And we are. She's skittish and bashful. Two traits I've never been able to claim." Margaret's eyes twinkled as she spoke. "I sometimes wonder how it is I created a child so wholly different from myself."

Penny fiddled with the letter to Dinah that she held in her hand. "I feel very different from my mother too. When I left, we were barely speaking to each other. She didn't approve of this trip." Her shoulders drooped. "It's been years since we've agreed on much of anything. I hated leaving her that way."

"I'm sorry to hear it." Margaret added more salt to the pot. "I hope that's not always the case. But it may be. You still ought to write her. A mother's heart is always warmed by news of her children's good fortune. You've been smiling since you came, so I'd say things are going well enough for you."

"I suppose it wouldn't hurt to tell her I'm safe. I'm not sure she'd care for the particulars, as she despises mud and Honey."

"Even a small note is better than nothing. Then you'll know you've tried. Does your mother want what is best for you?" Margaret stirred her soup with a large wooden spoon.

"In a way, I believe she does. But I don't think she knows who I am well enough to know what's best for me. She only knows what she had dreamed of for me when I was little, before life changed and I changed."

"So, you've run away because you don't agree with her?"

Penny pushed a stray hair from her face. "That was part of it. I didn't run exactly." She looked down at her boots. "Leaving was more than me being an angry child trying to get away. I assure you of that. I plan to face my problems, but first I needed some space so I could decide which cage to accept when I return. It's complicated."

"Cage? You've come with more troubles than I believed when I first met you." Margaret looked up from her cooking. "Picking a cage sounds frightful."

"It is." Penny moved toward the door. "But I vowed to think of pleasant things while I'm away. At least as often as I can."

"It's a nice day for a walk. That's always a fine way to think of pleasant things. Enjoy yourself and don't rush back."

"I will. Come, Honey," Penny called. The dog didn't rise from her spot near the cooking stove. Instead, she lifted her head and then turned it away from Penny. "Come."

"She can stay with me if you'd like."

Penny stared at the dog. "Behave," she said in her firmest voice. Then to Margaret she said, "Thank you."

Once her letter was posted, she again found herself with nothing pressing to do. To fill her time, she stepped inside the town store with the intention of buying paper. If she were to write a book, she would need something to write upon. The prospect of writing did excite a desire within her that she hadn't known before.

"You must be the author," the man behind the counter said. "My daughters devour everything they can get their hands on. I'll wire an order today if you'll tell me the titles of your books."

"I'm not actually published yet. I'm more of an aspiring author." Her eyes roamed over the shelf of books behind the man. Their gold lettering and smooth spines were enticing, and the idea of a story she'd written sitting among them made her heart race. "Big dreams and all that."

"We all begin as dreamers." His voice was slow and kind. "When your book is in print, I'll make a display for it. What can I help you find?"

"I'm looking for paper and ink. I didn't bring nearly enough with me." She looked around the store. "I see it. I can fetch it."

At the stationery display, she ran her hands over the smooth paper. Every day at the dead letter office she'd touched paper, smelled it. She'd devoured the written word. And now she would write. The dream was new, but the seed was already sprouting.

The bell above the door jingled. A man approached the counter. From the corner of her eye, she saw him. A small groan escaped her lips. It was Thomas! She lowered her head and pretended to busy herself with the paper.

"I went to make a biscuit last night and the book said I needed baking powder. I didn't have any, so I went ahead and made them without it." He smiled as he spoke. It was evident these two were on friendly terms.

"It didn't go so well, did it?" the man asked.

Both men laughed. The man behind the counter was older, with plump cheeks, a slow, easy voice, and a ready smile. She surveyed Thomas's tall frame and dark hair, which hung in his face as he shifted his weight from side to side. Underneath a beard and mustache in desperate need of a trim was a smile more reserved than the man's behind the counter. But small as it was, she couldn't take her eyes off of it.

"You've got to come to the social. It will be a welcome change," the older man said. "I don't know how you're managing out there. A light, soft biscuit will do you a world of good."

"After last night, any reservations I had about coming have faded. I'll be there, and if you come looking for me, just follow the scent of food. I'll be eating more than my share. Besides, I'm still needing that farm help." He reached for a tin of baking powder and placed it on the counter. "You suppose I'll have better luck with my next batch? I'm liable to lose a tooth if I keep eating the rocks I made last night."

Eavesdropping was not something Penny normally did. Well, that wasn't entirely true. She never listened in on conversations, but she was forever reading mail that was not hers. This wasn't so diffcrent. And this was Thomas. He may never be able to look her in the face without picturing her sprawled out in the mud, but she wanted to see him and hear him and know him so badly that she couldn't turn away.

"I think that's all I need," Thomas said. "Actually, I'll grab a bit of paper. I'm also about out of ink."

Panic seized her. She looked to her left and her right. There was nowhere to run and no place to hide. She pivoted and there he was, only feet away from her. She jumped and the stack of paper she was holding leapt from her arms. The thin sheets floated in the air before scattering across the floor.

She groaned.

Bending quickly, she began gathering the papers. Heat rose to her face. *This is not happening. It can't be.* Her eyes darted to the door. She could push past him and run back to Margaret's, but that would only add to her list of humiliations. There was no undoing the situation.

"Let me help you." Thomas closed the distance between them.

"I can manage." She stood quickly, knocking into the stationery table and shaking its contents to the floor. "Oh! How clumsy!"

He laughed. Not a menacing laugh but a good-natured one. Penny's eyes found his.

"The dog," he said.

She grimaced. "That was me. I've had a run of misfortunes today."

"I thought you handled your fall in the mud quite gracefully."

Penny pointed toward the mess of papers. "And this? Was this graceful as well?"

His eyes twinkled, and despite her present predicament she smiled at him.

"I'll help you clean it up," he offered again.

The older man approached. "It's not the first time something's been knocked over. We'll set it right. No harm done."

"If anything is broken, I'll pay. I'm so sorry." She grabbed large handfuls of paper and put the sheets on the table. "I'm not sure why I'm so clumsy today."

Moments that felt much too long passed before the floor was clear of debris.

When at last Penny stood, she looked at the table she'd bumped. The display wasn't nearly as aesthetic as it had been before, but she felt better knowing she wasn't leaving a pile on the ground.

"Thomas, I'd like you to meet the town's own budding author." The older gentleman nodded at her. Then to her, he said, "I'm Abraham Howell. I own this store. You let me know if you need anything while you're in town and I'll find a way to get it here. I didn't catch your name earlier."

"Penelope." Her voice came out as a mere squeak. She cleared her throat. "Penelope Ercanbeck, but most everyone calls me Penny. Except my mother." Mustering the smidgen of courage she had left, she held out her hand first to Abraham and then to Thomas. "It's a pleasure to properly meet you both."

Thomas took her hand. She could feel the roughness of his palm against her skin. "It was a pleasure meeting you. I'm pretty new here myself. I suppose you could call me a budding farmer." Underneath his unruly beard, she saw what could only be described as an amused smile. "I'm glad you've come to town. Now there's someone in town newer than me. Maybe the gossip will shift."

"If I continue to swim in the mud and throw things around in the store, I think it's safe to assume the wagging tongues will be busy keeping up with me." Penny tried not to stare, but despite her best efforts her eyes lingered on him. His eyes, his face. All of him was real. This was the man she'd prayed for. The man she'd thought about and wondered over. The man whose loss she'd felt so deeply. He wasn't an old codger, and he didn't look like a drunk or a villain. He was young, mid- to late twenties perhaps, with so much future ahead of him.

Only when the bell above the door rang did she pull her gaze away. She focused then on the space beside him. Where Clara should have been. Would he smile broader if she were there, standing near him? That thought sent a stray tear running down her face. This poor man. How his heart must ache.

"The paper didn't matter. No one minds." Thomas took a step toward Abraham. "Did we say something wrong?"

"No," she answered in as calm a voice as she could muster. "I must have gotten something in my eye when I was crawling around on the floor." She pulled a handkerchief from her pocket and wiped at the traitorous tear. "A bit of dust, I think. Oh, I didn't mean to be rude. Your store is not dirty. It's my fault." She bit her lip and forced her breath to come slower. "It's a pleasure meeting both of you."

"How long you planning on staying?" Abraham asked before she could leave.

She fidgeted with the worn piece of lace that adorned the cuff of her sleeve. "Three weeks. Or maybe two. It depends."

"Depends?"

"It depends . . . on . . . on the writing. How fast it goes. I don't have a solid plan."

"It'll be right nice having you. I'm not sure if we should hope your book goes quickly or drags on. The town's buzzing with excitement having you here. In fact, my girls were convinced you'd come all this way to see Thomas. Imagine that." Abraham moved back toward the counter. "At the social, you'll have to share a dance. You must have a great deal in common. Both of you being new in town and all." He waved as he stepped away. "I've a ledger to balance. I'll let you two get better acquainted."

Thomas bent closer to her and spoke softly. "You'd think we go way back with the way he meddles. His daughters, charming things, are just as bad. Maybe worse."

"I believe I've met them already. They greeted me on my way into town," she whispered back. "They seemed disappointed by my reasons for being in Azure Springs."

"Abraham told me it's a small town with a big heart. I think it might be a small town with a big imagination." Thomas stepped out of someone's way. "I'm still getting used to it."

"I've only been here just over a day and everyone I've met wants to know everything. I'm not used to the way small towns work. In DC—"

"I'm from Alexandria." He moved closer and she felt his eyes studying her. "We lived so close, but I don't recognize you." He paused. "I wouldn't though. I . . ." His jaw flexed. "I didn't take the time to meet all the people I should have."

"Of course you didn't know me." She wished she could ask him why he seemed so upset. "DC is large and I was not social. At least I hadn't been in a long time." She smiled, hoping it would ease his tension. "But here it seems everyone knows everyone. It's very charming. Although today it might have been nice to have gone unnoticed."

He raised a brow.

"Then no one would have seen me in the mud or disrupting Abraham's displays. I do seem to find myself in the worst predicaments."

At last his face seemed relaxed again. She could see the corners of his mouth raised. "It's true. In the city, we all tried not to see one another, but even there I believe I would have noticed a woman in the mud. Tell me, how is the boardinghouse?"

"Margaret is a dear, but she's already bossing me around. I've been wrangled into going to the social. And she's doing her best to pry every secret I've got from me. I'm afraid she'll be disappointed when she realizes how terribly ordinary I am."

"I stayed there for a few weeks. I admit she crowded me." He ran a hand over his beard. "I've nothing but admiration for her though. I think she kept me from falling into a deep pit."

"A pit?"

He shook his head. "I lost my wagon and my plans were thwarted. It was hard for me to admit defeat. That and other realities of life were hard to shoulder. Life's been a cruel teacher. But Margaret refused to let me withdraw. She's pushed me to face it all." He looked past her then. "It was a difficult time. Still is. I shouldn't be telling you this. It's not like me."

Every part of Penny wanted to reach out and touch him. To offer some comfort. Never had she yearned to be someone's solace in a storm as badly as she did at this moment for this near-stranger. And yet looking at him now, he did not seem like a stranger, for already she felt she knew what was inside of him.

Instead of touching him and holding him as she longed to do, she offered only a sympathetic smile. "If her persistence and attention kept you from slipping away, I am grateful. My father always believed we should look out for one another. Margaret seems to have a knack for it."

"A wise man." He cleared his throat. "I've agreed to the social as well. I need to find men to help me with my farm. I'm told everyone will be there."

"Margaret tells me the same."

"And will you be dancing?"

Penny's eyes met his. But only for a moment. His seemed to be searching hers and she feared he could see into her very soul. "I love dancing. I've not danced in years, but there was a time when I could dance all night and never sit a number out. I didn't tire of it a bit."

"I had a time in my life like that too."

Had Clara been his partner of choice? Probably she'd been his equal in looks. She sighed. The crowds had likely parted as the two had danced around in each other's arms.

He cleared his throat. "It feels like a lifetime ago."

"You were not always a farmer?" she asked, well aware she was baiting him. Fishing for more. For everything, if she could have it.

"No, I was not. I was a very different man." He stepped aside, opening the path to the counter. "But I'm a farmer now and the land is waiting for me. I'll see you at the social."

"I'll be there."

He walked to the counter, where he paid for his goods and thanked Abraham. With the small sack in his hands, he stepped toward the door.

"Wait! Thomas, would you carry a sack of flour to Margaret?" Abraham's loud voice interrupted Thomas's departure. "I promised I'd deliver it for her but won't make it over there until after her evening meal."

Thomas pursed his lips, then nodded before taking the sack from Abraham. "I'd be happy to help. Miss Ercanbeck, would you care to walk back with me?"

"Yes. Thank you." She stepped away from the paper and ink without purchasing anything.

With the flour on his shoulder and the small sack in his hand, Thomas left the store and Penny followed. A few steps later and they were walking at an equal pace. Penny tried to focus on the street ahead, but she couldn't resist stealing a few discreet glances in his direction. There he was, walking the streets of Azure Springs beside her. It was like a dream, a fantasy. And yet it was real.

"May I carry your baking powder and other supplies?" she asked.

He handed her the little bundle and shifted the heavier one onto his other shoulder. "Thank you."

Penny took a deep breath. "It smells better here than in DC, don't you think?"

"Much better. Here it smells like wheat and tilled earth."

She laughed. "It's better than stale air. I think I could get used to it here. I've never spent much time in quaint places like this. I didn't even realize people lived with so much space around them." She reached her arms out to her sides. "I love it. It feels freer, don't you think?"

"I do. But I wasn't as quick to figure it out as you. I showed up here and felt nothing but angry that my plans had been foiled. I didn't want to stay. I suppose I might have felt that way about most any place I'd ended up in. I wasn't too eager to put down roots." Thomas looked down the street. "There I go again. Have you some magical power that loosens my tongue?"

"I suppose we will have to keep talking in order to know for certain."

"Very well. I'll tell you this. Azure Springs is a good place.

137

One of the finest I've ever set foot in. I think you'll enjoy your visit."

"You came not wanting to stay and I came wishing I could stay forever." She looked up toward the Howells' home. "The twins told me they like to watch from their windows."

"I'll have to be careful what I do when I'm in front of their home." He chuckled under his breath. "Or I could have a little fun and see if I can give them something to talk about."

Penny put a hand over her eyes in an attempt to block the sun. "I don't see them now. Or else I'd be curious to see what you'd do."

"You'll see plenty of them. They like to follow me around and ask me all sorts of questions and then giggle. They'll likely take to you the same way."

"I'm quite certain they won't giggle around me for the same reason they giggle around you." She smirked at him, then looked ahead. Her eyes and mind were trying to reconcile the man beside her with the man whose letters she'd read. An involuntary sigh escaped. He seemed to be the very best version of all she'd imagined. "I do like the twins. There's something innocent and carefree about them. They told me you've a girl on the way here." She kept her eyes looking ahead to the boardinghouse and quickened her pace. Inwardly she chided herself for mentioning a girl.

He cleared his throat. "I don't have a girl. Not like they imagine it. It's probably for the best. I'm not sure my farm is a place anyone would want to live. They've got active imaginations and I'm guilty of humoring them at times."

"What's wrong with your farm?"

"The farm itself is a fine enough place. I'm just not much of a farmer." He shifted the sack of flour again.

"Why farm, then?"

"Well, I like it out there and hope to get better with time." He stopped then. "I want to succeed. Someday I want to be more than a budding farmer. I think I do at least. I want to plant seeds and know that because of my care they are growing. I don't know how to explain it, but it's the first place where I've cared about the process. Before, I only cared about my pocketbook. I don't know that I'll farm forever, but it's a good spot for me now. There's tranquility there that I've never known before. I've needed it."

"I believe you will tame the land."

"That's just it. The land is taming me." He started walking again. "Come and see it sometime. You're from the city. You know the constant ruckus of it. Come to my land and tell me if it whispers to you the way it does to me. I may sound foolish, but it's teaching me, and whatever lessons it has for me, I'm going to learn them."

"You've no idea how much I would like to see it and to hear it." If only she could ask him to take her now. What she wouldn't give to lay eyes on the old Dawson place. Instead, she schooled her tongue and said, "For my book, of course."

Thomas shook his head as he walked away. His pants were wet. His shirt was wet. Even his shoes were wet.

He'd carried in Margaret's sack of flour. His intention had been to leave it and then go on his way. He'd already spent far longer in town than he should have. But once he had opened the door, Margaret had come running, commanding them to catch the dog and get the filthy beast cleaned up.

"I thought you said not to hurry," Penny responded.

"I didn't realize your dog was so wild!"

Penny looked at him, her green eyes pleading. "Want to help? Again?"

"Of course," he said, unable to leave her helpless. The two of them chased the muddy dog through the boardinghouse until Penny finally cornered her and threw herself on top of the dog.

"I don't think you were properly introduced to my dog. Thomas, this is Honey," she said from her spot on the floor. "She seems to think rural living means no rules."

"You get that dog cleaned up," Margaret said. "You should have told me I couldn't leave the door open."

"I didn't know." Penny's voice was full of remorse. "I've never lived by a muddy creek. I had no idea she'd run for it every second of every day."

Margaret put a hand on her forehead. "Look at the floor."

They all looked. Muddy footprints dotted the floor and little brown spots were haphazardly strewn across the wooden planks.

"You're in such trouble," Penny said to the dog. Then she looked down at her own dress and laughed. "This will be her third bath of the day. And the third dress I've soiled."

"Let me help you," Thomas said.

Together they'd taken the dog outside and cleaned the thick mud from her coat. A muddy dog and a green-eyed girl. Neither had been in his plan for the afternoon. He laughed under his breath. It had been the finest afternoon he'd spent since coming to Azure Springs. He walked away wondering why he felt what he felt. Something was different. She was different—or maybe he was different because of her presence. He felt strangely at ease around her, comfortable as though they'd shared a long and intimate history. It didn't make any sense. Perhaps it was the flush of her cheeks when she'd scattered the papers or the striking contrast of her fair skin and dark hair. Or was it the tenderness he felt when she looked at him? Her eyes were so attentive. She cared about what he said. He knew it. And then there was the way they'd laughed together as they splashed the wet and muddy dog with clean water. It had been a good day, and he'd needed a good day.

But now the farm was calling. Thomas pulled the reins off the hitching post. "Come on, girl."

The horse pulled away, fighting against his command.

"Trouble with your horse?" Jeb Danbury sneered at him from across the way. "If you can't even manage your animals, how will you ever succeed as a farmer?"

Thomas would've liked nothing more than to slug the rebellious horse and then take a swing at Jeb. Instead, he tugged harder on the reins and turned his shoulder to the man.

"I hear they're hiring on the railroads. Maybe you'd do better with a pickax," Jeb called to his back. "Or you could go back to where you came from. There might be a factory that'd take you on."

The slight slur of the man's voice told Thomas he'd been drinking. Arguing with a drunk wouldn't get him anywhere. Besides, he'd had too good a day to let a worthless excuse for a man steal that from him.

Thomas clicked his tongue and led his horse away. With his back turned, he waved a hand in the air.

*T*homas bent near the broken mirror the Dawsons had left on the wall. He ran his hands through his long hair and over the coarse beard that covered his face. For months now he'd cowered behind it.

"No more hiding," he said to the face in the mirror. Then, with dull scissors, he cut the scruff from his face and finished by sliding the edge of a razor back and forth until only the smooth skin remained.

From the bottom of his trunk, he pulled out a creased but otherwise perfectly preserved three-piece suit. Shaking it out, he felt a rush of memories. It had been tailor-made to perfectly fit the man he'd been. He pulled it on and the fabric clung to the muscles the land had awakened in him. The suit was the same, but he was different. Larger, stronger. He was changed. Inside he was not the man he'd been before either.

Once his tie was knotted, he stood back and looked at himself, struck again by both memories and realizations. He nearly tore the suit from his body, but the social meant hands for his farm and food for his stomach. It meant seeing Penny again. And he liked the idea of seeing her.

"You ready to go for a ride?" he asked his mare once he stepped into the barn.

She snorted and pranced in her stall.

In an effort to soothe her, he kept talking. "It's hay and grain for you no matter where we are. But I'm aching for something other than my cooking to eat. You wouldn't want me to starve, would you?"

The horse whinnied.

"I know. It doesn't feel right going. Like I'm cheating somehow. I ask myself if it's right for me to laugh or dance when Clara is not here dancing with me. But I can't change that, and I can't hide forever. I need men to help with the farm. Anyway, it's been too long since I've seen Margaret. And there's a newcomer who might be there. I could help her feel welcome." He lied to the horse. Welcoming her was not his motive. Dancing with her and holding her in his arms was. Was that desire so wrong?

He gently put his hand on the horse's neck, only to have her pull away. "You aren't much of a friend." He kept his voice smooth despite his growing impatience. "You think I'm wrong. That I ought to wallow in misery for the rest of my life. I read you the letter, the one from the girl at the dead letter office. If I'm still here, there's work for me to do. Maybe I will even find some joy. Would you deny me that? Would you rather I live out my days waiting to die, and nothing more?"

The animal turned toward him.

"Of course you do. You may wish that upon me, but I like the plan where I find a bit of joy. If I'm alive, there's a reason for it. Don't you think I ought to look for that reason?" He reached for a handful of grain and offered it to the mare. "It's not easy though."

He hoped with time the mare would learn to like or at least

tolerate his voice and his touch. When she finished eating, he pulled himself onto her back. "Let's go. This is our home now. I think it's best if we at least pretend to sink some roots in."

Thomas rode across the rolling hills into town, fighting the mare's stubborn nature the entire way. As a young boy, he'd learned to ride. By age eight he'd known how to move with the horse. But this mare was not willing to accept him, and so he bounced along, swaying and knocking about until at last they reached the hall.

He eagerly slid off the mare's back and tethered her to a hitching post. "You stay out of trouble and I'll do the same." He patted her neck before walking away.

The closer Thomas came to the hall, the tighter his chest became. The memories of his last dance flooded back to him. Mere months ago he'd been in Alexandria and had attended the coming out dance of a wealthy businessman's daughter.

"Clara's over there," the matron had whispered in his ear when he entered the decorated hall. "She will look lovely on your arm."

He went to her then.

"Dance with me?" he asked, and she smiled up at him with her perfect smile.

"I'd be honored."

Thomas stood outside the little Azure Springs hall, but there still was not enough air. He took a quick lap around the building to clear his head. He didn't want to think of Clara and their days of dancing. He didn't want to think of the way she had clung to his arm and followed his lead. He didn't want to hurt. Not tonight. He wanted to be a different man, a better man. He wanted to pretend he had a future.

Hugh greeted him with a pat on the back. "You came. I hardly recognized you." Then he gave him another pat. "You going in or going to spend the evening out here?"

Thomas shook his head. "No. I . . . I just haven't danced in a long time. I was just about to go in."

"No need to be nervous. The crowd's fairly friendly. I'd hoped you'd come. I had no idea you'd shave and clean up." He let out a low whistle. "It's a good thing you came. If you hadn't, the town would've started gossiping about the recluse in the old Dawson place. Trust me, you don't want the town talking."

"Come now, that wouldn't have been all bad."

Hugh shot him a crooked smile. "It looks like you nicked yourself with a razor."

Thomas touched his freshly shaven jaw.

"It won't make a difference. The ladies will be flocking to you."

Suddenly, the three-piece suit and freshly shaven face didn't seem like such a good idea. "I don't want any ladies after me." He ran his hand back and forth along his jaw. "I thought we were supposed to clean up for a dance."

His friend laughed. "We do our best to spiff up, but no one in town owns a suit that fine." He pointed toward his mostly clean shirt and loose trousers. "You look like you're headed to see the queen."

"Seems I can't win around here."

———

Penny admired the garlands and flowers that adorned the simple whitewashed walls. The arrangements were bright local flowers with heather woven between them, giving the decor the perfect touch. Such detail. Such devotion. The sight of it all, the smell of the food—her senses jumped with excitement.

A long table ran along the back wall and upon it sat mountains of food. Mouthwatering, enticing food that smelled of home and love. And then she stopped. Her hand came to her heart.

Penny thought back to years ago when she would eat with her mother and father. Their cook, Cordilla, would serve them course after course. She breathed deeply, surprised by the memories flooding back to her. Memories of food and laughter. Memories of family. Of life before her father had died and everything had changed.

"You're looking at that food as though you've never eaten before," Margaret said.

"Your food has been delicious. Truly, it has. I'm not sure what I smell, but something here tonight smells like home. It smells of better days. That sounds silly." Penny looked again at the table of food and inhaled the sweet aroma. "I was merely remembering."

"When I hear the sound of the violin, I think of my late husband, Wyatt. I think God knows we need reminders from time to time. He wraps up a little blessing in a sound or a smell. A testament of his love. That smell, that memory is a gift for just you." She reached for a molasses cookie. "He even knows how to touch my old heart. Molasses reminds me of my mother."

"I did need it tonight." She took in another deep breath, relishing the smell of the food. "I feel so out of place and confused. I'm unsure at times of why I've come here. I promised my father years ago I would enjoy life, and tonight I will do my best to feel that way."

"Chin up, then. You look stunning, and if you can peel your

eyes away from that table you'll see everyone is staring right at you."

"At me?" She touched the lace around her neckline. Why would they stare at her?

"You've chosen well with that green dress. It matches your eyes." Margaret reached over and smoothed Penny's collar. "And your black hair piled perfectly. I'd say I did a fine job with that masterpiece. You're a sight." She pushed at one of her own curls and sighed.

"Your curls are looking especially . . ." Penny thought a moment. "They look lovely. They are Margaret curls, and I don't think you'd look right with them any other way."

"You're sweet. Tonight be sure to enjoy yourself. Don't worry about the past or the future."

"I believe you're right. There will be time for my worries tomorrow. Tonight I'll dance with anyone who asks." She tapped her toe on the ground to the beat of the music. "My father would've liked to know I was twirling around on the dance floor. It's been so long."

"And your mother?"

"She'd be appalled I was dancing in a little country hall. She thinks she has a sophisticated sense of enjoyment, but I think she's rather narrow-minded. She spends far too much time worrying about which rung of the ladder we are on."

"My own mother found me rather shocking at times. Be true to yourself and have a loving heart and somehow it all will be made right. Tonight you are in Azure Springs and very few of us care about ladders. Just dance." Margaret put a gentle hand on Penny's cheek. "And don't you worry about having a partner. They'll ask!"

Thomas stepped farther into the hall and headed straight for the table of food. It was his excuse for coming, and judging by the smell he was not going to be disappointed.

"My, my, look at you. All clean-shaven." Margaret whistled at him when he approached. "You look like a new man. Penny, take a good look at him. Doesn't he look fine tonight? I've always wondered what was under that beard."

Thomas tried not to squirm as Penny's eyes quickly looked him over. Her lips curled into a smile.

"Very fine indeed," Penny said. Their eyes met for a moment and he noticed the green of them. Green like gemstones. Sparkling. Lively. Her cheeks were pink from the confession and the rosy hue only added to her charm.

"It's good seeing you up and around," Margaret said.

"Abraham said there'd be good food here." He smiled. "I know what you're about to say. And I would have come to the dining hall and eaten your cooking, but I've been busy. Between you and me"—he leaned in closer to Margaret—"my cooking leaves room for improvement. I'd have been at your table every night if my farm could have spared me."

"At least I have Penny at my table now. She even comes down without a fuss." She winked at Penny. "I had to drag him from his room morning and night just to get the man to eat. You're a dear for coming down with no complaints. He wouldn't move until I threatened to swat his backside. It was like having an ornery child around."

"I'd imagine any child would be ornery if they'd lost what Thomas has," Penny said. "I imagine it was hard."

Thomas shifted uncomfortably. "What do you mean? What do you know of my losses?"

"I heard . . . I heard you were in a wagon accident," she said in a low voice. "I heard you were bound for Montana."

Had he told her it was a wagon accident? Or of his dreams of the frontier? He couldn't recall.

"It seemed a greater loss when it happened than it does now." Thomas had to break his gaze away from the green-eyed woman. The look on her face was unnerving. Sympathy seemed to emanate from her and he wasn't sure whether he ought to step toward her and soak in the compassion or run from her. He turned toward Margaret and did all he could to keep the conversation light. "Look how much more agreeable Penny is than you. She understands the pain I was in. I think you're right, she is sweet. Perhaps she'll rub off on you."

Margaret shot Penny a conspiratorial look. "His sense of humor seems to have come through his wagon accident unscathed."

"If only I'd injured my humor and not broken my axles. I'd be settled in nowhere Montana by now," Thomas said. "And you'd have to spend your night tonight trying to get someone else riled up."

"I suppose you've a point." Margaret laughed and patted his shoulder. "We're all glad you've bought the old Dawson place. Well, all of us but Jeb. And going up and down those stairs and dragging your hide down for dinner did keep me from sitting around wasting my time. There are some benefits to your being here." Her face became serious and her eyes lost their playful sparkle. "You look much improved and I am glad to see it. How is farm life?"

He shrugged. "Lots of solitude and thinking. Abraham gave

me a Bible. I'd be lying if I said it'd done nothing to help. Truth is, I'm finding some solace in it. More than I expected. I wish I'd cared more when I was younger, but now I'm drawn to it. I even wake up some mornings eager to start my day."

"I've turned to that very book often enough when my burdens have felt too heavy for me to bear. You keep reading it. Seems every time I read it I find something new in there." She took two plates and forks from the table and put them in Penny's hand. "You two ought to eat. I see you both drooling. Then I want to see you two young people dance. I've spent enough years observing people to know sometimes the best remedy for what ails us is a night of friendly companionship. Besides, you'd make a lovely couple." Margaret waved across the hall at an older woman with a cane. "I need to go and say a few more hellos. Be good to each other."

Margaret left him then with Penny.

"She seems to think you are in need of sustenance. Can I dish you up something?" he asked. "Did they not feed you in DC?"

She handed him a plate and fork. "Not like this. Not made by the hands of the neighbors, brought together just to be shared." She reached and ran her hand over the edge of the lace tablecloth, admiring the intricate handiwork. "In recent years, I've not had food nearly as succulent as this. In my youth, we went to parties and ate very well, but the cooks were all brought together to fix the meals. The food was mouthwatering, but this . . ." She pointed to the piles of food in mismatched dishes. "I think I like this. It suits me."

"I've never thought much about where my food came from until I moved to my farm. I've been cooking on my own since then. It's been, well, I'm not sure what is the right word. *Interesting*." He scooped a slice of pie onto his plate. "I think I ought to write my former cook and thank her. I'm not sure I ever did."

"You should write to her. Letters are so powerful." Penny looked down. "I think she'd love to receive word. And if you wait . . . there's no guarantee you'll be able to send it later."

He put a hand on her arm. "You've lost someone?"

"My father is dead. Life is always changing and you adapt and then it changes all over again. You ought to write while you can." She offered a weak smile.

"I'm sorry about your father."

"It was five years ago. Circumstances changed for us. They're always changing, even now. We did our best, but my father's money was mismanaged. I found work and we carried on, but I've missed him. You don't need to listen to my problems. I'm rambling on and on."

"I thought you were an author?"

Her gut twisted like it always did when she thought of her false occupation. "I do wish to write."

"If you've a mind to share, I'd listen to your other worries. What's changing for you now?"

"Well, now I can choose. I can keep working and barely getting by or I can move to my uncle's, where I wouldn't have to worry so much about making ends meet, but I'd have to abide by all his wishes. I would simply be moving from a wooden cage to one made of expensive iron. It might look better, but it'd be just as strong. Perhaps stronger."

A dull ache pounded in his chest. He looked at her and realized the ache was for her. "I'm very sorry. I think I lived in a cage too. For me, though, it was one I created around myself."

"Tonight I feel free. I don't feel caged and I don't even want to think of the trials ahead. Margaret has instructed us to have a happy night. I think we ought to follow her advice."

"Let's do. Let's talk of other things. Like what food I can get for you. What looks best?"

"Pie! Every kind there is! But I'm not sure we're supposed to eat yet. No one else is eating."

He raised a brow. "Someone has to go first. Are you sure you want every kind?"

"Perhaps I should take one slice at a time." She stared at the pies. An easy smile played across her face and two dimples added to her loveliness. "I think I should start with apple. It's my favorite. But I don't want that one there with the flaky crust to be gone before I can try it. I don't know what it is, but it looks delicious." She put her hands on her hips. "I do wish I could try them all. I'm not sure how to pick when I don't even know what they are made of."

He stuck his fork into the pie with the flaky crust and quickly cut a thin slice. Now that the inside was exposed, he declared, "It's blueberry. Did anyone see me?"

"I don't think so. Our backs were to the crowd." She pointed to another pie. "What's that one?"

He laughed. "Stand there a little to your left and I'll find out." She took a big step, closing the gap between them. He glanced over his shoulder. "There's a woman with a sour expression not far behind you. I'm not sure she'd approve of us taking a piece from each pie."

She made a face for only him to see. "Was it like this?"

"More severe," he said as he cut a slice from another pie and put it on his plate.

She laughed. "I wish there had been someone standing in front of me when I'd fallen in the mud so you'd not seen that."

"We have found something we disagree on. I, for one, am glad no one was blocking my view. Azure Springs does not offer much by way of entertainment. That is, until you arrived."

Penny laughed again and he found himself smiling at the sound of it. "I locked Honey in my room tonight and am praying I do not return home to another catastrophe."

"If she does cause a catastrophe, will you tell me when I see you next? I've smiled more since meeting that dog than in the many months prior to her arrival." Thomas stuck his fork into the pie.

"I am glad my dog makes *you* smile." She pointed to the slice he had cut. "What flavor is it?"

"It's rhubarb with"—he moved the piece around on his plate to get a better look at the pie filling—"peach, I think. It looks rather good."

"Rhubarb and peach? I might want to try that." She looked down the length of the table. "There are several more down that way."

"If you'll be my cover, I will get a slice of each."

"Of course. But let's go slowly. We don't want anyone to realize what we're doing. I saw an old woman earlier staring at this table like it was the finest work of art. She walked over occasionally and moved a platter to the right and then to the left. I'd hate to see her face when she realizes tiny bites have been taken out of each pie."

"You don't think she'd find it amusing?"

Penny's dimples flashed. "No! She looked to me to be a very somber woman." The pair meandered down the length of the table. "Let's pretend we are deep in conversation. I think no one will suspect us then."

"Very well. Tell me, Penelope Ercanbeck, about your novel.

Perhaps it will sell so well you will be an independent woman who's free of all cages." He found his question was not a mere facade. He did want to know about her writing—and so much more. "I've never met an authoress before. And I think I'd very much like knowing one."

She pulled her gaze away and hesitated a moment. "It's a work in progress. I'm still deciding on the story line. When the thought of writing a novel first came to my mind, it seemed absurd, but then I mulled it around in my heart and now it truly has become a desire of mine." She laughed a little. "I really can't tell you much about it yet. When I get further along, I'll tell you."

"Something else, then. Tell me, why Azure Springs?"

"Would you believe me if I said I felt like I was called here?" She fidgeted with the fork in her hand. "I needed a change. Something new. Why not here?"

Without thinking, he reached out and put a hand on her arm. "I do believe you. I too needed something different."

"Have you found it?"

He paused before answering. "I will. I get closer every day. And I can think of nowhere else I'd rather find it than Azure Springs. I hope you find what you need too."

"If nothing else, I'm enjoying myself. Except that my dog will not stop jumping in the mud. The rest has been delightful."

"She's done it again?" he asked. "Since we last bathed her?"

"Yes. If I or anyone else leaves the door open so much as a crack, she bursts through it and runs straight to the creek. And not to the clear water but to the muddy banks. I don't know what to do with her. I hate to lock her up all the time." Her eyes darted from his. "Oh, let's see what that one is." She pointed to another pie. This one had a lattice crust and was oozing red. "I think it's cherry, and I love cherry almost as much as apple."

"It is cherry," he said after cutting into it. "It looks good too."

"I think I've decided. I want a slice of the peach with rhubarb and the cherry."

He took her plate. "At your service, ma'am."

Penny ate her pie slowly, savoring each bite. She scraped the final morsel from her plate and lifted it to her mouth. When the last of it was gone, she sighed. "That may have been the best pie I've ever eaten."

"I'm surprised you haven't gone back for more." Thomas smirked. "I've never seen a woman enjoy her pie so thoroughly."

"I had good manners once." She laughed. "But that was before I was kicked out of high society. Now I appreciate good food when I can get it. And if you promise not to tell, I'll whisper a secret."

"I'm intrigued. I promise." He leaned in closer.

"Here is my confession. I have very little desire to ever have manners again."

"That is a truly scandalous secret."

"My mother would be ashamed. But doesn't it seem that if life is so short, we ought to be able to enjoy a slice of pie without worrying if we are using the right fork or not?"

"A woman, or man for that matter, ought to be able to enjoy a slice of pie with their fingers if they wish. May I take your plate?" He held out his hand. Penny's only reservation was she didn't want the moment to end. The pie had been delicious but the company better. Their laughter and conversation had been so easy, so comfortable.

The moment Penny put her plate in his hand and he stepped away with it, a man approached. "A new song should be startin' up real soon. I . . . I thought you might . . . well, would ya dance with me?"

"Yes. Of course." She forced a smile. The small man before her had rosy cheeks and a bulbous nose, but his smile was kind. He held out his hand, introduced himself, and led her to the dance floor. His hand was nearly as small as her own.

"I heard you are only in town a few weeks," he said with a bit of a lisp.

"Yes. It's a charming city. I'll be sad to leave it."

"It's an all right place. I live a few miles out of town. It's pretty much just me and my animals. I got four cows, two goats. I got a bunch of chickens. One of the hens hatched some chicks, so I don't know how many I got. Maybe twenty. Or it could be a few more." He stepped on her foot. She winced but kept right on dancing. "I might lose a few chicks to hawks or rodents. But with any luck, a few of them will grow and give me eggs. Every farm needs some good, reliable layers."

They went around and around the room in much the same fashion. Dull conversation and clumsy feet. When Margaret had suggested dancing, Penny had felt a secret thrill. But if all men in Azure Springs danced like this man did, she'd never make it through the entire night. Her feet would not be able to endure the abuse and her mind would grow numb from the simple chatter.

Looking away from her partner, she watched the other couples. Most of the faces were new to her, but she was able to pick out a few familiar ones. Abraham's plump arms were around a lovely woman who must be his wife. She recognized several people from the boardinghouse dining hall. Daniel Prewitt danced with a fair-skinned redhead and Marcus Bennett with a brunette. And Eliza Danbury, Abraham's oldest daughter, who Margaret had pointed out to her but not introduced her to, was dancing with a tall, handsome man she could only assume was her husband. They were a lovely pair despite their solemn faces. Many of the other couples seemed to be having better luck with their partners than she was having. Perhaps the night would improve with time.

She scanned the room looking for Thomas, only to find him still beside the table of food. Several women were near him. The pace of her heart picked up when one of the women put her hand on Thomas's arm. She scolded herself, remembering that she had no special connections to the man. Sure, she had come to see if he was well, but he didn't know that. If she were being honest with herself, she'd be forced to admit that she had already done what she came to Azure Springs to do, at least in regard to Thomas. He was well, or at least on his way to being so. Her mind should be at peace knowing as much, but she didn't want her purpose or her trip to be over. In fact, if she had her way, she'd extend it indefinitely.

When her heart would not slow, she turned her attention back to her partner. A private tutor had coached Penny in etiquette and presentation. "Be attentive and engaged," she had instructed. Who knew those skills would be utilized in a place and time such as this? Penny counted the moles on his face while she listened to his less-than-stimulating conversation and made sure she nodded occasionally as any good conversationalist should.

"I'm so glad you bought the old Dawson farm." One of the three women who surrounded him put her hand on his arm. "You'll make it into the best farm around. I just know you will."

"I'm going to do what I can." He took a step back, freeing himself from her touch. "It's certainly not the finest farm around."

"All it will need now is a woman's touch." They all giggled.

He cleared his throat. "Well . . ."

The tallest of the three stepped forward. "I hear you have a woman you write to. But now that you've been here and seen all we have to offer, you aren't still waiting for her, are you? She let you leave after all. I can't imagine she's a very loyal woman."

"I can't rightly say." He shifted about. Were all country women so bold?

"Do you dance?"

"I do," he said, "but my leg is paining me at the moment." He slapped the side of it. "Strangest thing, it just started acting up. I hope it passes quickly."

"I've watched you about town. You don't move like you're in pain." The tall one stepped even closer to him. "I think you're being coy."

Margaret must have sensed his needs. Someday he was going to thank the woman for being there for him during his many trials. She walked up beside him and winked discreetly.

"Anna, Alene, Leah, it's lovely seeing you this evening. You've all blossomed overnight." They laughed on cue. "I believe I heard the pastor asking for volunteers to help with the children's games. I've seen you three with the youngsters before. I told him I'd come get you. You don't mind taking a turn with them, do you?"

Thomas watched as the women looked at one another.

"Well," one of them said, "I guess we could."

Another shrugged and turned to Thomas. "Mrs. Anders is right. We do love the children. We are happy to help however we can. We are always helping with something."

"That's very selfless of you." He smiled. "The children will be lucky to have you."

"I guess we'll go, then," the tallest of the three said as she took a reluctant step away. "We'll come back, though, so we can get better acquainted later. And so we can dance."

He nodded but said nothing. Only when they were well out of earshot did he speak. "Thank you. I used to be so comfortable in large groups, but I find I'm a bit unsettled tonight."

"Maybe the new you is still getting his bearings."

Now that he was free of the women, his eyes wandered to Penny.

"She's something, isn't she?" the overly presumptuous woman asked.

"Her looks are unique."

Margaret Anders rolled her eyes. "Unique. She's gorgeous. Look at her black hair and fair skin. And her curls are staying in, just like I'd hoped they would. She's more than that though. Something about her is endearing. There's a good soul inside that beautiful woman and plenty of spirit to go with it."

"I think you're right. I've been to parties with beautiful women before. There's something else about her." He leaned against the wall. "I've never met a writer before. I had no idea they'd travel so far to work on a story."

She turned and watched Penny dancing. "I'm not sure."

"You don't think she's a writer?"

Margaret watched Penny with intense eyes. "I just think there's more to her than she's told me. Something she's not ready to share yet. You run a boardinghouse long enough and you realize most people have something they keep to themselves. Hers is different though. I don't think it's a dark secret. I sense genuine goodness in her. I can feel it when I'm around her. Her secret is something else."

"I suppose we're all entitled to a few secrets."

"Secrets and heartache. We all seem to have them." She rubbed her upper arm. "I believe I said we were to talk of happy things tonight, and didn't we agree we were going to dance?"

"I believe you *told* us we were going to."

"Of course I did. Come, then." She held out her hand. "Dance with me. I love a good partner, and I can tell from the way your foot's been tapping to the music that you know your way around the dance floor. And don't you dare tell me your leg's paining you. I won't believe it. I'm not one of those young spring chicks."

"I've not danced since I left Alexandria."

"It'll do you good," she said.

Thomas took the hand of the widow woman, who had to be twice his age, and led her to the floor.

"How do you do it?" he asked as they began to move to the music. "You claim to have heartbreak in your life, and yet you are always happy."

"No, I'm not always happy. I allow myself to feel the pain too. When I need to and when I believe it will help me. Otherwise, I choose happy because I prefer it." She tilted her head toward him. "Wouldn't you rather smile than cry?"

"I would."

"Then smile. And lead us over to that green-eyed girl so that when the music stops you can dance with her through the next number. She's caught your eye. It won't hurt to find out why." Margaret grinned. "Try to pry a secret or two from her.

160

I haven't wanted to scare her off, but I'm more than curious what her story is."

"I'll do what I can." He took the older woman in his arms and began moving to the music, each step taking him closer to the intriguing Penny.

When the music stopped, Margaret patted his arm and stepped away. He was near Penny. So near he could have reached out and touched her. Instead, he waited. His breath caught in his chest as he stood in the center of the dance floor, hoping she would turn in his direction. Time moved slowly as he waited for her partner to end the dance.

And then it happened. She was without a partner. He was as well. She looked over her shoulder. A smile spread across her face. Then she turned and approached him.

"Dance with me?" He reached out a hand to her.

"Yes."

Dear Dinah,

I have danced with Thomas Conner. He is a fine-looking man. I am not prone to fainting, but when I saw him walk into the social with his freshly shaven face I very nearly did. He was handsome before, but now he's ever so much more. If propriety would have permitted me to do so, I would have reached out and touched him. You will be proud to know I did not act on that impulse. He's more than a dashing physique though. He's funny. Not in a loud way, but subtly. We shared a laugh over the pies. For the first time in a long time, I felt young again.

And later we danced. Never could I have imagined a man could be so skilled on the dance floor. I've danced with so many partners but no one has ever been like he was. I felt like the belle of the ball when I was in his arms. I may sound as though I'm exaggerating, but I'm not. The crowds parted for us. I could feel everyone's eyes on me. But then I looked into his eyes and all others were forgotten. He moved so smoothly. Every moment of the dance was one I wish I could live again and again.

I came here to see for myself how he was faring and

to have time to decide my fate. Truly, that was my intention, but I find myself wishing I would cross paths with him every day. Every moment of every day, if I could. We spoke often throughout the social. Over the food and later while I was in his arms. Our conversation was so easy, so natural. Not a bit like the conversation I shared with my other partners. I felt as though I'd known him for months, years even.

But I do sense a sadness about him. His heart, I fear, may still be wounded beyond repair. His eyes grow dark from time to time, but I believe he is seeking the light and I can't help but hope I'm here long enough to see him truly embrace it. I suppose it's only normal that the news of his lost love is hard for him to recover from. It's a blow I can only partially empathize with. I know the loss of a parent but not of a love. He fares better than I had expected, and for that I am grateful. Everything about him is better than I could have hoped for. Oh, Dinah, is it wrong that my heart flutters when I see him? All night my gaze wandered back to him. Wrong or not, I couldn't seem to stop it. When he touched me, I was certain fire would burst from within me. I am a glutton for punishment. I know I am. But it feels good to be living a life of freedom even if it's short-lived.

Azure Springs has not been disappointing. It's small and quaint but friendly. I've been welcomed by everyone from the shopkeeper to the ticket man. I feel at home here in a way I haven't felt in Washington, DC, for so long. There I feel like I don't fit in. I'm no longer wealthy, yet I'm not entirely accepted among the working class. You being the exception, of course.

At the social I watched as farmers with dirt-stained hands danced with the schoolteacher and then with the mayor's daughter. I don't doubt there are sour grapes among them—there must be. But I can feel the camaraderie. There is a warmth here that soothes my aching heart. Tell me all the news from back home.

Your dancing friend,
Penny

She folded the letter, put it into her reticule along with a brief note to her mother assuring her of her safety, and set out for the post office. Her steps were light. If no one had been around, she'd have danced her way there, the music from the night before still so fresh in her mind. The sun was shining and the air was warm and inviting. Her spirits felt lighter than they had in so very long.

I leapt, she whispered as she walked. *Father, I leapt and you were right. I feel better for it.*

"Ah, Miss Ercanbeck. What can I do for you today?" the postmaster asked when she stepped through the door.

"I've two letters to mark," she said as she pulled the letters from her reticule and placed them on the counter.

"Florence Ercanbeck? That must be your mother. And another for Dinah." He looked closely at her letters.

"You're very observant." She refused to let his prying bother her, despite the fact that she knew postal workers were not to comment on the mail that passed through their hands.

He took the letters, then looked past her toward the door. "Thomas. Another letter?"

She turned to look behind her. His eyes met hers. She thought he was going to speak to her, but he did not. The letter in his hand shook slightly as he neared the counter. *Was it Clara he had written to? Even now, after the news of her death?*

"Just the one." He held out the letter to the postmaster. Penny looked at it as discreetly as she could. Clara's name was written across the front. His penmanship as neat as always.

"Who's the gal you keep writing to?" The postmaster took the letter. "I'm not supposed to ask, but we aren't one of those big towns. Here we like knowing about one another's families and whatnot."

"A woman from Alexandria," Thomas said in a low voice. "It's nothing anyone would want to know about."

Penny fiddled with the button on the cuff of her blouse. She kept her eyes down, but her ears were alert. This didn't make any sense. Why was he writing to her?

"I haven't seen a single one come back to you. She angry or something? Seems strange to send so many letters to someone if they don't even care enough to write back. We got girls here. Why keep sending these letters?"

Thomas leaned forward and snatched the letter out of the man's hand. "You're right. I don't need to send this."

It was the first time Penny had ever heard anger in his voice. Surprising even herself, she stepped closer, wishing for a way to calm him. "Let him mail it if he wants," she said. "It's his letter and he's paying for it. It's not our business who he writes to or whether they write back. I believe you've taken an oath to deliver the mail. Honor it."

"No." Thomas crinkled the letter. "It's a waste of time and postage. It's not worth sending."

"I didn't mean nothing by what I said." The postmaster looked visibly distressed. He tried reaching for the letter, but

Thomas pulled it away. "I can mail it. I was just wonderin', that's all. I was just making conversation."

"No harm done," Thomas said through gritted teeth. "It's about time someone told me how foolish I'm being."

Penny watched as Thomas turned to leave.

She put money for the postage on the counter and followed Thomas out of the post office without waiting for her change.

"I'm sorry I said anything about your letter," she offered as she approached Thomas. "I shouldn't have pried. He should have mailed it. It wasn't right of him. I wanted to help."

"He's just being like everyone else in town. They're all curious. I can hardly blame him. I showed up out of nowhere and bought a house. Of course they think I'm odd."

"I doubt he'll ever question a customer again," she said. "He shouldn't have even asked you about it. It was wrong of him. You should be able to mail your letters or buy a house, for that matter, without anyone getting in the way."

Thomas slowed his pace, took off his hat, and brushed his hair from his face with his forearm. "When I got here, I started seeing the world a bit differently. My whole life had been about having more and being more. But when I came here . . . that didn't matter as much. One night I woke up in the middle of the night and I had this pressing memory."

"You did?" she asked when he grew quiet.

"I remembered being a boy and having my favorite aunt leave. She was the only one who spoke to me like she cared about me. She promised she'd write. I waited for days and then weeks for a letter to arrive. I knew if a letter came, it would be filled with kindness, and that wasn't something I had experienced much of. With my father and mother, it always felt like I was simply a product, something to be molded and shaped.

I was the son destined to take over their shipping empire and that was all that mattered."

"I can see why you wanted to hear from her. What happened?"

"She never did write." He looked down at the ruined letter in his hands. "I'm trying to find myself all over again. I suppose I'm trying to discover the sort of man I am for the very first time."

With his head down and shoulders stooped, he didn't speak for a long time. Penny could almost see his pain.

"Your aunt should have written." Penny's voice quavered as she spoke. "I'm sorry she didn't. Every child should feel loved."

"It was a long time ago." He straightened his shoulders a little. "I didn't think of it again for a very long time. Not until I left that world behind and came here. I decided I wanted to be the type of person who *would* write. There's so much I can't undo, so many regrets, but I thought I could at least write a few letters." A terse laugh escaped him. "It doesn't matter if the letter is sent or not. No one will ever read it."

"I think sending letters can matter a lot." *Your letters brought me here.* She longed to say the words aloud. *They touched my heart and soul.* "I like to think my letter will make my friend smile when she reads it. Surely, someone from your hometown would like to hear from you."

"If you were to go to Alexandria, you'd soon learn that not a soul misses me. I left for the West and there was not a tear shed." He shook his head. "I shouldn't be telling you all this. It's my past. I brought my problems upon myself."

Sensing his vulnerability, she reached out her hand and rested it on his arm. "We all have a story. I'll listen. And if I could, I'd share the burden. If not, at least tell me about your farm. Tell me something."

They walked together away from the post office, stopping when they were in front of the stables. He laid the letter on top of a hitching post. "It's a beautiful place. My farm is peaceful. There's a gentle rise in the land. If you walk up the path, you get just high enough that you can see miles in every direction. I go there sometimes when the sun is setting and the whole sky lights up in color. It's like a painting. It's so vibrant. I believe the good Lord took mercy on me when he landed me there." Thomas took a deep breath, then let it out slowly. "I'm behind in my planting and fully expect the harvest to be abysmal, but I'm learning from the land and the solitude. I see the world differently now. I'd never noticed the colors of the setting sun before."

"It sounds beautiful."

He leaned over and put a hand on the gray mare tied there. She moved her head away. "This animal doesn't like me."

"She's stunning. I'm hardly a horsewoman. I used to think dogs were more my expertise, though more and more I'm realizing I still have much to learn about them." She reached toward the horse and stroked her mane. "I think she's lovely. Don't you think she looks like a storm?"

"She acts like a storm too. Unpredictable and destructive," he said. "I can't seem to win her affections."

"What's her name?"

"I haven't given her one." He folded his hands across his chest. "She's just been 'the horse' to me. Sometimes I call her 'the beast' or 'the blasted animal.'"

"I think she needs a better name than that. How can you win her affections if you don't even know her? She's not going to be impressed by your good looks or big-city manners. She's not one of those young girls from the dance. No, this horse needs to trust you and know you." She leaned over the post and cooed at the mare. "Hello there. Tell me, pretty girl, what name would fit you?"

"I didn't realize you spoke horse."

"I'm only just now learning horse." She mimicked a whinny, earning her a laugh from Thomas.

"You've a gift with languages." He tried to make the noise himself, but it didn't sound a bit like a horse. "I concede you speak horse far better than I do."

"Why, thank you."

"It'd be easier if she were one of those young girls from the dance and would follow me around no matter what I did."

"My father liked to tell me life wasn't meant to be easy. He was forever saying that the best things in life require time or sacrifice. I think an animal, or a woman for that matter, ought to take a bit of effort to woo." She rested her arms on the hitching post. "This horse will come around."

"All right, then." He put a hand on Penny's shoulder. "What name seems fitting?"

Penny clasped her hands together in excitement. "I do love naming animals. When Honeysuckle was a pup, I—"

"Your dog's full name is Honeysuckle?"

"Yes. I remember thinking hard about it as I tried to pick the right name. A sweet flower seemed the perfect name for a sweet pup. I'll help you think of the perfect name for your horse too."

"Hmm. I admit I'm a bit nervous. I'm not sure I could ride around town on a horse named Darling or Sweety."

She took a step back. "Are you not fond of endearments?"

"I . . . well, I don't know. I haven't much experience." His face flushed with color. With no beard to hide it, he looked red as an apple. "Just go on and tell me what you'd name the horse. I'm sure I'll like it just fine."

"Very well. I think she looks like . . ." She paused and pretended to be thinking, but it was the color in his cheeks that had caused her to stall. Thomas was a man who blushed! "She . . . she looks like a Josephine. And one day you'll be glad she's not absently following you. I think she's a smart horse." Then to the horse she said, "You're a smart girl, aren't you? You wouldn't mind if Thomas called you Darling from time to time, would you?"

Thomas stared as the horse nuzzled Penny.

"I think she likes it, don't you?" she asked as she stroked the animal.

"Josephine? For a horse? I thought you'd suggest something like Smoky or Thunder."

"Look at her. She's practically smiling." Penny ran her hand over the soft skin on the mare's nose. "It's a good name. She really is a darling horse."

He led the mare away from the hitching post. "I admit I haven't seen her this calm the entire time I've owned her. But Josephine? Josephine, Honeysuckle. I wonder what you'll name your children someday."

Penny crossed her arms over her chest. "I'm sure my children's names will be equally fitting. Keep calling her 'the horse' if you prefer. I was just trying to help."

"Don't go getting all high and mighty on me. I'll give it a try and see if it sticks." He put his boot in the stirrup. "I hired a couple hands to come help at my place. I need to get back out there and keep them busy." He swung up into the saddle. "I'm hoping to have them work from dawn to dusk until I get my place running a bit better. They need the money and I need the help."

"It's good of you to hire them. I hope your crops aren't the failure you think they'll be."

"Thank you. I'm not sure I'll be able to go back to my own cooking after last night's feast. Perhaps I'll see you at the dining hall one of these nights." The way he said it made Penny's heart race once again. She felt almost certain he wanted to see her at the dining hall.

"I eat there every night. Usually it's just me and a bunch of dirty men. I don't think most of them have ever seen a nail brush."

He put his hands out. "I'll fit right in. Save me a spot beside you?"

"I will."

*P*enny twirled her pencil between her fingers as she stared at the blank page. *How does one go about beginning a novel?* she wondered.

An hour later, she still had nothing written.

"What should I write about?" she asked aloud to Honey, who only raised her furry head and whimpered. "I know you want to go outside, but I can't let you. You'll run right for the creek and then traipse through Margaret's house with your muddy paws."

Honey's chocolate eyes pleaded with Penny, chipping away at her resolve.

"Oh, all right. But if you get loose and go in the mud, then I might just set you free like Mother was always threatening to do." Penny folded a blank sheet of paper and put it in her pocket just in case an idea came to her. "Come along," she called to Honey, who leapt to her feet and barked excitedly.

"Trouble with your story?" Margaret asked when they came down the stairs.

"Yes." She pulled out the blank sheet of paper and showed Margaret. "I want to write something compelling. Something about love and finding happiness. Those were always my favorite books. But I don't know what to write. Or how to start."

Margaret stopped dusting. "You just need inspiration. Something to get you going. I'd imagine if you picked the right idea, it'd get easier."

Penny scrunched up her nose. "Like what?"

"You're the writer."

"I'm not much of a writer. Do blank pages but plenty of ambition qualify me as a writer?" Penny scratched Honey's neck a moment, then stepped away from the dog and looked out the window. "I simply don't know how to turn my dream into something more."

Margaret studied her a moment. "One of these days I'm hoping you explain to me how you ended up here with nothing but a new dream." She pursed her lips and Penny could tell she was debating what to say next. "I won't hassle you. I've an idea though. I saw Em Reynolds earlier. You remember her, don't you?"

"I do. I spoke with her at the social, only briefly though."

"She's anxious to know you better. Why don't I ask her to take you around the town? She could help you meet more people and maybe one of them will spark an idea."

Penny nodded. "I'd like spending the day with Em. If she's willing, I'd gladly go with her."

"You could go out on one of the country roads after your time in town. See what farm life is like. It's what we're best at around here." Margaret smiled and Penny was sure she'd seen a bit of mischief in it. "You could stop by Thomas Conner's farm. He's new at farming. I don't think he could teach you much about the planting or harvesting, but you could deliver him some food. He talks of coming to the dining hall, but even if he comes in the evening that's only one meal. The man needs three square meals in him. I worry about him." Her eyes softened. "Most of my boarders are simply part of the job, but there are some like you and Thomas who become more to me. You'd take him a basket of food for me, wouldn't you?"

"Margaret! You can't fool me. You're scheming and I see it." Penny laughed as she crossed the room toward her friend. "You get that gleam in your eyes. It practically screams mischief."

The conspiring woman laughed. "I am scheming! I admit it. And you, dear girl, are loving it. I saw the way your eyes followed him at the social. You couldn't stop watching him, and I can hardly blame you. He's a fine-looking man. I'm merely giving you another chance to enjoy the Azure Springs scenery."

"He spoke of you with such admiration. I wonder if his sentiments would be as fond if he knew you were working behind his back."

Margaret reached up and dusted the top of the mantel. "I think he's come to trust me. In fact, I think he believes I have his best interests at heart. And I do now, just as I always have. I'm thinking of his stomach." She winked. "Do you want the man to go hungry?"

"If it's his stomach at stake, then I'll help." She pointed a finger at Margaret. "But don't go getting any other ideas."

"Oh, Penny, life would be too dull then." Margaret smiled. "I hope you find your inspiration."

Penny turned toward the door, eager for fresh air and anxious to pursue whatever inspiration she could. Only when she turned did she realize Honey was not there beside her.

"Honey!" she said. Then louder, she yelled, "Honeysuckle!"

A bark sounded in response. It came from the kitchen.

"No! No! No!" Penny ran from the front room. She'd just been stroking her head. How could she have gotten away?

"I told you to keep an eye on that animal." Margaret trailed Penny from the front room to the kitchen.

After she stepped into the kitchen, Penny stood completely still. Her feet would not move. Her mouth was ajar. The scene before her was too awful, too horribly awful for her to even know what to do.

"Stop that!" Margaret called to Honey. "Penny, stop standing there like a fool and get your dog away from the meat."

Penny jerked back to reality, raced to Honey, and grabbed her collar to pull her away from the roast she was devouring. "I'm so sorry," she whispered as she dragged the dog past Margaret. "I don't know what's gotten into her."

"I run a boardinghouse with rules and order." Margaret's voice was steady. "I gave your dog a chance, but between her leaving mud all over the floor and now eating the evening meal, I have to tell you she cannot stay."

"I understand. I'm so sorry." Penny's head was down as she spoke. She could already feel tears stinging her eyes.

"Chin up, girl, and hear me out. I like Honey as well as the next person. She's a dog full of life and personality, and that hair is something else. But I'd never be able to keep this place running if I didn't have a few expectations. I expect people who work for me to work hard. I expect guests to abide by curfews and avoid drinking. You know Robert was kicked out not long ago and I liked him, but he came into my boardinghouse intoxicated. I can't pick and choose which rules to enforce and keep this place running smoothly." Margaret walked over and patted Honey's head. "I expect all dogs to behave themselves. You may stay, but Honey can't."

"I'll figure something out," Penny said as she looped the leash around the dog's collar. "I'll take her out now, and when I get back, if it's all right with you, I'll tie her up behind the house until I have a plan."

"That'll be fine. I am sorry, Penny."

―――

"Sir," Trenton Stephens called when Thomas walked by.

"Yes?"

"I've been farming my whole life." Trenton threw down the handful of dirt that was in his hand. "And I've never seen anything like this."

Thomas stepped closer. "Like what?"

"It's normal for an animal to disturb a planting. They'll cause a little damage. A loose cow might kick up a row or two. But nothing like this." He pointed toward the fields. "Joe and Hector both agree. Someone's been in your field. Look at your rows. They're ruined. It's as though a herd of animals ran through, trampling all your new plants. But it was a horse, and my guess is that it had a rider. A loose horse on its own won't run circles like these tracks are testifying of." Trenton stepped closer. "Someone did this on purpose. There's no other explanation."

Thomas felt his muscles tighten. He took his hat from his head and crumpled it in his fist. Someone was out to get him. He could feel it. Here in Azure Springs, living off the soil and the sunlight, he had hoped he'd be able to sleep at night without watching his back. Maybe peace was something people dream of but never really have.

"All right." He shoved the wrinkled hat back on his head. "I'll hire someone to watch the fields at night. How do we salvage the harvest? What do we do now?"

Trenton shook his head. "We're getting too late to replant. You'll still get some from these fields, but it's not going to be a good year even if the weather works in your favor."

"Save what you can. Tell Joe he's to stay all night. I'll pay him extra wages for his time." He turned away from the hired man. "I'm going to get to the bottom of this. I'll find out who's behind it."

"You already know who's behind it. There's only one man who boasted of owning this place." Trenton pointed in the direction of Jeb's property. "You know it's Jeb."

"I don't know that it was him and neither do you until we can prove it." He felt his temper flaring. Through gritted teeth he said, "But if it is him, he'll pay for this."

"He'll fight you to the end."

"He's just talk."

"No. Look at your field. Besides, I've heard that Jeb's always talking big at the saloon about driving you out."

"I wouldn't stake too much on the words of a drunk man." Thomas looked again at his trampled field. The little plants were broken and bent. He felt the air go out of him. The heat and the rage left. He'd vowed to lead a different life. Before, he'd always entered every business deal with his fists up. Now here he was and all he wanted was a quiet life. Was that so much to ask?

"I'll sort this out. You just look out for my fields while I'm away." Thomas walked toward his barn to saddle his mare.

"Hey there," he said to Josephine once inside. "Looks like life's not going to be so easy out here." He reached out and tried to stroke the mare. She balked as usual. "I don't like it either," he said in a soft voice. "I was done fighting. I ran away from all that. It eats a man up. Changes him when he's always worried about who's out to get him or how to stay ahead of everyone else." He reached out his hand again. "What do I do though? Do I let whoever it is just come and take what is rightfully mine?"

Josephine stepped toward him.

"Well, look at that. I'm going to assume you're telling me we're on the same side." She let him pet her neck. "I think Penny was right—there's a good horse in there."

The mare came closer still.

"I think you liked Penny too. I can't get her out of my head." He walked to the mare's side and threw a blanket and saddle onto her back. "Let's ride out and see Hugh about our problems here. Then we'll go see if we can visit Penny. I'll tell her you missed her."

Josephine fought him less than usual as he rode hard and fast to Hugh's place. The roads were full of ruts and overgrown patches, but the ride itself went quickly.

Hugh approached when they neared his place. "What is it? Something's wrong."

"You told me Jeb wants my place. How bad does he want it?"

"Well, he'd tell everyone he was going to buy it and add it to his own property. He'd walk around and in his own Jeb way make sure we all knew his farm was about to take over the Dawson place and anything else he could get his hands on."

Thomas slid out of the saddle and jumped to the ground. "What lengths do you think he'd go to in order to get what he wanted? What would he do?"

"I don't know. His mouth was always going when we were boys, and even after. He would brag about what girl he'd get or how he'd own the town one day. If it wasn't one big plan, it was another. But he's just talk."

"He got the girl, didn't he?" Thomas fisted his hands at his sides, trying to contain his building frustration. But the anger left him when he saw the look on Hugh's face. "She's the girl you loved. That's why you hate Jeb."

Hugh's cheeks flushed red. "She never knew. I was never brave enough to tell her. I kept thinking someday I'd make something of myself and then I could tell her how I felt. I was too late. But long before he married Eliza, I knew what kind of man Jeb was."

Thomas walked over to Hugh and put a hand on his shoulder. "I hardly know Jeb, but I know Eliza would have been better off with you. I'm sorry."

"Don't be. I should have known Jeb, with his sly ways, would end up with Eliza." Hugh sighed. "Tell me why you've come."

"Someone's been in my fields. They were already late sprouting and now they're nothing but trampled rows." Thomas pressed a finger to his chest. "I was a sly businessman. I admit it. I was shrewd. I made deals that worked to my benefit, but I never stooped this low. I never sabotaged another man's property just to get what I wanted."

"Can you prove it was Jeb?"

"No. No one saw anything other than the ruined fields. I'm going to post a man to keep watch around the clock, but I don't know if whoever did it will be back." His crops were going to fail. All his hard work was going to amount to nothing. Maybe all his budding notions of hope and peace would be trampled like his tender plants had been. He kicked at the ground in front of him. "It's all ruined."

"It's your land." Hugh started walking toward the barn. "That's the good thing about land. You treat it right and it'll work for you. Maybe not this year, but it will. Don't give up on it."

"I plan to work it and fight on. But I wonder sometimes if I'll spend my whole life going from one problem to another."

"I wonder that too." Hugh laughed. "I'm going on twenty-six years of problems." Then he paused and scratched his head. "We could ask the new sheriff what he thinks we ought to do. He hasn't been in town long, though, so he won't know much about Jeb." Hugh looked down the road. "Caleb was the sheriff for years and years. He might help us. He doesn't have a badge anymore, but he has experience. And he knows Jeb. I think he's had a few other problems with Jeb over the years."

"Other problems?"

"Only minor things. A brawl at the saloon and a property line dispute."

Thomas leaned against the fence. "What could Caleb do?"

"He might have ideas. Maybe we could ask some of Caleb's hands if they've heard any talk." Hugh reached for a saddle. "I can go now."

"You're working. I can't take you away from that." Thomas shook his head. "You stay."

"If you were the businessman you say you were, my guess is that you had a hard time trusting people. But you told me yourself that's not who you want to be anymore. Here in Azure Springs, taking help from a friend doesn't make you weak. It only makes you stronger."

"You're a different breed of man." Thomas nodded slowly. "You're right. I want a new life. I thought I'd find it in my fields, but maybe I ought to be paying more attention to the people around me. You, Margaret, Abraham, even Penny. All of you are showing me who I want to become."

"Don't go getting too serious on me." Hugh rubbed his hands together. "I'm mostly just anxious to corner Jeb."

"Don't let your personal vendetta fog your thinking. He isn't worth it. That's one lesson I learned the hard way." Thomas reached for the reins of his horse.

"It's not just about my personal pain. If you had a rattlesnake in your house, you'd throw it out. Some things will never be friendly, and I think Jeb might be a serpent. I don't see anything wrong with wanting to keep people safe."

"First, let's make sure he did it." Thomas spoke slowly. "If he didn't, then I won't be the one to put space between him and me. I'm sorry about Eliza. I didn't realize she was the one. But I can't claim a new life if all I'm doing is exchanging one set of enemies for another. I'll give him a chance."

"You're a better man than you give yourself credit for." Hugh tightened the strap on his horse. "Let's go."

⟋⟍

"That's all I can tell you right now." The sheriff stood and walked to the jailhouse door, dismissing Thomas, Caleb, and Hugh. "If I hear anything or see anything, I'll let you know. But other than asking around, I can't offer you much help. There's too many needs in town for me to stand guard at your place."

"I'll help ask around," Caleb offered. "I know most everyone within a ten-mile radius of the city. I'll make some stops on my way home."

"Thank you." Thomas rubbed his jaw, grateful but uncomfortable to be the reason Caleb had left his fields. "I'll see if Margaret can keep her ears open at the dining hall."

"Glad to do it." Caleb put on his hat and headed for his horse. "Best thing I learned from being sheriff is we all got to look out for each other. If we all do, there's a chance we'll hear something that will tell us who ruined your fields."

"What did I tell you?" Hugh laughed as he readied his own horse to ride. "It's to everyone's advantage to help out a neighbor."

"I'm much obliged to have neighbors like you both," Thomas said.

The sun was well past the midpoint of the sky when he said goodbye to his friends. They'd declined his invitation to join him at the boardinghouse for dinner. Caleb wanted to make some stops and hurry back to Em. Hugh thought about staying but decided to return to his fields before all daylight was gone. Thomas did not feel eager to return to his trampled fields or empty home.

A noise startled him when he approached the yellow building. Cautiously, he stepped around the back in hopes of discovering the source of the sound. To his surprise, he found Penny sitting on the ground, sobbing, with her arms around her dog.

A noise startled Penny. She looked up and, through her tears, saw Thomas.

"Again."

"Again?" He took a step backward. "I can go. I just wanted to see if you were well. I heard a noise. That's all."

"You're always catching me in the worst of straits." She looked away and tried to wipe the tears from her face.

"Has something happened?" He took a few small steps toward her. "I thought my day was going poorly, but I'm certain it is nothing in comparison to yours. What has you crying?"

"Margaret has banished my poor Honeysuckle." Penny grabbed her dog's neck and pulled it into a tight embrace. "It's

Honey's fault. I don't blame Margaret, but I don't know what I will do with her. Margaret won't let her back inside."

"What terrible offense did she commit?" Thomas had worked his way to her side and now stood over her. "She's not covered in mud."

Penny stood up. She leaned close to Thomas and whispered, "Honey ate one of the dinner roasts."

"That is a terrible offense. Margaret takes her meals very seriously."

"I know. I tried to tell Honey to stay out of the kitchen, but she doesn't listen to me any longer." Penny wiped her eyes and looked down at Honey. "She's practically family, and even if she is naughty I don't want to part with her."

Thomas stared at the dog for a long moment. "Why not let her stay out at the Dawson farm with me?"

Penny's eyes shot up. "With you? You'd do that?"

"Of course." He shrugged. "It's awfully quiet out there. The place could use a good watchdog."

"Oh!" Acting purely on impulse, she threw her arms around him. To her great surprise, his arms came around her too. "Really and truly?" she whispered into his ear. "You'd really do that?"

"Yes."

She released him and looked up at his eyes as heat raced to her face. "I'm sorry. I seem to have left all my manners when I boarded that train for Azure Springs. But you don't know how grateful I am."

"It's nothing. She can help keep an eye on the place." He scratched the back of his neck. "You can come visit if you start missing her."

Penny put a hand on Honey's head. "She can be terribly

needy and she has a strange affinity for water. Especially if it's muddy."

"I think I've witnessed that. I can handle her." He held out his arm to Penny. "Honey seems to be tied up securely for now. Shall we go eat?"

"I believe you are a rather saintly man," she said as she took his arm. "I don't imagine I'll ever be able to repay you for your kindness."

"I'm anything but saintly. But I've decided I would like to be a good man."

*Y*ou don't have to look so down. Your dog is fine," Margaret said before handing Penny a bowl of oatmeal the next morning. "I think Thomas is quite capable."

"I *am* worried about her . . . and him."

"Of course you are." Margaret threw her a sympathetic look. "Em is going to be by soon to take you around and help you get better acquainted with the townsfolk, and then you promised to take Thomas a meal. You can see your darling Honey when you get out there. Until then, we will both hope your dog has not spent another morning in the mud."

"Margaret?"

"Yes?"

"Did you plot all this? I would not think it possible of most people, but I think you probably could orchestrate it."

Margaret chuckled. "You give me far too much credit. I may have prepared this basket of food for Thomas with the hopes that the two of you would share it, but I had no way of knowing he would volunteer to take Honey. And I can assure you I would never, ever give that good of a roast to a dog." Her features grew serious. "Providence may have had a hand in it.

185

But no matter how it came to be, your dog is now living with a very handsome and mysterious bachelor. Best get ready so you can be on your way."

~

Dear Dinah,

I wish you were here! I've been missing you and wanting to know what is happening with Lucas and if you've gotten any interesting letters at the office. Please write me and tell me everything. You know I enjoy lots of details. I haven't received even one letter from you and I've already written three. It's just that, for the first time in my life, I have so much to tell. I know I should spend as much time writing my mother as I spend writing you, but though I've written her I can't bring myself to share all the details of my days. I know she'll tell me what I'm doing is wrong. And so, my dear friend, it is you who gets to hear about my glorious day.

First, I must tell you that Honey was banished from the boardinghouse, but thankfully Thomas took her in. He rescued me in my moment of despair—truly, it was heroic. I was so grateful that I threw myself into his arms. I know it sounds terribly improper, and in my mother's eyes, it may have been, but I rather liked it. And since his arms came around me too, I think he must be at least partially to blame.

Today Margaret arranged for me to spend the day with Em Reynolds. Hers is a most unusual tale. When I am back in DC, I will tell you her story. It has a tragic beginning but a beautiful ending. Just hearing it made me believe happily ever afters do happen. There's no way

I could write it all out. If I did, it would be a novel no one could put down.

I'll keep it simple and tell you she is a good woman who took me around the area. We began in town, stopping to say hello to everyone we saw. My favorites were Mae and Milly Howell. I'd met them before, but this time I felt like we became friends. They are nine-year-old twins who are perfect replicas of one another. I believe my younger self would have very much liked them. Someday they will grow into terribly romantic girls who you would probably roll your eyes at but find charming all at once. I've also decided Violet Lane is someone I wish to know better. I imagine there are women like her in DC, but my mother never would have wanted me to meet them. Violet is old and poor. Her skin is weathered and worn. If I had to guess, I'd say she's seen at least eighty years of life. I think I'll go sit with her one day just so I can hear her stories. She's seen war, love, family, death, and so much more. She has a quick wit and an endearing smile.

Everyone we met seemed so eager to be not only my acquaintance but also my friend. You would've loved it, Dinah. So many of the rules that kept people apart in DC don't exist here. In Azure Springs, it seems anyone who wishes to be friends can be. It's a beautiful thing.

After our time in town, we went down the bumpy country roads. I was certain the wagon would split in two, it bumped so severely. But Em laughed my fears away. She took me to her farm. It's humble and peaceful. There are big trees and a babbling brook. The front porch has two identical rockers. I found it charming and serene. It's a place you could escape to and almost forget the rest of the world exists. We didn't stay long, but it was long enough for me to feel the love in the home.

Margaret had left us with specific instructions to drop off a basket of food for Thomas. She's a terribly meddlesome woman! And I confess I love her for it. The whole way to Thomas's I couldn't think a clear thought. I only felt. And what I felt was excitement. I was going to set foot on the old Dawson place. I could not wait to see it for myself. And, of course, I was eager to see Honey and had been praying that she'd behaved.

When we got there, Honey came running for me and I felt like I was being reunited with a part of myself that had been missing. Thomas assured me several times she had been no trouble. I wonder if he might have told me a lie. When my arms were around Honey, her fur felt damp and I thought I caught the faint scent of soap. I believe she may have had a bath recently.

Once I'd been reassured that Honey was safe and well, I looked at the land. I was swept away. It's the loveliest place I've ever seen. Truly, it is. A perfect little house, with a barn and a well, settled among the rolling green hills. A few trees blowing in the breeze. Fences and rows of crops. And, of course, Thomas himself only added to the setting. There he was standing in his fields when we rode in. Busy working the soil. It was a sight I could look at daily and never grow tired of.

Thomas seemed rather distraught when we first arrived. He confessed his fields had been disturbed just the day before. He said he'd have told me yesterday, but he didn't want to add to my worries seeing as I'd been in tears over Honey being kicked out of the boardinghouse. He doesn't know who tried to ruin his harvest. I was always drawn to the mystery of the dead letters and now I'm equally drawn, if not more so, to the mystery of his fields. I could tell he had suspicions, though he did not name names. He merely mentioned the dilemma and told Em he'd spoken to Caleb, Em's husband, about it. From what I gathered, Caleb had been unable to solve the puzzle despite his history as the town's sheriff. It seems entirely unfair that someone can do such a horrible deed and suffer no consequence for it other than the fact that his soul ought to be suffering wherever that good-for-nothing man is.

When Thomas saw the basket of food, his spirits seemed to rise. He was extremely gracious. Then he walked me across his fields, to his barn, and around the outside of his house. I wanted to peek inside but didn't dare. Someday I hope to see the inside of the Dawson home. Until then, I'll busy myself with imagining what it must look like inside.

Later, Em confessed a man in town desperately wanted Thomas's land. I wish I could help somehow. If the answer were tucked away at the library, I'd know how to find it. But this puzzle is of a different nature and I've not thought of a way to help. I can assure you I'll be thinking on it.

Leaving Honey was difficult, but Thomas has assured me I can see her whenever I wish. And when he is free enough to eat at the dining hall, he'll bring her for me to see. Perhaps Honey's troublesome ways are not all bad. I do enjoy my time with Thomas.

Write me, dear friend,
Penny

P.S. Can you believe how quickly the days are passing? I know I cannot stay forever. I will have to decide soon to either return to the dead letter office or go to Uncle Clyde's. I prayed last night that time would slow down. That extra hours could be in my days. That somehow I could stay longer in this beautiful place. My money will not last forever, though I wish it would.

Penny finished her letter, knowing there were so many things she couldn't fit on the pages. She could find no words to describe the way Thomas had looked when he'd stared with pride at his rolling fields. Even weary, he still looked like a man who was grateful for the soil he stood upon.

And he was so kind. When they gave him the food, he thanked them sincerely. Then Em, who was expecting a child, said she'd like to sit on his porch chair and rest for a spell. He pulled the rocker to the shade for her and brought her a drink.

"Show Penny around," Em said. "She's about to begin a novel. I think your farm will help her with her setting."

He turned to her. "Penny, may I show you around?"

Then, in a most gentlemanly fashion, he offered his arm. She tucked her hand into the crook of his elbow. "Thank you," she managed to whisper.

They walked—around the house, the barn, and the fields. Their conversation was easy. Hardly a lull, and when there was a lull it was peaceful as they both looked out at the vast and lovely setting.

"You've your own piece of paradise," she said as she admired the property. Honey ran around them enjoying herself.

Thomas nodded his head. "I didn't see it as that at first. I thought this was to be my prison. But I now realize what I left was a prison. This is freedom. I've found it, and though I cannot change the past, I see all this and have hope for a brighter future. My fields will grow again. I like to believe life still holds promise and can bear good fruits."

"My father always believed in good things ahead."

They stood side by side staring out at his land. He reached over then and put a hand on her shoulder. Penny took comfort in it and in his words. "I think I would've liked your father. Someday I hope you'll tell me all his wisdom."

"I think he'd have liked you."

"He must have been one of those people who likes everyone. I can be a difficult fellow to like." He removed his hand from her shoulder and tucked it in his pocket. "Tell me about your story. We've time now."

Her legs felt less stable then. If only he would put his hand back. Somehow she'd felt stronger when he was touching her. "I hope to truly begin tonight. I've decided only just now that I will write a story about a city man who heads to the country in hopes of a better life."

"A more fulfilling life." A faint smile played on his lips. "Write it about a man who carried a heavy burden. Tell how the Bible, the fertile soil, and a letter from a stranger changed him."

"A letter?"

"A few letters I'd sent didn't make it to their destination. Someone from the dead letter office retrieved them. A woman wrote me back. She said she'd prayed for me. I'd never had someone pray for me before." He paused for a moment. "Those words . . . just knowing someone out there cared. They lifted me up. I was in a dark place and they offered me light. I read the words so many times."

"Everyone should be prayed for." Fear kept her from saying

more. What would he think if he knew that it'd been his words, his pain that had brought her here? That she was the one who had prayed for him? "I'll be sure to include the letter in my story."

"Have it remind him that he has a purpose still. Have him feel less alone holding a stranger's words in his hand." He motioned toward the land. "Be sure to give your character a happy ending. Let him find joy after the pain. It's what I hope for."

"I will. The happiest of endings."

"Have your man meet good people. A pudgy shopkeeper, a wild-haired widow, and a good friend. Let them touch his life." He smiled down at her. His dark eyes were soft and inviting. "You could even have a girl with brilliant green eyes show up out of nowhere for a reason no one could quite put their finger on. She could be a perfect dancing partner. Someone who speaks horse and rides miles and miles on bumpy roads to bring him a meal. Make sure she owns a very hairy dog. One that cannot resist the water or a well-cooked roast."

"What will become of the girl and the dog?" she asked. "Did she find what she was looking for? Was there purpose in her coming?" Then she held her breath while she waited for his answer.

He didn't answer her right away. Instead, he merely stared into her eyes. She felt vulnerable and on fire all at the same time.

"I don't know. I would hope she finds everything she's looking for and more," he finally said.

She held his gaze. "Even I don't know how the story will play out."

"Whatever you do, give her a happy ending too."

Penny slowly let out the air she'd been holding in. Her whole life she'd dreamed of a happy ending for herself. But she was twenty-two now and had to support herself. Could something other than toiling day after day be in her future? Something other than Uncle Clyde and a strategic match with a stranger named Horace?

"I suppose in a novel anything is possible."

"I'm sure your father would say it's possible in real life too." He put a hand on her back and gently turned her toward the house. "Let's head back."

She agreed despite her desire to stay on that gentle rise and never leave it.

"If you start your story and can't decide what to write next, come walk this hill with me again."

"I'd like that." She nudged him. "I might get stuck often. I like it here in the open air with this view."

"You may walk my hill anytime you wish. Besides, your dog will want to see you. She moans from time to time and I have to reassure her you are coming back for her."

"Oh, my poor Honeysuckle." She looked at the dog. "She did that as a puppy too. I do hope she isn't a burden."

"Naw." He laughed under his breath. "But you really must come and see her as often as you like. Maybe then you can tell me why a city girl left her home for the country, why she picked Azure Springs, and why I feel like you know me even though we've only recently met."

"I don't know if I understand it all myself. Life did not go how I had expected it to. I'm merely trying to leap at the right moments and land on solid ground."

He reached down and took her hand in his and quickly pressed his fingers around hers. "I know that feeling." Then he let go.

Penny sighed now at the memory. Remembering the way his

eyes had beckoned her just as his letters had when they'd fallen into her hands. Every look, every sigh, even the smell of what was left of the crops on the breeze had been perfect.

With her letter to Dinah written, she left her little room and went to the dining hall. It was early yet. Margaret shooed her away and told her to come back in fifteen minutes. Obediently, she stepped outside into the evening sun, where she leaned her back against the outside of the boardinghouse and looked down the street. Couples, families, single men. These people who had been strangers to her only days ago now felt like much more.

"My, my, what a surprise."

"Thomas." She felt the breath in her lungs leave her. He was here. Again.

"With the men working my farm, I've time to come get a real meal in me. Besides, I needed to get away from those trampled fields. And Honey here was moaning again." He ran his hand through the dog's shaggy hair. Penny quickly looked the man over. He had cleaned up since she'd seen him last, only hours ago.

She put up her hand. "Wait here. Before I forget again, I have the letter you left on the hitching post the other day at the stables. The one you intended to send and never did. I believe it's for a Clara. I've not opened it. I meant to return it sooner."

"I don't need it. The postmaster was right. It doesn't need to be sent. Let's get into the dining hall before Margaret has our throats. I'll tie Honey out back until after the meal."

"She's not ready yet. I was just in there. She very firmly instructed me to go away for fifteen minutes. I try my best to follow her orders. It keeps me on her good side."

"I believe fifteen minutes is long enough for us to stroll down Main Street and back." He offered his arm. "You can tell me more about the city girl and her motives."

"I have a feeling you will badger me relentlessly about it." She didn't want to answer. All she wanted was to walk down the street on the arm of this handsome, intriguing man. But if she never told him who she was—who she really was—could they ever be more than mere acquaintances? Something deep inside her wanted very much to be more than a mere friend to him. "Very well. My father was Stephen Ercanbeck. He was a self-made man. The hardest worker I've ever known. He started as a store clerk and managed to work his way up until he owned several stores and had immense investments. He was brilliant. He knew where to put his money and, like magic, it would multiply. By the time he married my mother, he was one of the wealthiest men in Washington, DC. She had come from money and was several years his junior."

"You told me he died."

"He did. Five years ago. After he died, we carried on without him. For two years we carried on, living in the same circles. Unbeknownst to us, his finances were being ill managed. We lost everything. Even our own relatives were embarrassed by the scandal and would not help us. Or maybe they refused because we were poor and there was no advantage in being our friends or calling us family." She looked away. "It hurt at first. But I worked, and somehow we survived. Though my mother never accepted the losses. She's been living in denial for years. I learned the language of work and frugality, but she refuses. She's blinded by her goal of going home, back to wealth and the world she knew before. I don't know that I want to return to a world full of the type of people who shunned us."

"I wish I could tell you they were wicked and awful for betraying you and that I'd never do such a thing," Thomas said with a hint of regret in his voice. "I'd sound noble for saying it. But I am guilty of as much. When I was in the city, I spent far too much time mingling with only certain families. Until I came here, I didn't realize that being poor isn't a crime. I never knew so many fine people were out there."

"I like it here. I like how people are friends because of their shared goodness, not because of their shared status. I met Violet Lane the other day and that dear woman was so eager to have someone listen to her. I don't think I'll ever be comfortable living with fences between me and other people again." They reached the end of Main Street and simultaneously turned back around. "My Uncle Clyde's wife died and now he is alone and has asked me and my mother to move to his home. He's as unkind as I remember him being when I was a child and just as controlling. He's already lining up suitors for me. I don't have to see them to know there's no chance I'd approve of his choices. I must decide whether to move in with him or continue providing for myself. I couldn't think clearly in DC, so I went away."

"You came here?"

"Yes," she said quietly. "Only it wasn't that simple."

Thomas walked beside her, silently waiting. When the moment stretched on, he spoke. "You don't have to tell me. I admit I'm curious, more than I ought to be, but you don't have to tell me anything."

"I want to." She tried to think of the right way to tell him that she had come because of him. "But I know it will all sound so preposterous when I say it aloud."

Before she was able to pull together an explanation, they were back at the door of the dining hall.

"I will tell you exactly why I came to Azure Springs. I've never been good with secrets. But Margaret hates it when I'm late to her meals. I'm not leaving town just yet. There will be time for it all later. Anyway, I'm told a good story is meant to keep you wanting more."

"There's no way you'll tell me tonight? I find I'm in the mood for a good tale." He pled with her, not only with his words but with the tone of his voice.

"I'm partial to stories as well." She nearly gave in, but she wanted one more night of fantasy. "Let's wait. I think it'll be better tomorrow when I've time to think of the right way to explain it all."

"Very well." His eyes questioned her, but he said, "Let's eat."

They stepped away from the quiet of the street and into the ruckus of the dining hall.

"Look who decided to set his spade down and come put something nourishing in his stomach," Margaret declared when they walked through the door. "And you've found the charming Penny. Why don't the two of you sit here in the corner. I'm expecting a full house tonight and that'll be the quietest spot."

Penny slid onto the bench. "Thank you."

Thomas slid onto the bench beside her. The hall filled quickly, and he sat so close that they were nearly touching. He shifted on the narrow bench until he was looking right at her. "Penny."

"Yes?"

"Will you walk with me again tomorrow?" His cheeks had more color in them than normal. He looked younger, almost boyish. But the scruff on his jaw gave him away. "I know you aren't here long. If you were, I'd put time between seeing you. I'd wait. I do know the rules of propriety. But as it is, I want to spend time with you and your time here is limited. I'm not sure why, but I want to see you again." He winced. "That didn't come out right. I only meant it doesn't make sense me wanting to know you. My life is complicated and your visit is short. I've tried to pry out your secrets, but I have mine too. I'm not sure if it's right my wanting to see you again, but . . . well"—he took a deep breath—"something about being in your presence makes me want to be the character with a happy ending."

"I'd like to walk with you." She patted his hand. "For research, of course. I've got to get to know my heroic farmer better."

"Before dinner tomorrow?"

"Yes. If you promise to tell me more about yourself. I don't want to be the only one confessing secrets."

"I will. I'll be by an hour before dinner and I'll tell you anything you want to know."

"Is that a promise?"

"It's a promise." He reached out his hand and offered it to her. She took it and they slowly shook hands. Their eyes locked as they made the promise. "I'll keep my word."

*T*hroughout dinner, they talked only of trivial things. The food they'd grown up eating. The sounds of the country compared to those of the city. Simple things. Beautiful, easy things. And then all too quickly the meal was over and she was alone in her room.

Penny yearned to spend more time with him. To ask him countless questions. Ones that would peel away his exterior and expose who he was inside. What was in his heart? What dreams did he carry?

But he was gone now, and she'd have to wait until tomorrow evening to see him. She tried to recall all that had transpired between them. And then she recalled the crinkled letter he had written to Clara. She could read it now. His words could tide her over until she was in his presence again.

After all, he didn't want the letter back. At the dead letter office, they'd have considered it rejected. If he had mailed it, she'd have gotten it when it arrived at the office. What harm could there be in reading it now? The letter might give her another glimpse into his soul—and there was nothing she wanted more than that.

Penny walked to the window and looked out at the moon

shining brightly in the sky. She turned and eyed her closed door. No one could see her. No one would know. Several times she crossed the wooden floor. Back and forth she walked while she wrestled with temptation. A twinge of guilt grew within her, but she fought it off.

And then she knelt next to her trunk and pulled out the letter. She tore it open before she could second-guess her decision.

Dear Clara,

When I left Alexandria, I felt like a man stumbling under a heavy load. I knew not where I was going. I kept writing you even though the letters would never reach you. Still, it seemed like the right thing to do. It seemed like the only thing to do. There was no other way to say I'm sorry. I've said it before, and though I know your eyes will never see this letter, I'll say it again. I'm sorry.

If I'd done things different, you'd be here. I blame myself for your death. I should have been there to save you. I should have loved you more selflessly. I was the wrong sort of man then. And now here I am in a welcoming town, surrounded for the first time in my life by real friends. I am finally thinking with more than my account books in mind, yet my decision that night still haunts me. Forgive me, Clara. If I could go back, I'd be a better man. I'd be the sort of man who would have protected you. I'd have loved you how you ought to have been loved. I'll regret it always. My heart will always ache for you—

Penny stopped reading. All his words confused her.

The paper shook in her trembling hand. She shoved the letter back into her trunk and sat with her head in her hands. Why

200

did he blame himself? She died in a fire. Clara's servant had said so. Mostly, she hated the pain that shot through her heart as she realized Thomas was still grieving for Clara. He yearned for her hand, and rightly so. He'd loved her, had he not?

It was true that Penny's heart came alive every time she was near the man, but having one heart alive was not enough to build a life around. She'd been naïve to think there was a chance for love with Thomas. Her money would run out and he'd still be yearning for Clara.

She stood and walked again to the window. There in front of her was the town she'd come to love so quickly. This was her leap and she had taken it. A wave of sadness swept over her as she realized it was all going to end, and though there had been sweet moments, it wasn't her reality. What even was real? Not the fantasy she'd created about the man behind the letters. She had pictured him as the victim of a tragic misunderstanding. But he'd had some hand in Clara's death. Why had he written to her when he'd known all along she was dead? Penny felt as though she were walking through a haze.

But weren't the moments they'd shared real? Who was the man she'd danced with, the man she'd walked the fields with, the man she'd laughed with? Who was he? Would she ever really know?

Had the people of Alexandria turned their backs on him because he'd been cruel? Was he an evil man? A wicked man? Was *he* what Clara's family didn't want to be reminded of?

The line between what she wanted to believe and what she knew was a blur.

Mr. Douglas's voice echoed through her mind. *"The letters are not meant for you. Their contents are to be read and then forgotten."* Why hadn't she taken those words to heart? She should have thrown Thomas's letters into the bin. Now for the first time, she admitted it. All the letters. All the heartache and sentiment. None of it had been for her. She was never meant to worry about Thomas or cross the country to see his face. Sick with realization and heartache, she wrapped her arms around her middle. She'd been lonely and let her imagination get the better of her. Somehow she'd tricked herself into believing those letters, though not addressed to her, were for her. And now in the dim glow of moonlight she realized what a fool she had been.

She yearned for Honey or some other comfort. But she was alone. Very alone. Back and forth she traipsed, until at last she decided to break free from the barren room. Taking rapid steps, she rushed down the stairs only to fall into Margaret's arms when she reached the bottom.

"I heard you up there. You sounded restless." Margaret steadied her, then stepped back and searched her face. "You're pale as a ghost. Come tell me what's wrong." She stretched out her hand toward Penny, motioning for her to follow.

"I've . . . I've learned something. I think I have at least. I suppose I just realized something I should have known long ago." Tears came with the words and poured down her face.

Margaret stopped walking and pulled Penny into an embrace. Penny sobbed into the good woman's shoulder. "I've been so wrong and foolish. I thought I knew someone, but I realize that I don't and wasn't really meant to. I don't even know if they are as honorable as I want to believe they are. I'm so confused." She groaned. "I realize now what a simpleton I've been."

Margaret stepped back and held Penny at arm's length. "If you can, ask your questions of whomever it is you've changed your views on. Far too many relationships have been ruined simply because the right questions were never asked. Slow down." She squeezed Penny's shoulders. "Slow down if you can. The situation may not be as horrible as it seems right now."

Penny sniffled. "I do hope you're right."

Margaret pulled her back into her arms and held her close. "Remember too that mistakes are part of the journey."

"You don't understand. It's not just that I don't know who they really are. I've been careless with my heart and wandered down a path that is eating through my money and getting me nowhere. I fell in love with the idea of love, but now I see how foolish that was. I think I fell in love with someone else's love story. I was lonely, and I got caught up in something that wasn't mine." She shook her head, embarrassed and wishing she could run from it all. "If only I could go back and do things differently. I'd not be here, that's for certain."

"And this person. I'm assuming it's Thomas. Does he seem like a bad man to you?"

"No, he seems like a very good man. In truth, he seems better than any man I've known. But I would not be the first woman to be deceived."

"You're right." Margaret laughed a little. "No one will argue with you on that."

"It's not funny."

"No, it's not." Margaret's voice grew tender. "I should not belittle your pain. You have every right to feel sorrow or worry. Go on and cry if you think it'll help."

Penny allowed herself several self-pitying moments of fretting. Her handkerchief was soaked through with tears when Margaret put her hands on Penny's cheeks. "Dear girl, face whatever it is. You've been brave already. You've come here on your own. Only a brave soul would do that. Be brave again. Be brave until the end. You can't go back and undo this. It's one of the harsh realities of this life. If I could I'd go back and unsay every harsh word I've ever uttered. But I can't—and you can't change the past either. Look ahead."

Penny crossed her arms tightly against herself. "Margaret."

"Yes?"

"I wasn't brave when I came here. I was afraid and lonely most of the journey." Penny bit her bottom lip. "I was trying to do what I thought was right, but now I'm here and my money is dwindling and I'm no closer to knowing which path to take with my life."

"Something must have led you to Azure Springs. It's not exactly on the way to anything."

Penny felt a sudden need so powerful she could not contain it. Desperately, she needed a friend. A friend who knew her, who knew the truth. And so, in a few breathless sentences, she spilled her tale of loss and leaping, beginning with her father's death. She told about her mother, about their financial ruin and her years working as a clerk. "The letters Thomas was sending kept coming to the office. They were written to a woman. They were full of longing and regret. I could tell he cared for her deeply. I found his letters consuming. I thought about them all the time. There was so much feeling in them." She took a deep breath. "They spoke to me. Call me foolish if you wish, but they did. I've read so many letters, but none have ever affected me like his did. I know it was wrong, but it was almost as though the letters were for me."

"You came because of Thomas, even though he wrote to an-other woman? Is that why you said you fell in love with someone else's love story?"

"Yes . . . well, no. Not exactly. I did find his letters moving. So much so that I went to Alexandria to find his Clara. I wanted to help him avoid a life of loneliness. But once I was there, I learned she had died in a tragic accident." Penny put her hands on her heart. "I ached for him. I was sure he didn't know of her death, so I wrote him an anonymous letter telling him of the accident. Then when my uncle stepped back into our lives, the only thing that felt right was coming here. I needed to see for myself that Thomas was well. I'm not sure why. Maybe because I thought he would understand me. Azure Springs was the only place outside of DC I could think of."

"And now that you've met him?"

"Oh, Margaret. The moment I saw him, well, not exactly the moment I saw him. That moment was spent trying to pull Honey from the mud. But after that when he came to help me and every time after. Especially when I danced with him and when he walked me around his land. And when he helped me bathe my muddy dog. And even when he offered to take her into his home. All those times I felt my heart beating faster within me." Penny looked down. "I realize I'm too easily overwhelmed by emotions. I know I should not be, but sometimes feelings just capture me. And then when life falls apart, I'm left so hurt."

"Don't be too harsh on yourself. There's nothing wrong with a beating heart or even with one that feels pain." She stroked Penny's hair. "What happened? Did he learn the truth of why you came west?"

"No, he didn't. The truth is, I read a letter, well, part of a letter, that he had changed his mind about sending. Reading it, I was reminded of all I do not know. I have big questions about his past. I can't get the pieces to fit together. The one truth I'm certain of—he loves Clara. Even though she is gone, he wishes for her. I haven't the means to wait for a man to heal and no right to expect him to turn to me when he does." She stopped herself. Hearing her own words aloud only made the hurt grow deeper. "I suppose I realized this was all just a dream."

Penny took a steadying breath. "The letter awakened me to reality. I see now how wrong I was to come west. I need to start planning for my future. This"—she took a deep breath—"this is not my life. This is not my home. I can't stay here."

"I think it's time for a bit of honesty." Margaret nodded as though she were agreeing with her own idea. "You do have to think about tomorrow, and tomorrow you ought to ride out to the old Dawson place and ask Thomas all your questions. Remember, that letter wasn't meant for you. It might all make sense when he explains it. And when you've run out of questions, tell him the truth of why you came. Give him a chance to hear your story. Until then, stop fretting. It'll do you no good." Margaret walked to the mantel and took down a small painting. "This was my Wyatt."

"He's very handsome," Penny said, taking the image into her hands. The man in the frame had a thick beard and friendly eyes.

"The handsomest man who ever walked these streets." She took it back and stared at it. "Handsome and good." She looked up and smiled a crooked smile at Penny. "But before he was good, he was a man with a past."

"A past?"

"Mm-hmm. He gambled, even lost his family's prized horses once. He also got into more than one brawl over crop prices and who knows what. I remember watching him then. He was so reckless. But he turned his life around. He changed."

"How did you know?"

"Well, I didn't all at once, but it started with little things. He'd ask me questions and I could tell he cared about my answer. I could feel it. I knew deep inside he had become a different man."

Margaret ran her fingers over the edge of the little frame. "I don't know what Thomas's past is, but I believe he's becoming a better man. And there's nothing so fine as a man who knows to turn down a different road. Get some sleep, and when you see him next ask about his past. Be sure, though, to ask about his future as well. And tell him of your past and your future. Otherwise, there's little purpose in talking at all."

"Now the God of hope fill you with all joy and peace in believing, that ye may abound in hope."

Thomas closed his Bible as the words from Romans filled his mind.

Hope. Joy.

He had found both—in his growing faith, the town, the people, the land, the beautiful dark-haired girl. For a moment he wished he had found them earlier. It was a useless thought. He shook it away, not wanting to go where those dark memories often took him.

Instead, he retired for the night with his mind on the future.

Staring up at the ceiling, he found himself smiling at what the coming day would hold.

"Penelope Ercanbeck." There in the dark of his room he could see the curve of her lips when she smiled. The green of her eyes and her fair skin. She was kind and thoughtful. Funny and beautiful. More than that, he liked the way he felt when he was with her. Her spirits were bright. She seemed to have a laugh always near the surface. Penny made him want to smile and to dance. She made him want to be a better man. What he saw in Penny he'd never seen in a woman before. She was different from anyone else, even Clara. He didn't doubt many noble and good women were out there, but she was the first he had noticed since changing course. And he wasn't sure he ever wanted or needed to find another one.

He closed his weary eyes, reminding himself he'd see her tomorrow. Tomorrow would be another day to seek out hope, purpose, and joy. Sleep came easy. The nights of endlessly tossing and turning were past.

Penny tiptoed to the front door. It creaked when she opened it. Quickly, she looked over her shoulder.

"You thought you could leave without me knowing?" Margaret asked from the chair in the front room.

"Do you spend your time just listening?" Penny looked at the stockings on her feet and the boots she held in her hand. "I was so careful."

"I've owned a boardinghouse long enough to always have one ear open. You never know when someone's going to try sneaking out or sneaking in. I heard the boards creak and decided I'd get up so I could greet you."

"I wasn't sneaking. Not exactly. I just didn't want to wake you." She covered a yawn with her free hand. "I remember the way to Thomas's, but it's so far and I wanted to start early."

"Tell me, how did you sleep?"

"One moment I was lecturing myself on jumping to conclusions and the next I was jumping to conclusions." Penny fidgeted with a loose strand of hair. "I need to go there and confront it all. I'll feel better leaving town knowing I've asked what needed to be asked and told him the truth. He deserves that."

"I wish I could be a bird above you listening to the two of you bare your souls." Margaret motioned toward the kitchen. "Come get some food first. It's always easier to talk on a full stomach."

"Thank you. You're always good about seeing me fed," Penny said as the two stepped into the kitchen.

"Food is what I do best. What will you say to him?" Margaret asked while wrapping biscuits and putting them in a basket. She handed one to Penny. "Don't tell me you haven't thought about it."

"I believe I'll begin by telling him the truth about why I came. I'll tell him I'm sorry I concealed who I was. Then I'll confess to reading part of his letter. I will say whatever comes to my mind and my heart." She picked at the biscuit Margaret had given her. "I wish I were braver or at least one of those women who can command language and say the right thing in the right way. But I'm not brave or articulate, so I'll just be honest." She wiped a crumb from her mouth with a cloth napkin. "If he chooses to despise me, so be it. When it's done, I'll walk back and buy a train ticket. I'm really just here so I can delay what's to come. And that can only last so long. It's time to face it all and leave the fantasy behind."

"It's not fantasy. You are here in the flesh." Margaret continued filling the basket as she spoke. "Besides, you said you loved this town. You'd have never found that love if you hadn't come."

Penny rubbed her tired eyes. "You're right. I've never regretted a beautiful dream, so I will try not to waste time regretting this." She smiled at Margaret. "I do love it here. I love the people. I love that they share food at socials. I love the friendliness. I love the wide-open spaces. All of it is beautiful. This brief time away has been a precious reminder of all that is good. I only wish it could go on without ending."

Margaret crossed the room and put her motherly arms around her. "What would your father tell you right now?"

"I wish I knew." She sighed. "He always had the right words."

Margaret patted Penny's back. "Think. I've heard you speak often of his wisdom. What would he tell you? I'm certain his words are written on your heart. What would he say?"

Penny closed her eyes for a moment. "He'd tell me . . ." She tried to think back, to hear him again. "He'd tell me it is my job to do all I can in this life to make each day better. He'd tell me to get in and change what I can. And what I cannot, he'd tell me to hand over to God."

"A wise man," Margaret said. "Go today and change what you can and follow your father's advice with the rest. Then brush off your hands and go on living. No matter the outcome of the day, you'll carry on."

"I know the bread won't mix itself. I'll have to. It's time to go back." She stood and brushed a few crumbs from her skirts.

"You could stay here."

"I've thought of that. But I've no skills to earn money out here. I was raised to be nothing more than a genteel woman. Thankfully, my father thought languages should be part of my education. I believe that's why I was hired so quickly at the dead letter office. Working there is the best way for me to support myself." Penny tried to put on a brave face, but the thought of being a clerk again seemed daunting.

Margaret picked up the basket she had packed and handed it to Penny. "Go to Thomas. Take this so you aren't hungry. There's plenty in there for you two to share. If I've learned anything, it's that no one should have an important discussion on an empty stomach." She put a gentle hand on her shoulder and directed her to the door.

"Thank you," Penny said. "You've been so kind."

"You're most welcome."

Penny stepped out into the street, only to hear Margaret call to her. "I'm hoping you come back to tell me that it's all sorted out. I do love when two people I care so much about get to weave their lives together. Makes me feel like my meddling ways are worth something."

Penny waved as she walked from the safety of the boardinghouse toward the old Dawson place, where she was fairly certain Thomas would declare her a fool.

As she walked the long and dusty road, Penny filled the time with thoughts of Dinah and Lucas, of her mother and father, and of the story she hoped to write. She marveled that her fictitious alibi had become her real ambition.

Something caught her eye—a rabbit hopping for its burrow—and she paused. A hawk circled overhead. For no explainable reason she began to feel an urgency to get to the old Dawson place. Nature and its serenity no longer distracted her. Her heart raced, but she didn't know why.

She walked a bit farther and then there it was—just over the next little rise—the old Dawson place. Only something wasn't right. The sky was dark. A black cloud billowed above the farm, growing larger and larger.

Penny could smell smoke. Something was burning, something big.

Forcing her tired legs to move faster, she dropped the basket of biscuits from Margaret and ran as fast as she could toward the farm. Her heart pounded in her chest, telling her to slow down, but she would not. Confessions, interrogations—they did not matter now.

Only Thomas mattered.

From the corner of her eye, she caught a glimpse of a rider on horseback. It was a man, she could tell that much, but his face was turned away from her. His horse was still as he looked at the fire. Like a sentinel, he watched, then slowly turned and rode off into the distance. Why wasn't he helping?

There was no time to worry about the rider. Not now. Not while Thomas's fate was unknown. She forced herself to go faster still, despite her aching legs and raw throat. The worn and uneven road was the only thing that kept her from the blaze. She tripped, landing hard on her side. But as quickly as she went down, she got back up and hurried on.

A few more strides and she could tell it was the barn that was up in flames. She ran to it.

Where is Thomas? Where is Honey?

He had to be here. He had to be safe.

"Thomas!" she yelled as loudly as she could. The crackling, hungry fire muted her efforts. "Thomas!"

Frantic with worry, she raced around the barn, screaming as she went.

At last she saw him, his skin darkened from the thick smoke, beside a small, charred side door. His shirt was untucked and blackened.

"Clara!" he yelled as he pushed against the door.

She heard him, but she couldn't have heard correctly. She shouted again as she stepped closer. His head turned, and for a brief moment she saw his face. His eyes were wild and unfamiliar.

Like a madman, he flung the door open. Smoke poured from

213

within, racing to the fresh air with speed and mass. Thomas disappeared into the blackness. It was as though the fire had consumed him in one giant gulp.

She would not let it have him. Somehow she would save him. She ran into the smoke. Her eyes burned, but she would not close them. Not with him inside. Her eyes fought to adjust and soon she saw his dark shape moving deeper into the barn. Penny reached out and grabbed his arm, pulling at him with all her might.

"Stop, Thomas!" she screamed.

Penny darted in front of him and clutched the front of his shirt and pulled him toward her. "Stop this!"

He looked past her as though she were not even there. Penny let go, unsure what to do. A board crashed down only feet from them, launching burning shards of wood in all directions. There was no time to think. She had to act. She had to save him.

Penny looked to Thomas, hoping the caving roof would be enough to scare him from the barn. But his eyes were still wild. He pushed past her and took a giant step farther into the building.

She covered her mouth with her hand and followed. "Thomas, you have to stop. It's burning. We're going to die." Her lungs screamed for air, but she could not leave him.

A frightened horse cried from its stall.

"It's Josephine." Penny struggled to get the words out. She took Thomas's hand. "You can save her. Save Josephine!"

He said nothing but went to the gray mare and opened her stall door. Josephine reared and then ran for freedom, jumping over the obstacles in her way. She at least had the sense to leave the building. If only Thomas were as sane.

"We have to leave." Penny coughed. She felt weak. When

she tried to breathe deeper, her lungs only burned more. "Now. We have to go!"

A section of the roof fell. The already thick air became thicker still. Penny looked around her. They could still get out. She moved closer to him, searching for something or some way to bring him back to reality.

A beam fell from the rafters, knocking her to the ground.

"Thomas!" She cried out in agony. Sharp pain shot through her leg, stealing her breath and causing her head to spin.

Their eyes met for a fraction of a second. It was enough.

Something changed in him—like a bear awaking from his winter slumber. He lifted the beam and threw it away from her. Then he scooped her into his arms and ran from the dying building. Out of the mouth of the fire they emerged. Thomas ran with her to safety, then carefully set her on the ground. She felt him searching her body for injuries. All she could think was that she needed more air. And then she could think nothing at all. The world, the barn, even Thomas faded away.

*Y*ou carried her all the way here?" Margaret stepped from Penny's room and sat beside Thomas on a narrow wooden bench in the upstairs landing. The doctor was in with her and the two were alone for the first time since he'd stormed through the boardinghouse door with Penny in his arms.

Thomas kept his face buried in his hands.

"The doctor says her leg will be scarred from the break, but it'll heal. The smoke caused as much hurt as anything. I don't think she could have taken much more of it. But even her lungs will heal."

He didn't look up. His only movement was from the persistent cough that racked his lungs and sent his body shaking.

"Doc says she's lucky you got her out of there as quickly as you did. You're both lucky." She paused. "I can tell your lungs are hurting as well."

As the coughing subsided, he sniffled but said nothing.

She put a hand on his back. "You saved her. She's going to be all right."

"She saved me." Tears ran from his eyes, dripping between his fingers. "I was out of my head. I was mad. The fire awakened something in me. Something I've tried hard to forget." His body shook again as he remembered the events of the day. "If she hadn't come, I'd be dead. I know I would be."

"She did come though. The dear girl could not sleep all last night. And on her own, she decided to go to you."

"I ran in from the fields when I heard Honey barking. The barn was on fire, then the next thing I knew she was there beside me, pleading with me." He looked up at Margaret. "The whole way to town, she didn't speak once. She didn't even open her eyes. I was afraid she'd be lost forever. I thought I'd killed her." Then very softly he said, "I wish she hadn't come. I wish the fire had just taken me. Then she'd be well. I didn't mean for any of this—"

Margaret roughly put her hand under his chin and turned his face toward her. "Don't you ever say that again. Not around anyone. Especially not her. She's hurting now. You don't get to wallow in misery and regret. Get her well and she'll tell you why she came to you. But don't you dare make her feel bad for coming. She'll carry the scars of that decision her entire life. Give her a reason to wear those scars with pride. Let her be grateful she saved you. And she ought to be. And you ought to be thankful too."

She let go. "I don't know what tragedies you've seen. I don't need to. But I know this—you have a future. The good Lord's given you one and that girl in there needs someone. She has no family here. We get to be that for her for as long as she needs us. You can sit around lamenting about the past, the fire, and all your losses, or you can be the man she needs right now."

"I'll help her. I will. But I don't know how." He dropped his hands to his side. "I don't know how to make anything right. People who cross my path suffer."

"No! Life happens. No one can stop it. What you can do is be there for her." Margaret's face softened. "Put a smile on her face. Make those green eyes sparkle. Be near her. Hold her hand when she's awake. Soothe her when she coughs. Read to her. Take care of Honey. Do anything you like, but do it in a way that will make her smile and want to face each painful day."

"Like you did for me?" He stared at his feet. "When I wanted to give up because of my wagon and my past."

"I knew when you showed up with your hollow eyes that what you needed was a firm hand. I think a gentle touch might be more effective with Penny." She rubbed his back as he battled another body-shaking cough. "But I do believe there is something to smile about each day. Right now it's the fact that the charming Penny is still with us. Pain seems to have brought you two together, so you may as well enjoy the union."

The doctor stepped out from the bedroom. "Excuse me. I didn't mean to interrupt."

Margaret stood. "How is she?"

"She's sleeping now. I expect she'll wake up in pain before long. Often with smoke inhalation, there's a lot to clear out of the lungs. Her body will do its best to expel the fluid. I also expect she'll be tired and likely in and out of consciousness due to weakness and pain." He shifted the bag in his hand. "I've set and stitched her leg the best I can, but it'll scar. If kept clean, it'll heal. We can give her laudanum as needed."

Thomas stood. "Thank you for caring for her."

"It'll take more than me to see her through this. I'm sure we can get women from around town to help attend to her needs. Abigail Howell is a talented nurse. Rose Hewitt has experience as well." He looked at Margaret when he spoke. "I trust you can make arrangements."

"I'll enlist all the help I can get. Thomas plans to sit with her from time to time as well."

Thomas nodded. "I do. I'd like to help. I . . . I owe her that much."

"I'm not sure that'd be appropriate."

Margaret stood. "I will serve as a chaperone of sorts. You know the rules of this boardinghouse. I won't let anything happen under this roof that tarnishes its name. All things considered, I don't think sitting in the front room is an option."

"Very well. I'll trust your judgment." The doctor moved toward the stairs. "I'll come back again in a few hours to check on her. Until then, do what you can to keep her comfortable, and make sure she gets plenty to drink when she's awake. And, Thomas, you need to take it easy too. Your lungs seem to have fared better than hers, but don't push yourself too hard."

"I'll be careful."

"I'll keep an eye on him," Margaret said.

The doctor offered a few more bits of medical wisdom, then with bag in hand he left.

Margaret looked at him as though she were appraising him, judging his health and mental state. "I'd like to spread word of the accident. Penny hasn't been here long, but there are already many who will care. Will you sit with her?"

"Alone?"

"I trust you. Besides, I've a girl who helps me with dinner. She'll be downstairs in the kitchen prepping the meals. You're not truly alone. When she's better, I'll be sure I'm home if you're in her room. I meant what I said. This house is respectable, but there's a girl in there who needs a friend, so go."

Thomas swallowed the lump in his throat. "I will." Then he stepped closer to Margaret. "I didn't mean what I said before.

I don't wish I'd died. I'm only sorry she's suffering. I wish I could have stopped it."

"I know. But that's in the past now. Go on in there." She shooed him toward the door. "I won't be long."

He turned toward the door.

"Wait. How did the fire start?" Margaret asked.

"I don't know. The fire was already so large by the time I got there." He looked away. The loss of his barn felt trivial in comparison to Penny's pain. "I haven't given the fire much thought. It may have eaten my house by now for all I know."

"I'll have the sheriff get men out to your place."

"It's just a barn." Thomas leaned against the doorframe.

"No. It was *your* barn. And someone could have lost their life today." She looked at Penny's door. "Go see to her. I'll get the right people looking into the fire. Tell me, though, what has become of Honey?"

"I don't know. I heard her barking and came toward the noise. I didn't see her again. I became so worried about the fire and then Penny." He slammed his fist into the doorframe. "I promised Penny I'd take care of Honey."

"I'll tell the men to look for her. Go in there now." Margaret turned her back and descended the stairs, leaving him alone outside of Penny's room.

Obediently, he stepped into the room that had once been his. Penny lay on the very bed he had spent so many restless nights on. The furnishings were the same as when he had stayed in the room, but where his sparse belongings had been her more feminine ones now resided. A bonnet on the end of the bed, women's shoes near the door, and a hairbrush beside the washbasin. Still, there were enough reminders of his days in the room that a shiver ran through him.

Those had been dark days for him—full of agony and regret. Purposeless, hollow days. He'd make sure the days she spent in this room were better than his own had been.

"I'm so sorry." He stepped farther into the room and knelt beside her sleeping frame. "I wish I could take all the pain from your body. I wish I could go back and stop the fire from ever starting." He let his head fall against the edge of the bed. "I never expected to have so many regrets. I wanted to be a changed man." Then he lifted his head and looked at the woman who'd saved him. "I'll not make you sorry you came after me. I'll make sure you never regret that."

He took her small hand in his and held it, thankful she was able to find sleep despite the pain.

"You know," he whispered, "I was a successful businessman before I was a farmer." He filled the silence by quietly spewing whatever came to his mind. "Back then no one would have dared tell me I was wrong. But here I am, little more than a lost soul. But I'll be better." He ran his thumb over her knuckles. "I promise you, Penelope Ercanbeck, I will be attentive to you. If you need anything, I'll be there. I'll do anything. You will be my purpose."

He pressed his lips to the tips of her fingers before setting her hand down on the bed. "And my joy. This day and always." He sat up straighter, surprised by his own words, but he did not take them back. Instead, he found himself studying the fair-skinned woman on the bed. Dark smudges ran along the bridge of her nose and up her cheekbones. Her hair had come loose and lay in a mass of curls. He reached out and brushed them from her face.

"I'm afraid of fire," he confessed. "I thought the fear was gone. That I was a new man. I've felt so much better as of late, but when I saw the barn go up in flames it all came racing back to me. The memories and the fear took over. I didn't mean for it to happen. I didn't mean to run inside. I'm so sorry I did."

Penny moaned and turned her head to the side. He stood and took a couple steps away, unsure of how to help.

A washbasin with a cloth next to it sat in the corner of the room. He went to it and dipped the cloth into the cool water. Then he knelt again at her bedside and gently washed the black from her face.

"Fire is like a monster." His voice was low and steady. "It eats what it wants. Its appetite is always growing." He wiped the cloth across her forehead. "Devouring anything it can."

A tear ran from his eye. He did not move to wipe it. "I had a fire inside of me once—not a warm fire but a hungry, angry fire. It had no hearth around it to contain it. It was large and fierce. I could not see anything but the fire. I did not love well or even live well. All I did was feed it. I had to work harder. I had to grow my business. I had to have the town belle on my arm. I had to be better than any man around me. I fed the flames day and night."

He laid the washcloth on the bedside table and rubbed his face with his hands. "I let it rob me of so much. But you were only a victim. You ran into the flames for me. You saved me."

His heart swelled as the reality of her sacrifice settled over him. He leaned over her and pressed his lips to her forehead. "Thank you. Thank you for coming for me."

Her hand reached for his face, then dropped again.

Penny struggled to piece the puzzle together. She remembered the barn. The wild look in Thomas's eyes. And then the sudden pain. The searing, horrible pain. When the beam hit her, she'd believed she was going to die. In desperation, she'd called to him. She recalled that.

She opened her eyes. Thomas was sitting in a chair by her bed.

"You . . ." She tried to swallow. The words wouldn't come. Her throat was so dry. "You . . . the fire?"

"Shh." He stroked her hand. "You're safe. You're at the boardinghouse. It's been two days."

"Two days? What? How?"

"You're getting better. Don't worry. It's normal to sleep a lot when you're healing. The doctor has set your leg and stitched the injuries. He says you'll be back on your feet with time. Until then, we'll care for you. I'll care for you."

"But . . . the fire."

"It burned the barn and the cellar. I'm told the house was left untouched."

"Are you hurt?" she whispered. The more awake she became, the more she felt the throbbing pain in her leg. Pressing her hands into the bed, she tried to sit. "My leg. It hurts."

"I know it does. It'll get better. The doctor has assured us many times that it will." He put his hand on her shoulder and gently encouraged her to lie back down. "You have to take it easy. I know it hurts. But getting agitated will make it worse, not better."

She forced her eyes to focus on him. He looked tired. "You were here? All this time?"

"Yes," he said quietly. "Margaret has a spare room. She's permitted me to stay and help."

"Your farm?"

"Caleb and the sheriff are asking around. They hope to find

clues. But the fire may have been some sort of an accident."
He scratched his brow. "My crops weren't going to amount to
much anyway. Even if they were, I want to be here. I want to
be here with you." She watched as his Adam's apple bobbed
up and down. "You saved me."

"No," she whispered. "You saved me in ways you don't even
know. I wanted to tell you. I was coming . . . I was going to tell
you." She tried to clear her throat, but it was too dry. A painful bout of coughing racked her lungs. "I don't think it was
an accident."

"The barn fire?"

She nodded. "I saw a man. I couldn't see his face, but he
was not far off when I was coming." Another bout of coughing
shook her entire body. When it calmed, she went on. "Maybe
he was passing by. I don't know. I just ran to you."

His brow creased as though he too were in pain. "Do you
remember anything else? Did he see you?"

"I don't know if he saw me. I wish I could remember more.
I don't like thinking you're in danger."

He sat up straighter. His eyes looked at her with new urgency.
"I don't like thinking you're in danger. If someone is out to get
me, they can have me, but you've seen them." He ran a hand
through his hair. "I don't know who it is. If someone comes
for you—"

"No one will." Penny felt safe, comfortable at Margaret's. She
didn't want to entertain ideas that contradicted the peace she
had found. "No one will do anything to me. I'm never alone."

He flexed his jaw. "Rest now and get better. We'll have more
time to talk later. I'll tell the sheriff you saw someone. I'll sort it
all out later." He picked up a stack of books and showed them
to her. "Mae and Milly were so worried about you. They've

sent several books for you to listen to. I believe their words were 'She's an author. She must love books.'"

"An aspiring author." Penny struggled to get the words out. "I told them that."

"Nevertheless, they sent them. I've read you some already, but I don't think the words meant much." He put the books back down and picked up something else. "You've also received a letter."

"A letter!" She pulled herself up quickly, only to slide back down when her head started spinning. "Someone wrote me."

"Take it easy." He showed her the letter. "I can read it if you want."

"No! You can't." She tried to grasp for it. "Don't read it!"

He laughed and the sound made her weary spirits soar. "I'll set it on the desk for when you are feeling well enough to read it yourself. Why don't I read to you? Just a book, nothing personal. I'll let you keep your letter to yourself, though I am rather curious. It must be full of secrets. When you're better"—he paused—"we can talk of other things."

She sank deeper into her pillow. "I would like that."

She felt the bed beside her. Something wasn't right. "Where's Honey?"

A long silence hung in the air. Finally, he put his hand on her shoulder, leaned close, and said, "Will you trust me to care for her? You just get yourself well."

Instantly, Penny's chest tightened. "Is she hurt?"

"She is."

"Is she dead?" Penny's voice cracked. "Tell me. I have to know."

"No. She's hurt, but she's alive. We aren't sure what happened. Maybe part of the burning barn fell on her too." He

225

glanced toward the door. "You saw a rider. Someone may have injured her. The doctor's done what he can, but there's not much he can do if the injuries are inside of her."

"She may not get better?"

"She's not had much of an appetite these last two days. She's in my room. I can bring her in here if you want." Thomas moved his hand to her cheek. "I'm doing what I can for Honey. I'll make it right somehow."

The feel of his touch sent Penny's heart racing and tears ran from her eyes. He wiped them gently.

"I would not have offered to care for her if I'd thought it would end like this," he said.

"It's not over. She'll get well." Penny bit her quivering lip. "We'll all be well again." She put her hand on his. "Bring me Honey? We've spent many years together. She's shared my good and my bad times, and this should be no different."

"I'll bring her." He stood and left the room. When he returned, he was carrying Honey in his arms. Her normally energetic dog looked weak. For a moment Penny wondered if she was truly alive. "The doctor has stitched her up and done all he can for her. He didn't think she would make it when we first got her to town, but she has a fighting spirit."

He stepped so close that Penny could look into the chocolate eyes of her beloved friend. She touched Honey's nose with a weak hand. "Hello, girl." Honey whimpered in Thomas's arms. He held the dog even closer to Penny. Honey whined, then calmed when her head was resting on Penny's shoulder.

"Don't be afraid," Penny said while stroking her. She was so tired that even the small motion added to her weariness. "I know Thomas will take good care of you. And I'm here."

"I'll make a bed on the floor for her." Thomas set Honey beside Penny's bed, then gathered blankets and made her a bed of her own, all the while talking to the animal in a smooth, soothing voice. "Now I can look after both my charges at the same time. Won't that be nice? You can be in here with Miss Penny."

"Thank you, Thomas. My father gave me Honey. In a way, he feels closer when Honey is here." Penny lay back on her pillow and closed her eyes. "Promise me you'll get her well. I don't want to lose her."

"I can't promise that." He took her hand in his. "I can't promise it even though I'd like to."

"Please," she whispered.

"I promise you I will stay with you and with her. I promise you I will do all I can to keep you safe. Those things I can promise you, and I do promise them."

Penny forced a grateful smile, but even as she did, another tear slid from the corner of her eye.

Dear Penny,

I've received two letters from you and hope to receive many, many more. I want to hear all the details of your adventure. Every day I eagerly rush to the post office in hopes of finding a letter from my faraway friend. For the first time, I've letters there for me. You were right, letters do brighten people's day.

I knew when you opened this letter you would want to find news of my wedding. I can imagine you holding it with eager anticipation. So, I'll spare you any further suspense. I am married to Lucas!

We met last Friday night after work and hurried to the pastor's home. He had agreed to marry us and Lucas had arranged everything. I wore my yellow dress. The one with the blue flowers. It's the nicest dress I have. I was worried it was not nice enough for a wedding, but Lucas said I looked lovely. And I never sensed a moment of hesitation from him.

I believe the pastor was in a hurry. He said very little, and once I heard him mumble under his breath about us being too anxious. Even if he wasn't the most eloquent *pastor, he still married us. We each promised to love and cherish each other. We signed the certificate and walked away husband and wife. It's such a simple thing, yet I knew in those brief moments that the entire course of my life had changed. I am married because of those vows. And I will honor them always.*

We spent our wedding night in our new home. I know if you were here, you'd whisper questions about being with a man. I'd tell you too. I'd tell you being with a man is beautiful. At least being with a good man is. I cannot write more than that. (I know if this does not reach you, someone at the dead letter office will read it, and I could never stand for my secrets to fall into the hands of the clerks.)

I was afraid I'd have regrets or fears, but I have none. Lucas is quiet, but he is kind. We told my parents the next day. My mother brushed her hands together and then asked me if I'd change the baby. It was strange and heartbreaking. I suppose I had hoped marrying would somehow change me in her eyes. We stayed and I played with the little ones and then we left. I'd always hoped my mother would see me differently. I've wanted her approval since I was a little girl. And though I'd still like it, I will not change my course in order to gain it.

Lucas's parents are poor but kind. They gave us a set of four tin mugs as a wedding gift. I know it's a simple gift, but it felt like a welcoming embrace. His mother pulled me aside and told me how she had prayed that her son would find a good woman. She had tears in her eyes when she said it.

I live in my own apartment now. We walked for hours yesterday looking for flowers. We walked together through the city, all the way to the outskirts. I told Lucas my hopes for our home. I told him I wanted to make it bright and happy. I don't think he understood it all, but he took my hand and walked with me until we'd found a handful of bright flowers, then he bought a little vase to put them in and set it on our table. That gesture won my heart completely. I could not have found a better man. I knew then that our love, though different from some, was just as valid and real.

The only thing missing here is you. I am happy, though, knowing you are following your own heart and doing what you felt led to do. My heart soars knowing you have met your Thomas and that he is not a grumpy old man. Your words about his handsomeness and dancing have left me longing for more details. I feel as though I am missing the second half of a novel. I must know everything. Have you brought him hope? Has he fallen for you? I like to think he has. I hope your heart is fluttering around like you always imagined it would.

I have laughed over your stories of Honey and her troublesome ways. She was always begging you for more freedom, and now she has it.

Last night I sewed buttons on a shirt for Lucas. He sat in a chair beside me, balancing an account book. And in that moment, I was very grateful this is my life. I spent many years lamenting the hardships of my youth. I know your heart aches too. You lost a great deal. Your fortune and your father. I hope you'll one day have a beautiful mo-ment when it all makes sense. I hope you have a moment when you know the road you've walked was not a mistake but a route leading you to happiness despite the bumps

along the way. My moment brought a smile to my face. I
imagine you'll be ever so much more dramatic. I miss you.

Your friend,
Dinah

"That's all it says." Penny turned her head toward Honey, who lay convalescing on the floor. "I wish there were more. I've missed her so. More now than ever before."

Penny closed her eyes. The peaceful moments Dinah spoke of seemed out of reach. Impossible, even.

She had spent four days lying in bed, fighting the pain that screamed through her body. Thomas had visited often. He had mostly read to her or sat silent as he held her hand. She had overheard him talking to her while he thought she was sleeping. Over and over again, he apologized. Normally his ramblings only left her with more questions. She had planned to ask them, but she'd been so exhausted. Only now was she able to read and think clearly.

Lifting the blankets, she looked down at her splinted and bandaged leg. The pain was becoming tolerable. If she kept it still, she could pass the time in relative comfort. But sitting still all day presented different challenges. A heaviness invaded her chest as she worried over the fire, who started it, and the expense of being laid up. The doctor alone would cost her the meager savings she had left.

A knock sounded on the door. She dropped the blanket back down.

"Come in."

"You're awake." Thomas opened the door and stood with a tray in his hands. "May I?"

231

"Of course. I was just reading the letter my friend wrote."
She put Dinah's letter on the little bedside table.

"Was it happy news?"

Penny managed to smile despite her melancholy. "She's married. There was a time when she had given up on that dream.
I'm happy for her. She had feared she would never have a house
and life of her own." She looked down, afraid if he saw her eyes
he'd see the pain in them. He'd see her fears of being alone or
married to a man of her uncle's choosing. Already, he worried
too much over her. "I've not met her husband, Lucas, but she
says he's a good man."

"I'm sorry you missed her wedding." He set down the tray
on the bedside table. "I can fetch you paper so you can write
her back."

"I'll write her soon. I'm not sure I feel up to it yet. I promised
I'd write her about everything, but I don't want to send bad
news." She tilted her head back and looked up at the ceiling.
"My friend married in secret."

Thomas settled into the chair beside the bed. "I'm sure her
parents were sorry they couldn't be there."

"I don't know if they were. When Dinah lived at home,
her father drank all the time and her mother was so busy
caring for all the other children that she rarely did anything
but order Dinah around. They probably miss the income she
brought in." Penny picked at her rough thumbnail as she tried
to imagine Dinah a married woman. "She's going to make a
different sort of home for herself now." She turned toward
him. "There was a time when my parents would have thrown
me the largest wedding in DC. My mother still dreams of it.
The newspapers would have talked about it on the front page.
I don't care about such things now. But I do miss my father

232

and my friend, and I long for the mother of my youth. I suppose I'm just feeling sorry for myself." She shifted on the bed. "We're all entitled to a blue day every now and again, are we not?"

"I know I've had my fair share. I won't begrudge you as many as you need."

"Life has turned out so different than I imagined. Not just because of my leg, but all of it."

He took her hand. Her heart fluttered even though she knew it was not a romantic gesture.

She looked at her hand in his. His skin was rough and darkened by the sun. She felt the calluses that covered the underside of his palm. Since her injury the two had grown closer as they shared in her recovery and divulged bits of themselves. She longed to be closer still.

He pressed his fingers tightly around hers. "I'm sorry," he whispered. "I wish I could fix it all."

"My father liked saying that pain was not the enemy." She lifted her gaze to his eyes. "But sometimes it feels like it is. Loneliness hurts, my leg hurts, and my heart hurts. I don't think any good could come from it. And yet, I am grateful you are here holding my hand."

He swallowed. "I don't understand how it all works. I'd go back and change so many things in my own life if I could. But I'm glad I'm here now."

"You are?"

"I am." His hand tightened around hers as he scooted his chair nearer to her. "I'm a better person in Azure Springs than I was in Alexandria. And pain brought me here. I'm still making peace with it all, but I'm grateful I got here even if the road was rocky and marred with pain."

"Someday, will you tell me about Alexandria and why you left?"

"I will. You get well first. I think you still have much convalescing to do."

She groaned. "I don't think I'm the sort who was made for convalescing."

"You'll be back to dancing before you know it. And I think Honey might just be back to running for the mud before long. She won't even stay on the bed I made her. She's always scooting toward you. You were the medicine she needed." He lifted a bowl from the tray. "Margaret has sent instructions. She says you are to eat all of this. If I bring it back with even one bite in it, she'll have my head." He handed her the bowl. "Do you need help?"

"I can manage." She stared blankly at the bowl.

"Would you like me to go?"

She shook her head. "No. I enjoy having company. But if your fields need you—"

"They don't." He ran his hands along the arms of the chair. "Buying that farm was a wise decision. One that didn't make sense but I'm grateful for. I'm not a farmer, but I was a man who needed solitude and something to keep me busy while I found my way. But I don't think I'll be a farmer forever."

"What will you do? Will you leave Azure Springs?"

"I suppose in some ways it depends on who burned the barn. I won't stay in town if I am putting anyone in danger." His shoulders rose then fell as he shrugged. "I came here knowing I could come or go as seemed right. But I like it here. And I like the Dawson place. I just don't know that I'll be there forever."

Penny pressed her lips together. She tried to imagine Azure Springs without Thomas, but she couldn't.

"Go ahead. Say what you're holding back."

"Very well. Don't you need to work? How can you survive if your crops have failed? It doesn't work like that. At least not for most people." Penny winced. "I shouldn't have said that. It's not any of my business and terribly unladylike of me to ask."

"Nonsense. You can ask me whatever you wish. The truth is, I still have some money coming in from Alexandria." He shifted in his seat. "Money's not been a worry, not ever."

Penny shook her head. "It's been so long since I could live like that. I've been busily counting coins for years."

"But you're not working now."

"I saved for many years. Just a few coins here and there. I've been using that money to live off of since I've been here. It will not last forever." She had Margaret dig her money box from her trunk early today. She would not make it much longer. "The day will come when I'll have to return to work or live off my uncle's charity." She took a deep breath and let it out slowly. "Someday soon I'll have to head back. Once I'm well enough to travel, it'll be time to decide what to do—work or a marriage of my uncle's choosing are my options."

"And your book?"

"It's still a dream. But dreams don't pay for doctors or for board." She squirmed uneasily. The room felt warmer and she wished she could stand up and go to the window for fresh air. Instead, she changed the subject. "Tell me, have you found Josephine? Or learned more of the fire? Did you catch the man? I feel as though I've missed everything. I have so many questions now that I'm well enough to ask them."

"We've asked around. A few people have passed through town lately, but no one who would have a reason to go to my place. The sheriff hasn't been able to find anyone with a motive." He leaned closer to her and took her hand again. "There's really no evidence of anything. There's the man you saw and that's all. I don't like it. I won't sleep soundly until I'm sure this town and you are safe. Have you remembered anything else?"

"I want you safe too." She wanted that most of all. "I've tried to remember what I can about the man I saw. I think his horse was large and black." She looked at their hands. His touch was distracting and comforting all at once. "You held my hand. It was you, wasn't it? When I was in so much pain."

He brought her fingers to his lips. "It was."

"I took comfort in it." She smiled. "I wish I knew more about the man. I wish I had answers for you."

"Don't worry over it. The sheriff is bound to find a lead."

"Your barn—and Honey. It makes my skin crawl to think someone did this intentionally. We could have died out there."

Thomas shushed her. "It's all right. Try not to get upset. I promise everyone in town is talking about the fire and trying to put the pieces together. I trust them to help me find answers."

"Did you not have someone watching your fields that night?" She let go of his hand, then ate a spoonful of the soup he had brought. The rich flavors of beef and onion awakened her stomach. "This is so good."

"Margaret will be pleased. You've rejected most everything we've offered you." He sat silently while she took another spoonful. "I did have a watchman, Joe, but he had asked for the night off. He'd been so eager to go, I couldn't say no. It was such short notice that I couldn't find anyone else. I thought with Honey there I'd hear someone if they came."

He handed her a glass of water and she took a sip and handed it back to him. "At first I suspected Joe, but his story holds up. He was invited to dine with the Marlinskis. I believe he is sweet on their daughter. They say he was there. I can find no holes in his story."

"But was he there in the morning? Surely, he was not." She felt the same eagerness to solve the mystery of the fire that she'd felt so often before when she read an intriguing letter. "Whoever did this must know the Marlinskis well enough to know they were having Joe as a dinner guest."

"I've thought that too. Or someone could have been watching for the right moment. In the morning, he was at home with his family. His parents and sisters all vouch for him. I don't know who else to ask. I suspect Jeb's involvement, but there's been no proof. The sheriff even asked his wife. She says Jeb was at home with her during the time of the fire." He grimaced. "It's all very puzzling."

"What of Josephine?" she asked again while handing him her bowl. "Have you found her?"

"She showed back up on her own. Hugh brought her into town and put her up in the stables for me. For a horse that doesn't like me, she's proven to be either dim-witted or loyal." He rubbed the back of his neck. He opened his mouth as though he were going to speak, then shut it again.

"What is it?"

"You've . . . you've not looked this well yet. Your face has so much color today." As did his. A rosy blush darkened his cheeks.

"Who knew I'd come out of the fire a different woman? Normally people only remark on how fair my skin is." She laughed quietly. "I am glad to be feeling better. Though I do long for the day when I can move with ease."

He continued to squirm in his seat. "I wanted to. I've . . . I've been wanting to tell you that I am grateful for what you did. I . . . I was somewhere else in my mind. The fire . . ."

"You are afraid of fire," she whispered. "I dreamed you told me the other night. I dreamed many things."

He brought her hand to his lips again and pressed a kiss to it. "I *am* afraid of fire. So afraid I could not think clearly. But you were there. You saved me. I don't know why you were there that morning, but you were. And now you're sitting here looking at me with your green eyes and I see nothing but sweetness and goodness despite the pain you've endured. I don't deserve it."

How was it that she could feel the touch of his lips throughout her entire body? "I've thanked God I was there. I'd do it all again for you. I would. Even knowing my leg would break. I'd still do it."

"I am sorry about Honey too." He looked toward the sleeping dog.

"I have never seen her so docile." Penny's eyes lingered on her four-legged friend. "Last night when neither of us could sleep, she crawled across the floor and laid near my bed. I told her I was going to be all right and she in her own way told me she would be too." Penny took a deep breath as she tried to suppress the storm of emotions she felt. Excitement. Relief. Warmth. "Even if she were not to be, I would not blame you. I've seen a glimpse of your heart and it's not wicked. You wouldn't hurt her by choice, and I cannot blame you for an accident."

"You don't blame me?"

"No. Bad things happen. And since the fire you have taken care of us and we will be well again. That's what you could control. You were there for us when we needed you. I felt you holding my hand when I was lost to the pain. You gave me something to hold on to."

"I am here. I want to help you pass the time while you recover.

Whatever it is that will help, tell me and I will be your faithful servant." He winked. "What is it your heart desires?"

She scrunched up her face while she thought. What did she desire? A good many things, but she could not voice them all.

"Go on. You can ask for anything," he said. "I want to help."

"You don't have to feel guilty. You owe me nothing." She could still hear him screaming for Clara. "You don't have to take care of me. I didn't go into the barn expecting anything from you. That's not why I ran to you. I will not hold this over your head."

He leaned forward and put a hand under her chin. Gently, he turned her face toward him. Their eyes locked. "I *want* to be here. I've never wanted anything so badly. Tell me what I can do to make your days better. Let me help. Please."

She took a deep breath, then latched onto a desire she felt safe enough now to say aloud. "Write me a letter."

"A letter?" he said as he brought his hands to his lap.

She nodded. "With my name on it."

"I can do that," he said. "I don't have a lot of experience though. I can't promise you'll enjoy it."

"I know you've written before."

He sat back in his chair. "I have written before. But I never intended for most of the letters I wrote to be read." He cleared his throat. "That sounded far more mysterious than I intended."

"It's all right. You don't have to explain to me. It was a silly idea."

"No. I will write you." He pointed to the letter from Dinah. "Was that not enough?"

"I loved it. It made me long to see my friend. It made me happy and sad and so many other things all at once." She swallowed the lump that rose in her throat. "I miss her. Now I have her words to revisit as often as I like. But I want more. And don't you just feel like a letter is a special gift?"

"My experience with receiving letters has been primarily limited to business correspondence."

"I confess, I love letters. My father used to write my mother. I believe my fondness for letters began when I first discovered that he addressed his letters to her 'my darling.' Since then I've always loved the written word."

"Then that is what you'll get." He stood up suddenly. "I'll write you friendly correspondence. I . . . I wasn't saying I'd write a letter like your father wrote." He bent over and picked up the water glass. "Here. Have another drink."

"Thank you." She took it and brought it to her lips for a long sip. "I wasn't asking for a letter like the ones my father wrote." Such a silly request. She chastised herself for being so bold.

He sat back down. "I'm sorry. What would you like it to be about?"

"I don't know. My favorites are letters that tap into the soul. The written word has a way of capturing emotion in a sweet and profound way."

"I'm not sure I can write a letter that opens my soul."

She smiled, remembering the letters he had written to Clara. The longing, the sadness, the pain. She had felt it all when she read his words. "Try?"

"For you, I will."

*T*homas sat much of the night at his desk with a blank piece of paper in front of him. Writing to Penny felt so different from writing to Clara. The words he wrote would not be for his own healing but for another's. Penny's presence, even when she was in pain or sleeping, was incredibly pleasant. *What words does one write to an angel?*

My Dear Penny,

He wadded the piece of paper into a ball. She was not *his* Penny even if he had begun to think of her as such. He began again.

Dear Penny,
When you arrived in town, you brought sunshine with you. My life had been so dark and then there you were. I was climbing out of a deep hole, and I felt like if I followed the light, I'd be all right. I was searching for a hand to hold, someone to help me figure out how to go on and how to live. I was seeking purpose and joy.

And then there you were with your green eyes and dimpled smile. You've been in my head and heart since that first day. You were so charming, all flustered as you struggled to pull Honey from the mud, then later when you stumbled about trying to put papers and books back on the display. Something about the way you smiled, or perhaps it was the way you made me laugh over the pie at the social. Or was it the way you listened when I spoke or the way my heart raced when you were in my arms? The truth is, I don't know what it was about you that changed me. I only know that you did. And even now, as I plead with God to ease your pain, I am changed. I've never cared for another's wants and needs. I didn't know the purpose that could be found in acts of selflessness until now. I find myself wanting to care for you always. If I could choose a course to lead, I'd choose one that included holding your hand forever.

Your very presence makes me believe I can be more than what I was before. I am not sure what led you to Azure Springs. But I believe God was in it. He must have been. There is no other way something so beautiful could be born of so much pain. And you and I both have walked our own tear-stained paths.

He looked at his words on the page. They were true. Every word was true. He had felt different since he met her. And he did wish and pray and hope there could be a way for him to enjoy Penny's presence always. But he could not put that letter into her hands. Not now. Not when there were still so many unspoken words between them. Not when he'd just made a fool of himself letting her know he would not be writing a love letter.

He took another clean sheet of paper and laid it on the desk.

Dear Penny,

As you know, I live on a beautiful farm that I know will produce next to nothing this year. It's strange, though, that I care so little. Don't get me wrong, I am a man who believes in hard work. But I've learned so much from the labor, from the unpredictable nature of farming, and even from the loss that I don't mind. I never knew I could fail and succeed at the same time. I have reaped a great deal despite my abysmal harvest. My little farm has taught me about life. About planting good seeds and riding out the storms, and for the first time in my life I see value in my failure. I don't know what course I'll take next. I think I'll walk the streets of this town and see what I might offer it. I owe it that much. It's given me a new start and welcomed me with open arms.

My life as a farmer and the lessons I'm learning are probably not what you were hoping to read about. But if you want to know my soul, then you must know I am a man navigating a new road. A path I never planned to travel. A path I found as I struggled with remorse, loneliness, and uncertainty. A path I wish I'd found some other way but that I am grateful to be on.

You in your own way have been part of my journey. Even before you saved me from the flames, you were there reminding me to smile. I thank you for it. And I pray for a swift and full recovery for both you and your mud-loving dog.

Prayers for healing,
Thomas

For a moment, he stared at his words. They would do. His soul was exposed but not as completely as in his other attempt. He slept then, grateful that Margaret had arranged to have people sit with Penny during the night.

At first light, he crossed the hall and rapped on her door. He had heard someone leave not long ago and hoped to find Penny alone.

"Come in." She had been awake already. He could tell from her now-familiar voice.

"I've your letter," he said as he opened the door and entered the room. Penny was propped up in bed. Her dark hair was loose, hanging around her shoulders. He walked to her bed and held out the paper. "I'm not the best with words."

She clasped her hands together. "You wrote it! Already?" She smiled and took the letter from him.

"I did." He shoved his hands in his pockets. Everything in him wanted to reach out and touch her. "Read it when I'm gone. Save it for when you are tired of looking at these four walls. I know how it can be sitting around all day."

She pressed the letter to her heart. "I will enjoy every word of it. It's a beautiful gift."

"What will you do when you return to the city? I've wondered about it since you told me your two options." For a second he wished he could take back the words. Asking her, though he craved an answer, meant facing her impending departure. He swallowed against the lump in his throat. *If only she would tell me she was staying.*

Penny pulled the blanket tighter around herself. "I've struggled with this decision. I hope to have my job still. Margaret has sent word to Mr. Douglas at the office telling him of my injuries and asking him to be patient while I recover. I will attempt to find a boardinghouse or room to rent. I might be able to board with a girl from the office. I haven't been able to work all of that out yet. I feel tired whenever I think of going back."

"What of your mother?"

Penny looked away. "I asked Margaret to send word of my injuries. We've heard nothing back, but it may be she hasn't gotten it. My uncle has always been fond of traveling, so perhaps she's away. I don't know her schedule. Anyway, I think working is a better choice. I may not have financial freedom, but I will have the freedom to choose how I live. I don't think I could find joy in a forced marriage. If for some reason Mr. Douglas will not take me back or for some reason I become desperate, I suppose I'll have to submit to my uncle to survive."

"Where did you work?" Thomas asked. Talking of wages seemed far safer than discussing marriages of convenience. "Tell me who you were before you came. I'd like to know."

She fidgeted with the letter in her hands. "I worked at an office. I sorted papers." Her eyes would not meet his. What was she trying so hard not to tell him?

"What sort of an—"

"Thomas," someone shouted up the stairs. "Thomas, are you here?"

He stepped away from the bed and went to the door. "I'm up here." Then he turned toward Penny. "It's the sheriff. I forgot we were meeting to talk about my barn. Can we talk more later?"

"Go. That's where you need to be." She waved the letter in the air. "I'll just read this letter while you're away."

He hesitated at the door. Everything in him wanted to stay. "I'll be back. I want to know more."

"I worked at the dead letter office," she blurted out, then covered her mouth.

"You worked at the dead letter office?" He didn't mask his surprise. It couldn't be true. The dead letter office was where his lost letters had wound up. His letters to Clara. His stomach twisted into knots. "The dead letter office?"

"Yes."

"What? H-how?" He'd already had questions for her, but now he didn't even know where to begin. When he had thought privately about her past, he'd never once thought to include the dead letter office in his speculations. He tilted his head back and stared up at the ceiling. "You—"

"Thomas." The sheriff's voice traveled up the stairs again.

He stared at her. Who was she? Who was she really?

"Go," she said. "Go be with the sheriff. I'll be here when you return. I'll tell you anything you wish to know. I'll tell you it all."

He stared a moment longer, torn between leaving and staying. Finally, he stepped away from the room. "I'll be back," he said before shutting the door behind him.

What had she done?

She put her hand on her chest. The hand he'd held so often these last few days. Tears sprang to the corners of her eyes. "I had to tell him," she said to Honey, knowing it was true. The dog's face turned down. "Don't look at me like that. I had to. I can't pretend forever." But the truthfulness of it all did not make it easier to swallow. Honey staggered across the floor until she was sitting at Penny's bedside. "I didn't mean to care for him so. I don't know how it happened."

Honey whimpered, and the sound of it pierced her heart. Why couldn't she have met Thomas in some simple, ordinary way?

246

"Shall I read his words?" she asked. Honey cocked her head. "I hope they are not the last words we read from him." She took a deep breath, trying to brace herself for the very real chance that they may be. "I'll not think of that now. I'll just read them and enjoy them. Let's just be happy we have them. All right?"

Penny unfolded the letter. She didn't read it right away. Instead, she allowed her eyes to admire the fine penmanship.

He wrote to me. Thomas Conner wrote to me.

She pushed herself up higher in the bed so she was sitting and brought the letter closer. Slowly she read his words. Savoring each sentence, devouring them like one consumes a rich and delectable pastry. *This is what I wanted*, she reminded herself. Her purpose for coming to Azure Springs was to know he was well—and he was. Only now she wished there could be a different purpose in it all. A longer, more lasting purpose.

Another knock.

Penny folded the letter and tucked it beneath her pillow. "Come in."

"I'm sorry to come by unannounced. I'm Eliza Danbury. I've wanted to meet you but have not been able to until now." The woman looked back toward the door, her eyes like those of a skittish deer. "I hope it's all right that I've come by."

Penny had seen Eliza at the social. This beautiful woman was Jeb's wife. Why was she here? "It's nice to officially meet you. I'm Penelope Ercanbeck. I'd get up and give you a proper greeting if I could."

"Please don't even try. I can't stay long. I have to get back before . . . I just have to be back soon. I wanted to stop by and see how you were. I heard you were hurt in the fire."

Penny nodded. "I was. A beam crashed into me. Thomas lifted it off and pulled me out of the burning building. I'll be all right with time. I expect I'll have scars, but I suppose we all do. Only some cannot be seen." She watched as Eliza tugged at the sleeve of her dress. "The doctor said I'll be fine."

Eliza seemed to relax. She clasped her hands together. "I was so worried." Her voice was thick with emotion. "I was afraid you'd not be able to walk. When I heard, I was sick inside."

Several women from around town had been by to check on Penny since she'd been injured. All of them had showed concern, and she'd been touched by their generosity and compassion. But none of them had looked as troubled as Eliza, whose brow was marred with worry lines. But why?

"Thank you for caring. It means a great deal. Especially since I am but a visitor here."

Eliza brushed her hands over her skirts. "What of Thomas? Is he all right? Is he angry over his losses?"

"He's confused and wants to know what happened, but he does not seem angry. Mostly, he's been worried about me." She studied the woman. She was near her own age, but she looked so tired. "His barn is lost, though, and his cellar. His horse would have died if he had not gotten her out. And we believe someone hurt my dog. We can't say for certain, but she was injured at the same time as the fire."

"His horse was still inside? Someone hurt your dog?" Eliza muttered something under her breath that sounded like the words *cruel and hateful.* She crossed the room and knelt in front of Honey. "I'm so sorry." She scratched Honey behind one of her soft ears. Honey nuzzled closer to Eliza, whimpering in contentment as she went. Without looking up, Eliza asked, "His horse is well?"

"Yes. His horse was in the barn when the fire started. Thomas could have died saving her. Do you know anything about the fire? Do you know who started it?"

Eliza stood up and took a step backward. "I'm glad you're recovering. And I'm very sorry about your dog. It all seems so horrible. I-I wish there was some way I could help. I have to go though. I'm due back."

"Tell me. Do you know something?"

Eliza bit her bottom lip and shook her head. "There's nothing I can do. I'm so glad you're recovering," she said as she backed out of the room.

We haven't been able to put together any clues about the barn. I'm sorry I don't have better news. We've all been asking around, looking for any information we can find. But everyone we suspect has an alibi. The color of a horse isn't much to go off of." The sheriff slowed his pace. "I wish I could tell you more. Unfortunately, there's really no way of knowing who started the fire or hurt the dog. When I talked to Penny, I tried to get more out of her, but she doesn't remember anything else."

"That's not good enough." Thomas's voice rose. "Whoever did this is still out there. You're supposed to keep this place safe."

"I'm sorry."

"What do I do now?" Thomas said through gritted teeth. "Pretend it never happened? Wait until the person strikes again and hope they don't go after my house next time?"

"Rebuild your barn." The sheriff spoke in an even tone. "There really isn't much else you can do. Get on with your life. I used to be a sheriff in Comish, and we had things happen there that we couldn't solve. Just like in this case. If something comes up, I'll revisit it. Right now there's just nothing."

Thomas didn't mind rebuilding. It was what he was doing with his life right now, so he might as well rebuild his barn too. But more was at stake than just wood and nails. "Who's to say it won't happen again?"

"I wish I could say it won't. But I can't make you any promises. Let's hope it was some sort of an accident. The man on the black horse may have been a coincidence."

"So, that's it? Someone gets to burn my barn and I get to spend the rest of my life wondering when it's going to happen again, praying it was just a fluke? I'll have to watch my back all the time. I thought I was done living like that." Anger was boiling inside. "Do I let them win? Tuck my tail and run?"

"Get a few men to work out on your land. Build a bunkhouse. The more eyes, the better. But that'll cost you money. I wish I had a better solution for you. Mishaps are part of the cost of living this far from the civilized part of the country."

"Mishaps." He shook his head. "It's not the farming I care so much about. I could give that up. It's feeling at ease with my neighbors. I'm after a peaceful life and I'm not sure that's possible without putting an end to this. What if I'm blessed with a family someday? How can I keep them safe if I don't know who the enemy is?"

"We'll do what we can. You've my word."

Thomas looked around in frustration. Through the window of the sheriff's office, he caught a glimpse of a woman leaving the boardinghouse. "Isn't that Jeb's wife?"

The sheriff's eyes followed Thomas's gaze. "Sure is. That's Eliza."

"What's she doing at the boardinghouse?" Thomas left the office with the sheriff on his heels.

Eliza must have seen them, because she changed directions and stepped into her father's store.

"Excuse me," Thomas said after following her inside.

"Yes." Eliza offered a weak smile. "What can I do for you?"

The sheriff took the lead then. "I've been wanting to talk to you again about the fire."

"I told you I don't know anything." She grabbed a tin of beans off a shelf. "I came into town to pick up supplies, not to be interrogated."

Her eyes darted about the room. Thomas could tell she was looking for an escape. An uneasiness overpowered him. He would not be a man who frightened women. That's not who he was.

He put a hand on the sheriff's shoulder. "If she says she knows nothing, let her be. She knows a woman almost died in that fire. I don't think she's the type to sit by and do nothing."

"Thank you," Eliza said, her eyes downcast. He couldn't help but wonder what she must have been like when she was the young, carefree woman he'd heard so much about. She set the tin back down. "I'll be on my way, then."

"You don't have to go." Abraham was making his way from the back of the store. "Stay, Eliza. I didn't know you were coming. Please stay."

"I can't," she said. "I'll try to come again soon. I want to see the girls, but I need to get home and take care of the house."

"Be safe," Abraham said as he watched his daughter hurry from the store. "She knows something. She didn't even buy the beans," he said quietly. "I can tell she knows something. She hasn't admitted it, but I can feel it. Fear's keeping her from talking."

"What can we do to keep her safe and get her to talk?"

"I don't know." He shook his head and Thomas felt the weight of his sadness. "I ask myself that question every day. I see her now—since she married Jeb—and she's not the little girl I raised. The Eliza back then was fearless. She wasn't afraid of anyone or anything. She cowers now."

The sheriff stepped toward the door. "I have to go check on the men in the jail. Be sure to tell us if you hear anything else. But if no new leads show up, I'd say it's time to move on. If Eliza's not coming forward, there's nothing else to go on." He left then, walking as though he were in a hurry.

Abraham smiled sadly at Thomas. "When you have a wife someday, treat her with gentleness. Don't give her a reason to be afraid."

Thomas swallowed. Only recently had he aspired to gentleness and meekness. He had watched Penny tossing about in a fitful sleep and had yearned to hold her, to soothe her aches. But now, with her confession, he wasn't sure what to think. Gentleness was right though. It was always right. "I will," he promised, knowing his vow was sincere.

"You're a good man, Thomas Conner." The older man looked near tears. "There is no shame in kindness. There is no shame in thoughtfulness. Remember that. Anyone can be angry and forceful. Takes a humble man to rise above that."

Thomas wished he could ease Abraham's worries. But he could not. All he could do was promise to live by the good man's advice. "I'll do that. I give you my word."

"Do you think Eliza knows anything about the fire?" Penny asked Margaret later that day. The woman's peculiar visit was still fresh on her mind. "Why won't she tell if she does?"

"I'd be willing to wager that she knows a great deal." Margaret sat near the window, sewing new curtains. She set her work down in her lap. "But she's afraid."

"Why?"

"Jeb's a smooth-talking man, always has been. As a boy and even as a young man, few of us saw him for the snake he was. Even my Scarlett thought he was charming. But there was always something wicked behind his words, and if things didn't go his way, he'd mope around or drink. I'm told he's been going to the saloon often since he was little more than a boy. But none of that was enough to keep the girls away. He had his good looks and all that land."

"Why did Eliza marry him?" Penny winced in pain. She had moved too quickly to sitting.

Margaret walked to the bed and helped her shift her legs until they were comfortable again. "I'll change these bandages again tonight."

Penny straightened her blankets. "I look forward to the day that I can get about without being at everyone's mercy. I'll be happy to leave this room and get a taste of fresh air again. I think that will be good medicine." She let her head rest against the pillow. "Will you tell me more?"

"About Eliza?"

Penny nodded. "Eliza and anyone else. I want to know about everyone."

"Eliza was the town belle. Everyone, even Caleb Reynolds, found her enticing. She flirted with them all too." Margaret slapped her leg and laughed. "You should have seen the way she danced about town. Smiling and waving at everyone. Not so different from Jeb, but for the most part her actions were innocent enough. Those of us who were out of the marriage game found it all entertaining. Things changed and there was a time when Eliza seemed to be maturing into a fine young woman."

"What happened? Why Jeb? It sounds like she could have had any man she wished."

"I'm not in Eliza's head, but I think she had played hard to get so long that everyone had started giving up on her." Margaret took her seat again at the window. "That may not be true. I don't know the whole story. I only know something changed. It's like she made up her mind she was going to get married and she was going to do it soon. That's just me guessing though. I'd love to hear her side of it all. I think her story would be laced with regrets and pain."

"Whose isn't?"

"You've got a point. But unfortunately for Eliza, I don't know how she'll overcome it all. But with Jeb . . . well, I'm not sure what to hope for."

Penny sighed. "I used to believe love was simple."

"I don't know a couple yet who would call it simple."

"What will become of Eliza?" Penny didn't really expect an answer. Who could know the future of the poor woman? Penny had spent much of the morning trying to imagine a happy ending for Eliza. She'd not been able to think of one.

"It's a tragedy for sure. The poor girl settled for Jeb, and since the day she wed him she's not been the same. I worry that he hurts her. I see her sometimes pulling at her neckline like she's worried we will all see something. Even if he's not, I don't think there's much kindness in that home." Margaret stitched on the curtains, her stitches small and consistent. "I hope things will turn around for her. Some men change when they have a good woman in their lives."

"And others?"

"They don't. Some become even worse." Margaret set her sewing in her lap.

"So she won't tell what she knows about the barn because she's afraid of Jeb." Penny folded her arms across her chest. "It's not right. Eliza shouldn't have to live that way and Thomas shouldn't have to suffer his loss and live in fear all because of one hateful man. I don't understand why Jeb's so cruel."

"It's not fair at all." Margaret held up her curtains for Penny to see. "Almost done."

"They're lovely." Penny managed a smile.

"Don't be so glum. Eliza's a strong woman. She might surprise us yet. She was brave enough to venture into town and check on you." She patted Penny's hand. "Thomas will be fine too."

"It's not safe out there for him."

"I promise you, that man cares little for his barn. His heart is here, helping you recover."

"It may have been, but I told him this morning I used to work at the dead letter office." Penny wrung her hands together and groaned. "I think I may have scared him off."

"And what did he say to that? What did he do when you told him?"

"Nothing. He just stared at me for a long moment and then left with the sheriff. I haven't seen him since. I can imagine, though, that he's questioning every word I've ever spoken to him. And rightly so. I never meant to be dishonest, but in his eyes I'm sure that's how he sees me. I only kept it to myself because I feared he'd think me foolish, and now I fear he thinks I'm nothing more than a liar."

"He'll have questions, but I don't think he'll turn his back

256

on you. I'd guess he'll be back by your side nursing you until you are up to dancing. And I have a feeling he'll want the first dance. He's not so blind that he can't see your heart."

"You really think he'll come back?"

"I do."

I was out to your place earlier today." Hugh slowed his horse when he saw Thomas walking the street in the late afternoon. "I've been trying to keep an eye on it and look for any clues."

Thomas smiled at his friend. "And how is the old Dawson place?"

"The barn's a charred ruin, but the house is in good shape. I saw a rider on a black horse when I rode in. I didn't get a good look at him, but he didn't look like one of your hands." Hugh swung off the side of his horse.

"Just the same hands as before. You didn't know the man?"

"No. I've never seen him. He left in a hurry when I got there. Rode toward Jeb's place. I started to follow, but I was unarmed and something in the pit of my stomach told me if this man was connected to the fire, then he probably wouldn't hesitate to take out a nobody like me."

"Penny saw a rider on a black horse on the day of the fire." Thomas ran a hand through his hair. "It's got to be the same person. The sheriff's all but given up, but I don't think this is over."

"What are you going to do?"

Thomas wavered between heading to the boardinghouse or the jail. "I don't know. Penny's not better yet."

"You care for the girl, don't you?"

"I don't know. If you'd asked me a few hours ago, I'd have said yes. I'd have told you that I planned to spend all the time with her I could and possibly forever, if she'd have me." He shook his head. "But now I don't know. She said something that has me wondering about the past and the future all over again." He squinted in the direction of the yellow boardinghouse. "I do know she ran into the burning barn to save me. I promised her I'd stay by her side while she recovers. I promised her that, and I won't go back on my word." He let his hands fall to his sides. He had allowed himself to imagine a future with her. It hurt thinking that may never be more than a dream. "She plans to leave town as soon as she's able. I might never have time to sort it all out."

Hugh tied his horse to a hitching post. "I hope she's on her feet soon, whether she's the girl for you or not. Think we should tell the sheriff about the rider?"

"He was here not long ago. We should let him know, though I doubt much will come of it. He's pretty well told me the case is closed. If Eliza won't talk . . ."

"It's not her fault."

"I wasn't meaning it was. I think she might know something about Jeb, but I don't blame her for keeping it to herself. I'm tired of his smirk, and I only have to see him when he rides by. She has to live with the man."

"It's not—"

Thomas reached out and put a hand on Hugh's shoulder. "Hugh, I don't mean to interrupt you, but I think I know what I should do."

"About the fire? About Jeb?"

He shook his head. "No. I love what I've learned on the farm, but I'm not really a farmer. I'm a businessman. Does this town have anyone who helps sell all the harvest?"

"What do you mean?"

Thomas pointed toward the railroad. "You told me that everyone sells their crops when the train comes through. Everyone sells it for whatever price he gives you. Am I right?"

"That's what I've always done."

"This is prime farmland. And with people moving in all around and towns popping up, there's going to be more and more demand for what we're growing here."

"We're all hoping the prices go up. I sometimes wonder if I'll be able to keep my farm going long enough for that to happen though."

"I was a businessman before. I'd imagine the companies that are buying what you're producing aren't thinking too much about you. It's just a game. Give you a few cents more and keep you happy when they're likely making dollars more." Thomas looked out at the golden fields. The timing of his realization struck even himself as strange, but the idea seemed sound enough. Adrenaline pumped through him. "There has to be a better way. I've been out in the fields now. I know it's backbreaking work. Farms like yours ought to be able to bring a fair price."

"How would you change it?"

"I'd have to think about it. But I've some money, and I could buy a thresher and a combine. We could have them here in Azure Springs. Then people wouldn't have to beg and plead with Jeb to loan his. People could use them for a reasonable fee and work faster. We could band together and seek out buyers rather than wait and take whatever is offered. Right now only men like Jeb have the new equipment. The rest of you are working hard to make your land produce but can't get the best prices because you don't have the quantities the big farms do. I could help change that." Thomas rubbed his hands together. For the first time, he envisioned a business that would help others. "It might work."

Hugh slapped him on the back. "I don't know where that idea came from, but I like it. It's going to work. As long as you can find a way to keep everything you own from going up in flames or being trampled, I think it'll be a big success."

"You tell the sheriff what you saw and tonight at Margaret's I'll ask around. Maybe someone else also saw the rider on the black horse. We'll put an end to all this."

"Our town isn't going to stand by while someone sabotages one of our own." Hugh reached for his horse's reins. "Tell Penny I'm wishing her well."

"Are you sure this isn't too much?" Thomas looked at the little table with its cloth and fancy dishes. A private table outside. What would she think of it?

"Of course not. She's been eating off of a tray in that stuffy upstairs bedroom long enough." Margaret set a dish filled with boiled potatoes on the table. "Celebrating the little things is what keeps life thrilling. Besides, I've a feeling you two need to sit and have a nice, long conversation. You might as well have that out in the open air."

"What makes you say that? Did she tell you?"

Margaret narrowed her eyes. "You've been spending every waking minute by her side until today and now you've been walking laps around my boardinghouse all afternoon like you're afraid to go up there. You've both been keeping secrets long enough."

"You're probably right." He glanced toward the upper windows and groaned. "I'd still rather be the server. I'm sure I could find my way around the kitchen."

"You've been by her side day and night. Under my supervision, of course." She winked at him. "You deserve this meal as much as she does. Now run up there and fetch her. Be a gentleman."

"I was planning to ask around about a man on a black horse. I need to do that. Hugh might have seen the same rider Penny saw. We have to stop whoever's out to get me. But I'm sure Penny will enjoy eating out in the fresh air."

"Nonsense. I've lots of practice asking around about things." She shot him one of her don't-even-think-about-arguing looks. "If there's anything to be learned from those in the dining hall, I'll find out. You take care of Penny. I know her secret and it's not so horrible as you've tricked yourself into thinking. It's all rather sweet and innocent."

"She worked at the dead letter office. She hasn't said so, but I believe she read all those letters I mailed. All day I've been worried about what she must think of me and wondering why she never told me she was the woman from the dead letter office. I don't understand it."

"She was on her way to tell you the day of the fire." Margaret's eyes softened. "Don't judge her too harshly. She was lost and confused. We all run to the place we think will welcome us when we're afraid."

"She ran here," Thomas said.

"She ran to you."

"To me? But if she read my letters, then she knows the man I used to be." Thomas's hands shook. He folded them across his chest. He hated knowing that the tender Penny knew what sort of man he'd been before.

"And she still came. I know she's confused and has questions, but that shouldn't scare you off—it should draw you to her. A woman who you can trust your past to is the type of woman you want to share your future with. Answer her questions and ask her yours, but don't turn your back on her just because she came."

"She came for me?" he asked.

"Yes, now run up those stairs and fetch her for dinner. Abigail said she would have her all ready to come down."

He rubbed his freshly shaven jaw. Margaret had convinced him to clean up for dinner, and now he understood why. "Still seems like too big a fuss."

"Not another word of that." She reached for his arm, then pulled him closer. "She received a telegram from her mother this morning, not long after you left. I'd sent word of her accident and her mother finally wired back. She said she was sorry about the accident and Uncle Clyde would see to her care once she returned. Penny's mother said she had this coming by being so foolish and headstrong. Can you imagine? Her own mother blames her. Penny cried while she read it. Go get her. Have a wonderful night with her. She needs it. Now, go." She shooed him as she would a bothersome fly. "Enjoy yourself."

"She cried?" he asked, ignoring her waving hand. She had cried and all he could think was that he should have been there to comfort her.

"Yes. But you will make her smile. Go up there. The food is ready."

He went slowly up the stairs, his heart heavy and uneasy. When he got to Penny's door, he knocked and waited. "Penny, it's me, Thomas."

Abigail opened the door a crack. "Wait a moment. I've almost finished her hair. I decided to try something new, and it's taking a bit longer than we expected. With Eliza grown and out of my home, I'm out of practice. Mae and Milly still wear their hair so simple."

"I'm sorry to keep you waiting," Penny called from within. "I didn't know Margaret was going to insist I dress for dinner."

"No hurry," Thomas said as Abigail softly closed the door.

He leaned against the wall and waited. Muffled voices met his ear. He wished he could decipher them. Knowing she knew about his past made him nervous and vulnerable. Was she telling Abigail about Clara? About all his foolish letters?

He thought about the letter he'd received in return. The letter that'd been from her. From Penny. It must have been her. She was the girl who had prayed for him. And she'd come here, to him. He reached out and put a hand on the doorframe to steady himself.

Abigail opened the door again. "She's ready. I have to go back to my girls now. Enjoy the evening."

"I will. Thank you for all you've done."

"She's a remarkable woman. I've enjoyed every moment I've spent with her."

He waited while Abigail walked out of the room and down the stairs, then he stepped through the door. Penny sat propped up in bed. She was dressed in her green dress—the one that brought out the green of her eyes. Her hair was curled and pinned. "You look lovely."

She smiled at him. "Why, thank you. It's nice to wear something other than my nightdress."

The apprehension he'd had was gone. This was the woman who had written him. She'd known his heartache and she still sought him out. She was beautiful. Now and always.

Penny motioned for him to come farther into the room. "I'm sorry I didn't—"

"Don't be sorry about anything. I'm the one who owes you an explanation. But you . . . you reached out to me. The letter—it was from you?"

She nodded. "I couldn't put my name on it. I wasn't supposed to care about the letters. My job was to redirect them and then forget them. But yours were different. I heard your voice as I read them. They spoke to me."

"Thomas! Penny!" Margaret hollered up the stairs. "Come down. The meal's ready. You know how I feel about punctuality."

"We'll be right there," Penny answered.

He held out his arm. "Margaret's been busy down there. Go enjoy her meal and then I'll tell you everything."

Penny sat very still.

"What is it? Have you decided you don't wish to leave your room?"

Penny shook her head. "No, it's just that I can't put any weight on my leg yet."

"Oh." He froze.

"You'll have to help me. If you don't mind."

His throat tightened. "Of course." He slowly stepped toward her. Being as mindful of her injuries as he could, he lifted her up. She put an arm around his neck and then she was so close to him—their faces only inches apart. He could smell the soap her hair had been washed with and see the faint freckles on the bridge of her nose. Her eyes, her cheeks, her lips. She was so close.

"Am I to dine with the men in the hall?" she asked.

He shook his head but did not speak.

"Where, then?" she asked. "Are you keeping a secret from me?"

"It's not my doing. I wish I could claim this was all my grand plan, but Margaret has set up a little table outside for you to eat at. She's even found someone to watch Honey so you won't have to worry about her."

"She thinks of everything."

He pulled her a little tighter against him. "Yes, she does."

"She knows me so well. I've longed for fresh air since being sentenced to my room. I don't think I could ever tire of Azure Springs and its prairies and beautiful sky. I'll miss them when I go. I'll try to soak in all I can before then."

"Must you go?"

Penny turned her face away from his and nodded.

"I suppose I better start walking. If I just stand here with you in my arms forever, that will really get everyone talking."

"I'm told this town loves good gossip."

He forced a smile but didn't take a step. "Yes, they do. I'm willing to oblige them. It's Margaret I'm worried about."

"I suppose you'd better take me downstairs, then. I'd hate to be the reason she used the switch."

He forced his legs to walk out into the hall and down the stairs carefully and slowly.

"My father loved eating out of doors," Penny said as he reached the bottom step. "I feel so eager. Almost like I felt when I went to my first real dance. I remember that night so well. I was a mess of excitement. I cried when I went into the ballroom. I'd always dreamed of being announced at a dance and there I was. And now here I am, free of my room and about to be in the sunshine. I feel the same temptation to cry."

"Would you feel as eager if you knew I was to join you?"

Her beautiful green eyes sparkled with real excitement. "I'd be even more eager, especially if I knew it was your wish as well."

"It is." He grinned, holding nothing back. "I confess, it was Margaret's plan. I felt uncertain, but now, right at this moment, there is nowhere else I'd rather be."

Penny squeezed his arm. "Let's go! Let's enjoy every moment of it. I want to fill the rest of my time here with as much happiness as I can. Dinah always tells me I am too easily swept away, and she may be right. But don't you just want to be happy sometimes? I feel that way."

"I do know that feeling." He smiled as he set her down into her seat and helped her prop up her leg on an extra chair. The small table was covered in an embroidered tablecloth. Blue and yellow flowers adorned the edge. He took a seat beside her. "It's easier when I'm with you. May I ask you again? Must you go?"

"As I see it, there's no other choice for me." She leaned in closer to him. "But that is not a pleasant thought."

"We will talk of it later." He shifted in his seat and looked around. Green grasses blew in the breeze while birds circled overhead. The boardinghouse ruckus was far enough away that it was nothing but a muffled din. "Let us talk of happy things and honest things."

"It's time?"

"Yes."

⌒

By candlelight, Penny worked on a detailed letter. Her mind and heart would not settle down after the perfect night with

267

Thomas, so she propped herself up in bed and poured her heart out onto paper.

Dear Dinah,

I should have written sooner. Especially because I am so thrilled by your news. You are married and you love your husband. I can think of nothing more wonderful than that. I do long to see you and whisper all my questions to you. Someday, I hope, that wish will come true. And now, dear friend, I will tell you why I haven't written and all that's happened.

I've put off writing you for many reasons. The first being I broke my leg. I'll tell you the tale, but first I must assure you that I am recovering and have had excellent care.

I broke my leg while trying to save Thomas from a burning barn. Actually, it was Thomas's barn that burned. Margaret discovered just tonight that the man we believe is behind it may be a visitor from out of town who is staying above the saloon. I'm getting ahead of myself. The day of the fire, I happened to be there at the very moment that Thomas walked into the flames. I believe divine intervention led me there. Tears come to my eyes whenever I think of what could have been if I'd not decided to venture to his home. When I got there, he was mad. Out of his head screaming for Clara. I was able to stop him but not before a beam fell and broke my leg. He pulled me from beneath it and carried me back to town. I don't remember him carrying me. I wish I could. It would be lovely to remember being held in a man's arms for so long, and don't you think it's terribly romantic to be rescued? Don't tell my mother I said that—she'd be even more convinced I am a heathen.

My poor dear Honeysuckle was hurt and very nearly died. Thomas has been nursing her back to health, with the good doctor's help, of course. I watched him once from my sickbed. Thomas sat beside Honey and brushed her tangled hair. When it was somewhat less matted, he coaxed her to drink. I found it sweet and touching that he would so gently care for her.

Since the accident, Thomas has endeared himself to my heart even tighter. No man has ever sat beside an ailing woman as Thomas has sat beside me. He holds my hand, he reads to me, and when my eyes are closed I hear him pray for me.

Tonight, for the first time, I left my room. Thomas had to carry me from my room, down the stairs, and to the table for two Margaret had set up for us behind the dining hall. I know I should have been blushing in embarrassment, but the truth is, I liked it. I think being in his arms is the finest part of having a broken leg. I am tempted to complain day and night for a very long time just so he'll sweep me up into his arms and carry me about.

He knows now I have read the letters he wrote to Clara and that I am the one from the office who wrote to him. My stomach was sick as I told him the truth, but I didn't let my nerves stop me. I told him everything.

It was his turn then to talk. I think he may have been as nervous as I'd been. He kept fidgeting with his fork, and there were moments when he had a strange, far-off look in his eyes. I was nervous too. I've wondered so often about his past. Tonight I learned he had been a businessman who had been extremely successful but had cared for little else and had many enemies in his hometown of Alexandria. I believed him when he told me that he did nothing illegal but that he did nothing noble either. He put many out of business and only associated with people if it was advantageous to him. I don't think I would have liked him very well then. Tonight as he told me, I knew he was no longer that man. He was meek and humble as he shared his dark past.

I had wanted to know what sort of a man he'd been. And he told me. Though some moments were hard to hear, I am grateful that the secrets are no more. I asked about Clara. The silence was so long. I've never seen a man so in pain. I reached out and touched his arm. I wished I could calm him. In a hushed voice, he told how he had first sought her because of her family's wealth. She was a sweet girl, young and naïve. He says he knew how she adored him and he soon began to care for her too. But he wasn't the man he should have been, and he didn't love her like she deserved. Mostly he had liked the way she looked on his arm, and he'd been proud of what a sophisticated woman she was. Poor Thomas was near tears as he confessed it all. The town gossips were sure the couple would marry, but Thomas says he doesn't know if they would have.

The night she died, he'd taken her to a fancy restaurant. While they were eating, an associate of his came in and asked to speak to him. He promised he'd be right back, but he stayed away an hour or more. When he returned, the building was lost to a fire. It all happened so quickly. The fire trapped eight people that night. The roof caved in and they couldn't get out. He said if he'd been the man he should have been, the man he likes to believe he's becoming, he would have been there to protect her. But it had always been business first for him. Until that night when he watched that building burn and realized what a monster he was.

Dinah, he wept. He sobbed when he told me of running at the building and trying to save her, only to be too late. He blames himself for her death. Everyone blamed him. Clara's father, people who worked for him, everyone. He didn't care that they were being unjust. He said when he was standing there looking up at the burning building, he saw his many sins and wanted to hide. He wanted to run away and free everyone from his own presence.

My stomach churned just hearing him say it all. He doesn't seem like the man from his story at all. The man I know is kind and thoughtful. He helps Margaret in the kitchen if he's here early, and he loves the sight of plants creeping from the ground and the smell of rain on a warm day. Margaret told me people can change. I know my father would say the same. I think Thomas has changed. I feel I witnessed the change all those months ago when I read his letters. He says when he came to Azure Springs, he thought it was all an accident, but now he cannot imagine another place. He's found himself here. He's found his true self.

The letters to Clara were a way for him to try to heal. I think it is a good thing I am not a detective. I was wrong about so many things. But I believe I was right to come here. If I had not, I would not have been here to save him. And despite his past, I love the man he is today. I love his

271

tenderness. I love his gentle voice and his laughter. I love it when he holds my hand. I love that he left his city home in search of a better road. I love his toil for goodness. I love it all. You told me I was too easily swept away, and you were right. It's all happened so quickly for me, but it's real. What I feel is not a lie. I do love him.

I could not tell him that, but I did tell him I was sorry for his pain. I told him I believed what I wrote so long ago. His life still has purpose and he can have joy. I believe Clara and my father wouldn't want us to sit idle just because they are not here. He should have been with her that night, but he was not. That does not make him a murderer. I told him that. I told him it was wrong of anyone to blame him.

Our conversation was quieter after that. We spoke of loss and how hard it is to go on. We spoke of pain and grief. I always dreamt of a fluttering stomach and tender kisses, and I don't think I'll ever stop loving such things. But tonight, sitting beside a man as he bared his soul, I realized there is more to giving your heart to someone than I ever knew. I believe my father was right when he told me love can come in many forms.

The sun was gone when we finally left our spot at the little table. He carried me up the stairs. At the top, just outside my room, he held me a moment longer than he ought to have. I thought he would kiss me. I had hoped he would, but he did not. He merely tightened his arms around me and pulled me close and thanked me for listening. It was over before I was ready. Tonight was difficult and perfect all at once. The distance between us is not as vast as it had been. I know Thomas Conner now. I really *know him. He has trusted me with his burden, and I've trusted him with my own scarred heart. I know not what tomorrow will bring, but I do know that I love Thomas—past and all. No matter what happens, I'll keep that in my heart.*

I long to see you and meet your Lucas. I want to whisper with you and hear all the things you are not telling me. I was so happy to hear that you are enjoying married life. Your letter lifted my spirits. I should have trusted you more when you first told me of Lucas. Love can be quiet and simple and beautiful all at the same time. Love can be many things. It can be born in grief and pain. I am happy you have your love and a man who will walk the city looking for flowers with you.

> *Your tirelessly romantic*
> *friend,*
> *Penny*

*P*enny." Margaret stepped into her room. "I've brought you a telegram."

She sat up and wiped the sleep from her eyes. "What do you mean? Is it another one from my mother?"

"I didn't open it. Stuart brought it over. They usually bring them right away. He said the boy who was supposed to deliver this two weeks ago dropped it behind a counter and he didn't find it until he was cleaning today. He ran it over himself and apologized at least a dozen times."

"I don't know who it could be from." Penny tore it open.

Someone looking for Thomas. Came to DLO after you went to Alexandria. I think it's bad. Roland.

"Where's Thomas?" Penny asked with an urgency in her voice she could not mask. She'd feared he was in danger since the fire, but this telegram reinforced her fears. "I need to see him. Is he here?"

"He went with the sheriff this morning to the saloon. They are hoping to talk to a stranger staying there who rides a black horse. He told me to tell you he'd be back soon. He was all smiles this morning. I think he must have enjoyed your dinner last night." Margaret reached into her pocket. "He left a note though. Said something about your liking letters."

"I've never had so much mail." She took the letter. "Will you get Thomas? I think it could be important. The telegram has to do with him. I think he's in more danger than we imagined. Will you go to the saloon and get him?"

"I can't stand Silas. He's the serpent who owns the saloon, but for you I'll go in that wretched place."

"I'd go myself if I could." Her leg muscles twitched. She longed to run to Thomas.

"I don't mind all that much. It'll give me a chance to give the man a piece of my mind. You read your letter and I'll find Thomas."

"Thank you."

As soon as Margaret left her room, Penny tore open the letter from Thomas.

Dear Penny,

You told me you love letters that expose the soul. I've never felt more exposed than I did last night. Until now I've always kept any grief or pain I've had to myself. Sharing it with you unnerved me, but you were so kind. You calmed my fears.

I don't understand why I've been blessed after all my years of selfishness, but I have been. Every moment in your presence is a gift.

I'd be remiss if I did not thank you. And I'd have to live with deep regrets if I did not plead with you to spend more time with me. Penny, will you dine with me again tonight? Margaret rolled her eyes when I asked her if we could share the outside table again, but then she laughed and said yes.

Join me tonight?

Thomas

Penny set the letter from Thomas on the little bedside table and busied herself by sewing the hem on a set of dishcloths for Margaret. Her mind kept returning to her fears. Would life ever be peaceful? If only she could eat outdoors with Thomas each night with no worries.

"Penny."

"Come in," she said when she heard Thomas's voice at the door a few minutes later.

"Good morning." He walked across the room and sat beside her. Honey limped over to him and rubbed her head against his leg. "Good morning to you too."

"At the dead letter office, we put the envelopes we never thought would be redirected but that we had managed to solve into a little book. It was always fun looking through it. A man named Roland was the very best. He could figure out addresses no one else could." She held up her thin stack of letters. "I think someday I'll love flipping through these. Not for the same reason, of course, but because I'll want to remember it all. Every moment of it."

"I'll have to write you often."

She smiled. "I hope you do. Margaret brought me the one from you this morning. I'd love to dine with you again tonight."

Thomas's cheeks turned a faint pink. "I didn't want to sound too forward."

She was tempted to tell him to be a little more forward. She had so little time. This glimpse of romance, if she could even call it that, was to be short-lived. If only she could tell him to take her in his arms and hold her. If only she were bold enough to tell him how she felt about him. "It was a perfect invitation to dinner."

"I was over at the saloon trying to find the man on the black horse. Did you need something? Margaret said it was important."

Penny reached for the telegram and put it in his hand.

"It came days ago, but I only got it just now. I'm afraid we've been wrong this whole time. Maybe it's not Jeb."

He read it quickly. "What do you think it means?"

Penny groaned. "I think it must be my fault."

"What? How?" Thomas's face scrunched up in worry. "What happened?"

"When I went to Alexandria to find Clara, I took a letter from the dead letter office. I showed it to the Alexandria postmaster. We told him where we got it. He yelled and practically threw me out."

"I remember him. He was a friend of Clara's father. I believe they were distantly related, or maybe it was by marriage. What happened then?" Thomas leaned closer, his foot nervously tapping the floor.

"Because I wanted to write you and tell you what I'd learned of Clara's death, I had to figure out where you lived. I had to search through records and find a town with a railroad, a store owner named Abraham, a family named Dawson that had moved, and a boardinghouse. In the end, I found Azure Springs. Several people in the office knew I'd found it." She gritted her teeth. "I think whoever set fire to your barn must have found you because of me. They must have come to the dead letter office and learned from the other clerks where you were. I'm so sorry. I never—"

He put a hand on her shoulder. "You didn't mean anything by it. They'd have found me eventually. I've moved money around and purchased land here in my own name. Don't blame yourself."

"I went to Alexandria to help. I never meant to put you in danger. Who would want to hurt you?" She grasped his hand. "Is there someone who would be angry enough with you to destroy your crops and burn your barn? Could all your troubles be traced to the same person?"

Thomas rubbed his jaw. After a moment of silence, he said, "It could be. If this telegram came weeks ago, then the man on the black horse could have done all this."

"Did you see him at the saloon?"

He shook his head. "No, he was gone. Silas, the owner, said he was a fine gentleman and not someone to be worried about. Neither the sheriff nor I know the man. When Margaret got there, she got more out of Silas than we had. She cornered him and managed to learn that the man's from out of town and goes by the name Jesse Bordeaux."

"Do you know who that is?" She pulled out a piece of paper from the bedside table and wrote down the man's name.

"No."

"I will send a telegram to Roland and see if he will look up the name. If it's an alias, then we won't find anything. Where was the man? Did Silas know?" Penny held her paper ready.

"You sound like a detective." He smiled at her. "I think it's charming. Silas didn't say where the man had gone. He only said he was gone for the day. That he was gone more than he was there. I'll check back later."

"When we find him, we need to find out where he's from. What if we asked one of the girls at the saloon to get some answers from him?"

Thomas rubbed his forehead. "It could work, but he might just lie. What else do you think we ought to ask?"

She twirled the pencil in her fingers while she thought. "Twice we've seen him ride off to Jeb's house. What do you think Jeb has to do with all this? Could Jeb know anyone from your past?"

"That's the part I can't figure out. Jeb hasn't liked me from the start, but now with your telegram and Silas saying this man's from out of town, I'm wondering whether the men have a connection or not. None of it makes sense." He stood up and paced across the room. "I think I'll go find the sheriff and tell him about the telegram. Will you write out what you want me to wire Roland and I'll take it?" He cleared his throat. "I'll pay to send it too."

"You don't have to." She began adding up what a telegram would cost her and figuring how much she'd have left.

"I insist. It's my mess to sort out. I'm grateful for your help. Besides, if I pay for a few things, it'll stretch your money and you can stay longer."

She looked up from her paper and held his gaze. "You don't want me to go?"

"No." He waited while she scribbled her note.

Her hand shook as she wrote. "Here." She handed it to him. "Thank you."

"Will you take Honey across the street to the Howells'? The twins said they'd take her outside and watch her for me today. She's getting restless just sitting here."

"Of course. Come on, Honey." Thomas snapped his fingers

and waited while Honey made her way over to him. "Are you sure she's ready to go out?"

"The doctor said it'd be good for her. She's tired of being trapped in here. I think she needs exercise."

He nodded. "Very well. I'll be back tonight."

"Thomas."

"Yes?"

"You will be careful? Margaret has told me stories of Jeb, and when she speaks of him I feel afraid deep inside. Something about the man worries me. And now with the telegram . . ."

"I'll be safe." He grinned. "So this is what it feels like to have a woman worry about me?"

"Is it so horrible?"

"No. It's something I could certainly get used to."

Dear Eliza,

Thank you for visiting me. I am often alone as I sit and wait for my leg to heal. I believe a visitor is the greatest gift an invalid can be given. I am writing you now not only to thank you but to ask you a question. You see, I have gotten to know Thomas Conner and he is a good man. Before he lived here, he had troubles in Alexandria. I will not make excuses for the man he was before. But I am afraid for him now. I worry his troubles have followed him. And I believe even if we cannot go back in time and undo the past, we can move forward and have a better future. I want that for Thomas. I worry, though, that he'll not be able to do all the good things he has planned if he is always haunted or even hunted by his past. I worry for his safety. He could have died in the fire. Will whoever did this take his life next?

I don't know what you know or if you know anything. But I beg you to come forward if you do. Help him if you can. There must be some way you can help without putting yourself in jeopardy. I don't claim to know your own struggles, and I'd never wish to belittle them, but are

*they so great that they would keep you from speaking up?
A man could die.*

*I hope someday to know you better. I'd love to hear
your story and share mine with you.*

> *Best wishes,*
> *Penny*

"Margaret."

"Yes?"

Penny folded the letter as she spoke. "Do you think there is
a way to get a letter to Eliza? I learned at the dead letter office
to follow up on any lead I found until it turned up dead. I still
think Eliza knows something."

Margaret set down the tray she'd been carrying. "There
might be a way. I know Norbert Frintz is a hand out there. He
eats here most every night. Do you remember him? He has a
scraggly blond beard and always wears suspenders."

"I don't recall."

"No matter. I trust him. He's been eating here for months
now, and we've shared enough small talk that I think he's a
decent man. If I told him you had a personal letter for Eliza's
eyes only, I think he'd get it to her."

Penny handed over the letter. "I'd appreciate it. I have to try."

"You're worried about Thomas, aren't you?"

Penny nodded. "I am. I wish my leg would heal faster so I
could be out there with him putting all the pieces together. I'm
afraid whoever did this will not stop. I may be only a guest in
this town, but I worry about the people here. I want everyone
to be safe, especially Thomas."

"I know the sheriff has a lot of his trusted men keeping an

eye out. Em and Caleb are staying with the Howells for a few days. He was the sheriff not too long ago, and he's agreed to help watch the town. I think Thomas will be safe enough."

"Safe enough is not good enough." Penny sat up straight. "I thought Azure Springs was without problems. It seemed so quaint and perfect when I first came."

"Every place has problems. We've our fair share of sickness, we've a wicked saloon owner, and we've prideful men. But if you look around, you'll see that everyone bands together when those hard times come. Thomas hasn't been here long and already people are quietly rallying behind him. That's what counts." She walked toward the door. "I've got to start the evening meal. You get some rest. I hear you're eating at the private table again."

Penny bit her lip. "I hope you don't mind."

"I will never mind watching two people I care about fall in love." She winked, then walked out and closed the door.

"He didn't return all day. The sheriff convinced someone to notify us when he arrives back at the saloon." Thomas sat across the little table from Penny.

"I wrote a letter to Eliza. Margaret knows someone, a man named Norbert, who can get it to her. I'm hoping she'll decide to tell us something."

"It still doesn't make any sense to me. I can't reconcile the telegram with what's been happening around here." He sat back and let out a frustrated sigh. "Let's talk of other things tonight. My head has been spinning all day trying to figure this out."

"All right." She scrunched up her nose. "Hmm. If you capture the man who rides the black horse, what then?"

"When I've had time, I've been thinking on it. I even sent out a few inquiries. I think I'm going to invest in all the big harvest equipment and create a business that allows men like Hugh to farm their land faster and more efficiently. I'll rent out the equipment somehow. I don't know how yet, but I'll do it fairly. When I'm not doing that, I'll help them find good buyers for their crops and get the best deals on seed." He reached for her hand. It had become almost instinctual to hold her hand whenever he was nervous or excited. "I think it'll be good work—and it'll make a difference. Right now only men with deep pockets can afford the best equipment."

"I think it's a wonderful idea. Where will you live?"

He looked out at the vast and beautiful rolling hills. "I don't know. I like the peace at the Dawson farm, but I'm not sure if I'll stay that far out. I'll have to see if I can work the land and run the business."

She looked at him with her sparkling green eyes. "I think whatever you do, you'll do well."

"What about you?"

"I worked on a letter last night to my mother. I've officially decided I will go back to the dead letter office. I want to be near my mother, but I don't want to go back to the world that rejected us. And I'm not willing to court or marry just to please my uncle." She shifted about. "I think when the nights get lonely and I am tempted to feel sorry for myself, I will write my novel. I think I'd like that. When I read mail at the office, I learned so many fascinating life stories. Only bits and pieces of them though. I'd read about a new baby or a big harvest or a terrible feud. I think I'd like to write the rest of those stories. Fill in all the holes."

He squeezed her hand. "I thought you were going to write about a city boy turned farmer."

"That will be my first book. But I still can't figure out what the ending will be."

"Excuse me." Margaret approached them. "I've two bits of news for you. First, the twins have sent word that Honey jumped in the mud today. I can't decide if that is good news or bad news, but I do believe it means she is beginning to feel like her old self. The second is that this telegram came." Margaret held out a thin piece of paper.

Penny grabbed it and quickly opened it.

Dead ends on the name. Might be Finley. That name was in our guest registry.

"Finley. Like Clara Finley?"

Thomas reached quickly for the telegram. "What's the guest registry?"

"We keep track of who comes to the office. There are valuables in there, so the office isn't open to everyone. What do you think a man by the name of Finley was doing there?"

Thomas stood up from the table. "I don't know." He took a deep breath. "That's not true. I do know. It may have been Clara's father, Oscar. He was the angriest of them all when Clara died. Well, angry and hurt. I can't blame him. She was his only daughter. He went around town telling everyone how I killed her. His influence was great and everyone believed him. I believed him. I was exiled in large part because of him."

Margaret walked toward the back of the boardinghouse. With her hand on the doorknob, she turned back. "I have to go and serve dinner. Let me know if you need me."

"Thank you, Margaret," Thomas said.

"But would Oscar Finley come all this way? You left. Hadn't he already won?" Penny furrowed her brow. "It's not right to seek revenge like that."

"It's all right, Penny. It wasn't a war between good men and bad men. He was a hurting man and I was an easy target." He picked up his hat from a nearby bench. "I think I'll go over to the saloon and wait until he returns. I thought running away would solve this, but I think—I know—I need to face it."

"Will you be safe?" she asked. "I worry every time you leave. I think you should wait for the sheriff. If he's as angry as you say, he may have a gun. He could kill you."

"I have to do this. I have to make peace somehow. The letters were my way of finding peace for myself, but I need to fall at the feet of Clara's father and let him know how truly sorry I am."

"Promise me you won't do anything dangerous."

He sat on the edge of his chair, leaned toward her, and looked into her eyes. "I promise you, Penelope Ercanbeck, I'll be back. I have to. I don't want the city boy's story to have a sad ending." He inched closer and kissed her forehead.

She leaned into his touch. "I don't want it to either. I want it to have a perfectly blissful ending."

He pressed another kiss to her forehead. "It'll be blissful." He kissed her cheek then. With his face near hers, he whispered, "Your story will have a happy ending too. I'm certain of it."

She bit her bottom lip. "Dinah says some stories don't work out the way we want them to."

"But some do." He pressed his lips to her cheek again, this time letting them linger. With his face beside hers, he whispered, "Some even work out better than we expect."

She nodded. His hand came gently under her chin and tilted it upward. Their eyes locked. He leaned in so close he could feel her breath upon his skin.

"Penny," he whispered.

"Yes?"

He pressed his lips to hers. For one brief moment, there was no man on a black horse, no burnt barns or trampled fields. "Some stories do end with happily ever after," he said when their lips parted. He wrapped his arms around her. An almost desperate need to hold her overpowered him. He wanted a future full of Penny and her sweetness. "I'll come back. We'll figure out our story together."

Her head bobbed against him. When he pulled away, he met her gaze once again. And in her eyes he saw the same desire he felt. "I'll be back."

"here's Thomas?" Penny asked when Margaret stepped into her room with a breakfast tray.

"He's sleeping. He was out all night waiting for Finley, or whoever it was, to come back. Poor man had to spend the entire evening in the saloon."

"Was he . . . had he been . . . ?"

Margaret laughed. "He was as sober as ever when he walked in this morning. He was grumbling about the place. I wouldn't worry about his morals. Silas kicked him out, and since there was no sign of the man on the black horse, I sent him to bed." She reached into her pocket and pulled out an envelope. "This is for you. It's from Norbert. He was sent into town for supplies and dropped it by. He said he had to wait outside the privy for Eliza to meet him. Jeb doesn't know."

"Feels wrong asking a wife to lie to her husband." She took the letter. "I worry for her."

"We all do. Poor Abigail is beside herself with worry. None of us know what to do. I'm surprised she even dared to write you. Gives me a little hope though. Either things aren't as bad as I am tempted to believe they are or at the very least she's fighting still."

"I am glad she sent it, even if I do feel a little guilty about how I got it." Penny tore open the envelope. "I used to read other people's mail, about their troubles. I never thought I'd actually be in the middle of so many of them."

"I hope that someday you'll have a calm, peaceful season. One of those beautiful stretches when the letters you write are filled with nothing but good news." She sat in the chair by the bed and covered her mouth with her hand. "I'll stop talking and listen. What news does Eliza send?"

Penny read aloud.

Dear Penny,

I haven't long, but I'll try to tell you what I know. I too want Thomas to be safe. I never meant to become the type of woman who conceals the truth. Everyone should feel safe in their own home.

When Thomas bought the old Dawson place, Jeb was angry. He's always angry, but never like this. The anger just grew day after day. He started going to the saloon more. Most every night he went. One night he came home and was smiling all evil-like. He had a man with him. That night I heard him talking to the man. His name is Oscar Finley. He's from where Thomas lived before. Thomas played a role in his daughter's death. The man talked about how his life had been ruined. When Jeb stepped outside to work in the barn, I heard the man crying. I've never heard a man sob like he did. There was so much pain in it. I don't know if I'm ready to declare him an evil man, but the two of them together are not a good combination. They drink and they scheme. One day I heard them talking about how the night watchman was gone and that they'd go then. I didn't know what they were going to do until I heard about the barn catching fire. I didn't see what good would come from telling when it was already burned. I was afraid of Jeb. I've my reasons for my fears, but I'm sorry. I should have said something.

They are still together. Their anger is still just as raw and as deep. I had hoped it would go away, but now I hear them talk of burning the house when Thomas comes back or watching for him when he comes out of the boardinghouse. Jeb does most of the talking. He's fueled by a deep anger. I don't understand it. I never would have thought it possible for him to be so evil, but I believe it now. I worry for you all. I'm telling you, he is capable of the cruelest of deeds. Tell Thomas to be safe.

Burn this. Jeb can't know I sent it.

Eliza

"This is horrible. She can't live like this. Always afraid."

Margaret reached for the letter. "Do you trust me to take this to the sheriff?"

"Will you burn it then? I could never live with myself if something happened to Eliza on my account."

"I will. We need to act quickly."

Penny pulled herself up higher in bed. "Is there anything I can do from here? I want to help."

"You sent the letter to Eliza, and your telegrams, they've all helped. Besides, if you'd not been hurt, Thomas likely would be dead. Staying in this town under this roof is what's kept him alive all this time." She patted Penny's cheek. "Stay here. Start your story. Write a letter. Keep yourself busy so you aren't just sitting here worrying. We'll catch these men. You will get your peaceful stretch."

Penny bit her lip and nodded. Her insides twisted as she watched Margaret leave. She fidgeted with worry until, finally, she reached for some paper.

"I suppose I will write," she said to Honey.

A man with a dark and troublesome past wrote a letter . . .

"I've rounded up Caleb, Hugh, the Lenard boys, Abraham Howell, and a few men from the O'Donnells' fields. They're all armed and ready to go. Others might join us later as the word gets out." The sheriff caught Thomas up on what he'd been doing.

"I'm ready now. I'm worried though. I don't want *anyone* in danger." Thomas fastened his gun belt around his waist and put his gun in the holster. "I knew Oscar Finley. We didn't always see eye to eye, but he wasn't a violent man. Losing Clara must have changed him. Or maybe it's Jeb's influence."

"I can't speak for what happened to him, but he's here in my town and he's dangerous. A man can't just burn another man's barn and get away with it."

Thomas rubbed his forehead. "But what will happen to Eliza when Jeb finds out she told?"

"He doesn't need to know that. We will try to get a confession from him. I can't say for sure what will happen, but going out there is the next step."

"Will you wait a few moments?" An urgency to see Penny again filled his chest. He couldn't ride off toward danger without being near her once more. Even if only for a moment. He'd told her a great deal of what was in his heart, but he had more to say. "I need to give Penny a message first."

"All right. I'll make sure everyone is saddled and ready to go. Meet us near the livery."

Thomas thanked him and ran for Margaret's, where he rushed through the front door and took the stairs two at a time.

"Penny." He banged on her door. Just knowing he was headed toward danger put a desperate need in him to say the words he'd been holding back. She had to know how he felt.

"Come in."

Thomas opened the door. "Penny, I'm heading to Jeb's. There's a whole group of us. It's dangerous, and I couldn't go without saying what needed saying." He crossed the floor and stood beside her bed. "I don't want you to leave. Don't go back to DC. Don't go back to the mother who doesn't understand you. Don't go back and spend your days reading other people's mail. Stay here with me and I'll write you all the letters you want. You'll have so many—hundreds, thousands if you wish. Don't go back." He took a deep breath. "I couldn't leave without you knowing what I want."

"I can't stay."

"Why?"

"I have to be able to support myself. Even now I'm about out of money. I'd love your letters, but I can't stay."

He stepped closer. Then he knelt beside her bed. All walls were gone. In this moment, there was only truth. "No. You're not alone. While you're here in Azure Springs, we're together. We're stronger, better. Let me stay near you all my days. I'll be the man I was meant to be. The one who sits beside you when you are ill. I'll read to you, write to you. You won't want for anything."

She looked into his eyes. "You could have your pick. You're young and with money. You could do anything, have anything. And you want me and Azure Springs?"

"I do. You believed in me before I even believed in myself. You came here. You came knowing my heartache and remorse. You know my past and I so desperately want to share my future with you. I don't want anyone else." He put his hands on her cheeks. He kissed her forehead, the tip of her nose, and finally her lips. Her skin was soft, perfect. He felt hungry for more, but he stopped. "Penelope Ercanbeck, I love you. Providence brought us together in this town. When I'm with you, the pain from before is not so piercing. Life has purpose and joy. Ours is an unusual story, but it's ours. Can you feel it? How being together heals so many of the hurts from before?"

Tears ran down Penny's face. "I do. I feel it. My father told me to leap and I did and now I know why. Because here with you, I don't have to worry about fitting in. I can just be me. He was right about everything and about our lives being different than we plan but still being beautiful."

"And ours will be. I know it will."

She leaned her head against his chest. Never had anything felt so right to him as holding this woman in his arms. He kissed the top of her head, pressing his lips to her hair and letting them linger there. The scent of soap so soft and sweet. He felt himself sigh in blissful contentment. This woman, this beautiful woman in his arms, was the future he wanted.

The moments of tenderness ticked by. There were men waiting for him. An unreconciled past to attend to. He straightened. "I have to go. Someday soon I'm going to give you a future that is safe, but first I have to end all this."

"I know you do." She wiped at the tears in her eyes. "I cry a lot."

"Soon I hope to make sure you cry only happy tears." He picked his hat up off the floor. When he bent down, her stack of papers caught his eye. "You're writing?"

"Yes. I was so nervous that I had to do something."

He kissed her again. "Keep writing. I'll be back and then we'll start our life together."

Green tear-filled eyes looked up at him. "Be safe."

He moved to the door.

"Thomas," she called.

"Yes?"

"I want you to know that I love you. I have for a long time now. It started when I read your letters and I will go on loving you forever."

A lump rose in his throat. "You can't imagine what hearing that does to me."

"I will tell you so often you'll be tired of hearing it," she said through her tears. "I love you."

"If that is to be my lot in life, then I can assure you, dear Penny, my story will have a happy ending."

"As will mine."

He had to go. In four large steps, he crossed the room. His body, his heart begged to touch her again. She tilted her head toward him. Thomas pressed his lips to hers. He wanted to kiss her again and again, but he pulled away. "Write your story, and when I come back, we'll live it."

*I*t's all right, girl," Thomas said as he patted Josephine's neck. "Settle down. This will be over soon. Then we'll build you a new barn and Penny will feed you carrots. Can you imagine that? A future with Penny in it." His chest grew tight. The words sounded right, but he knew as he stroked the stubborn mare that there was a chance there would never be a new barn or a future with Penny.

"Let's head out." The sheriff motioned for the group of men to follow. Hugh rode close at his heels. Thomas had never seen his good-natured friend so distraught. Periodically throughout the duration of the ride he removed his hat and wiped his brow. On more than one occasion he smacked his hat against his side and groaned.

Thomas clicked his heels against Josephine and rode up beside him. "Hugh?"

"I don't like it."

"Going out like this?"

"Eliza's probably in there. She's living with Jeb. She rarely leaves the farm." Hugh's jaw flexed.

"We're large in number. We should be able to overtake them." Thomas tried to reassure himself and Hugh. They were quickly approaching the Danbury farm, and soon it would be too late to have second thoughts.

"We've got them in number, but they've got her." ·

"Every man here would give his life to keep her safe. We won't let anything happen."

"Can you guarantee that?" Hugh scowled. "Can you promise she'll get through this unharmed? You can't—and neither can I."

"Men." The sheriff's voice silenced their conversation. "Bring your horses around."

All the men rode up near him. Every face in the crowd was serious, concerned. Abraham Howell's chin shook. He was the oldest man in the group and the least qualified. But he was Eliza's father and not a single man tried to keep him from riding.

The sheriff paused a moment before he spoke. "I'd like to send in a scout to figure out their location. Then we'll approach in two groups. The first group will circle the house or barn. Wherever they are. The other group will hang back and come when there's danger or need. We'll have more power over the situation if we come in waves."

Caleb volunteered to go ahead and scout. "I've had experience tracking bandits and will be able to keep a cool head."

Before the sheriff could even respond, Caleb was riding away.

The others divided into two groups—six men in the first and five in the second—as they waited for Caleb to return.

A tightness gripped Thomas's insides. He wanted this over. Not just for him and for Penny but for all these men. This was his fight and they'd come to stand beside him. Their lives were in jeopardy because of him. He took several slow breaths. *Stay in control*, he instructed himself. He had to act rationally, not emotionally. When a wave of nausea threatened to make him sick, he turned away from the group to hide his disobedient body the best he could. Clara had died on his watch. Penny was injured. He looked at the men around him. These were his friends, his townspeople. Would he cause more pain?

"You ready?" Hugh asked. "Looks like Caleb's back. It's time to end this."

"They're in the house. All three of them. I didn't see any hands around." Caleb took a handkerchief from his pocket and wiped his brow. "Maybe we should wait. We could all watch different parts of the property. We could surprise the men when they're alone."

"No." The sheriff sat up tall in his saddle. "We go now. We'll surround the house. There'll be no waiting on my watch. These men are too dangerous."

"They have Eliza," Caleb said in a harsh whisper. "She's with them. Don't be a fool just so you can end this. Do it right. They'll use her to keep us from taking them out. Jeb's proven how little he cares. He'll use her to escape."

"We ride."

Thomas urged Josephine ahead a few steps. "I don't want anyone getting hurt. Maybe there's a better plan."

"No one is getting hurt," the sheriff shouted. "We're large in number. We end this now." He turned his horse and started toward the house. "Follow me."

Abraham hesitated, looking from man to man. "I'm going with him. I got to save her. That's my daughter."

Caleb nodded. "We ride."

Thomas urged Josephine after the other horses. First wave and second wave were forgotten. All the men rode together. Their eyes focused intensely on the house. Uneasiness was written across all their faces. Their knuckles were white as they gripped their reins. The thundering of hooves created a roaring din as they galloped toward the house.

Hugh passed Thomas and raced ahead.

Soon all the men were riding faster. Harder.

With his hand in the air, the sheriff drew a giant circle. "Circle the house!" he yelled. "Cover all the doors. No one gets away."

Jeb must have heard the commotion. The curtains closed across the front window and Thomas could hear muffled voices coming from inside. The blocked view into the house only caused Thomas's heart to beat faster.

The men took their positions, encircling the house.

"What's happening in there?" Hugh sat on his horse to the right of Thomas. "Come out!" he yelled. "Come out and face us." He pulled his pistol from its holster and fired it into the air. The ring of horses whinnied and pounded the ground with their hooves.

"Come out, you coward," another man said. Others joined in, yelling and baiting him to come out.

The echo of the gunshot faded away. The horses calmed. Still and quiet, they waited. Long minutes passed. Hugh's horse pranced back and forth.

"Hold him back," Thomas said. "We can't do anything irrational."

"We already have," Hugh said. "We trapped Eliza inside with those monsters."

Thomas flinched when the moment was broken as the front door of the house flew open. Jeb sneered at them as he emerged. "Here I am." His left arm was wrapped around Eliza's middle. Her hands were tied and her mouth gagged. She kicked her feet, trying to free herself. Jeb shook her and swore.

Thomas slipped a foot from his stirrup. He wanted to fly

from his horse and run with fists swinging at Jeb. But there was a gun pressed against Eliza.

"No," Thomas said under his breath. "No."

"You want me?" He shook Eliza. "Then it'll cost you her. Oscar, go get us a couple horses saddled up. Better yet, just take a couple of theirs."

Oscar Finley stepped out of the house with a gun in his hand. It shook in the air. A second pistol was strapped to his side. He didn't move toward the barn or toward their horses. He stood frozen behind Jeb and Eliza.

Abraham slid from his horse. "Take my horse. Give me my daughter."

"Stop right there," Jeb growled. "She's my wife. You get back on your horse. You're nothing but a worthless old man. The rest of you, drop your weapons." He pressed his gun against Eliza's temple. "Drop them."

Eliza's eyes searched them, pleading for help. Thomas looked away. There was so much fear in her eyes. Had Clara looked the same way when she'd faced death? Every man in the circle dropped his gun.

Abraham stood staring helplessly at his daughter. Tears ran from his eyes as he watched her suffer.

"Please," he begged. "Let her go. This isn't her fight." Abraham's legs gave out from beneath him and he fell to the ground. "Please. Take me. Let her go."

"No. She goes with me." Jeb kicked her again. "She's mine." Eliza whimpered beneath her gag.

He spat to the side of him. "Worthless woman."

Hugh flew from his horse. Thomas slid off his horse and grabbed Hugh, holding him back. Hugh fought against him.

A shot sounded. Thomas looked from Hugh back toward

Jeb. He lay on the ground. The men were all flying from their horses and running toward Jeb and Eliza. Thomas let Hugh go.

"What happened?" Thomas asked as they raced toward the house.

"Oscar." Hugh gasped for breath. "He saved her. He shot Jeb." Oscar stood in the same spot he'd been in. His hands still held the gun he'd used to shoot Jeb. "I-I had to save her." He repeated it over and over. "I had to save Clara. I had to save her."

"Drop your weapon." The sheriff held his gun pointed directly at Oscar. "Drop it."

Oscar's weapon fell to the ground. He collapsed then too. Shaking all over, he knelt on the ground with his hands on his knees.

The sheriff rubbed his jaw as he walked back and forth in front of the broken man. "You saved Eliza. But you . . . you burned the barn."

"I . . . I . ." Oscar looked around. Then his eyes locked on Thomas's.

Thomas pushed through the crowd.

"You killed her," Oscar cried.

Thomas stepped closer, his head bowed. "You saved Eliza."

The man's jaw shook. "No man should lose a daughter." He looked away. Thomas's eyes followed his gaze. Abraham was holding Eliza. Rocking her back and forth. Thomas felt relief and anguish. Abraham had his girl in his arms, but a man was dead. The cost had been high.

Oscar shook his head. "I had to stop him. I couldn't . . . I couldn't let that man"—he pointed again at Abraham—"feel the pain I'm feeling."

"I'm sorry," Thomas whispered. "I'm so sorry."

"I burned your barn—"

"We have a confession," the sheriff said. "Someone bring me rope. We'll tie him up and take him in."

"No." Thomas stepped in front of Oscar, blocking the way to him, and turned to the sheriff. "It's my barn. I don't want him arrested. He's a man hurting. I don't blame him."

Oscar stood and put a hand on Thomas's shoulder.

Thomas faced him. "I should have been there with Clara that night. I should have stayed by her side and found a way to save her. I wasn't Jeb. I never meant to hurt her, but I wasn't a good man. I wish I could fix it. I wish I could bring her back." Thomas wiped at his sweaty forehead. "I know it's asking a lot for you to forgive me. You don't have to . . . Burn my house. Do whatever you have to do."

"She was my girl." Oscar wept. The anger was gone, but the pain and heartache were still there. "She was my little girl."

"I know. I was wrong."

"I was supposed to protect her. I was supposed to give her everything." He let out a horrible sob. "I was her father. She was my girl."

Thomas stopped thinking and acted. He put his arms around Oscar. He held him. He sobbed with him. The two strong men became weak and vulnerable as they mourned together. "I'm sorry." Both men spoke the words, the life-changing words of forgiveness.

The sheriff cut in again. "Thomas." Thomas moved away from Oscar but kept his eyes on the heartbroken man. "I don't have to file this. But I don't feel I'm doing my job if I let a man who would burn another man's barn roam the streets of Azure Springs. Oscar Finley needs to leave our town and never come back."

"Go back to your wife." Thomas's voice was calm. "Go back

to your friends. So many people need you. They depend on you."

Oscar's face was red and puffy—tears, shame, embarrassment, relief all evident. "I'll go." He put out his hand toward Thomas. "I've heard you're a good man here."

Thomas shook his hand but remained quiet.

"I forgive you." Oscar dragged the toe of his boot back and forth in the dirt. "This was foolhardy. It won't bring her back. I'm ashamed."

"Don't be. You were grieving. It's forgotten."

Oscar nodded and looked Thomas in the eyes. "Thank you." Then he turned and walked away.

Thomas watched him go to the barn. Minutes later he left on the back of a tall black horse.

Hugh approached Thomas. "We saved her. Well, that man did."

"I can't talk," Thomas said. "I need to think."

He left the crowd and walked away from the Danbury farm. Jeb was dead. His mind raced as he tried to make sense of it all. Death had freed Eliza, but it still left an unsettled feeling. A sickening feeling. Oscar had come there to get revenge and now Thomas had his forgiveness. He pressed his hands to his forehead, wishing he could push the pounding away. Tears came and went as he walked the hill. He stopped at the top, overlooking green fields, and let himself feel it all. The emotions were so raw and real. Feeling them hurt, but he would not run from them. Not this time.

Abraham walked up the hill and stood beside him, his eyes fixed on the waving grass. "You aren't to blame."

"I brought trouble here."

"Jeb's problems started long before you." Abraham blew

his nose into a handkerchief. "I've been crying all day. But not because you came. You say you brought trouble, but I suppose we all bring a certain amount of trouble."

"You've your daughter back. I'm glad of that."

"I think it'll take some time. The scars of something like this don't fade all at once. You know that though. I'm not sure they ever heal, but I do hope she learns to smile again."

"I'm learning that even now. I tried to run. Before I came here, I tried to run from my pain."

Abraham's big chest rose and fell. He patted Thomas's back. "Stop running. You were a good man even before Oscar forgave you. Be a good man still."

"I want to be." Thomas watched as the sun moved lower on the horizon. "Tomorrow the sun will rise again."

"That it will."

"I'll rise with it." Thomas looked to the place where the sun would come to defeat the night. "Every time it rises, I'll rise with it."

"That, my friend, is one of the great secrets to a happy life. Face it. Whatever it is. Day after day. Face it and decide you won't let it knock you down. I've been hearing talk that you may have found someone to face it with."

Thomas closed his eyes, the last rays of sun warming his face. "I think I have."

"Go tell her you are safe. Take hold of your future and make it something worthwhile."

❦

"Penny." Margaret's voice came through the closed door.

"Yes. Come in."

Margaret opened the door and stepped into the room. She

sat beside her. "I wanted to see how you were. I was afraid you'd
be up here fretting over Thomas."

"I'm so worried. I've been writing and doing what I can to
keep busy, but I'm afraid. So often I've had dreams that haven't
come true. I think I could have a whole life with Thomas. I
think it could be a truly happy life. But if he doesn't come—"

"He'll come back."

"After my father died, my mother was never the same. I know
that just because I want something, that doesn't guarantee it
will happen." She rolled her pen back and forth on the desk.
"I'm afraid for him. He's only just learning to live with his
regrets. He's finding himself. I want him to have a beautiful
spring season in life. When everything feels good and right."

"We all long for that. A few men are down in the dining hall
still. They're having a meeting in there about some town business. What would you think about me asking one of them to
come carry you down to the front room so you can watch for
Thomas from there?"

"I'd be grateful. I've been worried something was happening out there that I don't know about. I don't want to be the
last to know."

"You wait here. I'll go get someone to carry you down."

Penny straightened the papers on the little desk while she
waited. Every few seconds, she looked over her shoulder toward
the bedroom door, eager to be free of the lonely room and
nearer the front door where news was surely to come. She didn't
like the idea of being in another man's arms. She'd seen most
of the men in the dining hall. A shiver raced through her.

The door to her room had a slight squeak. Most would
not recognize it, but Penny had trained her ears to hear it. She
heard it now.

Penny ran her hands over her skirt as she nervously braced herself for her trip down the stairs in the arms of a stranger.

"Penny."

She turned. In the doorway stood Thomas and Margaret. All the breath in her lungs left with a giant exhale. He was back. He was safe. "Thomas."

Margaret stood with her hands on her heart. "Go to her." She nudged Thomas. "This just makes my heart happy. I'll leave you two. Behave yourselves, but be sure to make all sorts of plans for the future."

"Margaret!" Penny felt heat rise to her face.

"I'm not blind. I know love when I see it." She patted Thomas's arm before stepping out of the doorway.

Thomas crossed the floor then in several large strides. Penny's heart quickened with his approach. He knelt beside her and grasped her hands. "I was afraid I wouldn't make it back to you. I'd never been so afraid."

Penny leaned forward and let her forehead rest against his. "You're safe," she whispered. "You're back. Is it over?"

He nodded, his head still against hers. "Let me get the chair." He stepped away only to seat himself near her. At first he just looked at her. She met his gaze. There was a new softness she had never seen in his features. Tears stung the back of her eyes. Looking at him, she knew he was glad he was alive. She had yearned for this moment since reading his first letter.

He took her hand and held it as he recounted the fear, the desperation, and the ultimate conclusion of the evening. "The whole way back I thought about my life. It hasn't gone how I wanted it to. I wanted to go backwards so badly to fix all that was wrong. I've been afraid to move forward. I'm not anymore. When I saw Jeb with his gun and I knew there was a chance I'd never come back to you, I realized how deeply I'd regret that. I want a future and I want it with you." He leaned forward, grasping her hand tighter. He brought it to his lips and kissed her palm. "I want to make plans for the future. Penny, I want to get married. I want a family."

"I prayed you'd come back to me. I want that future too."

"I believe your prayers have been heard." He buried his head in her lap. His body shook as he began to cry. Penny ran her hands through his hair and told him he was safe. She was home. Not in a physical abode but in spirit and heart. Thomas was her home. This was where she belonged. Love and home did not have to look the way she'd always imagined. They were born in joy and in sorrow.

"I love you," she whispered. "I love you. I love you for all you've been through and for all that is to come."

Thomas raised his head and looked at her with tear-filled eyes. "There's been so much pain. But you . . . you've been a balm for my soul."

Penny kissed his cheek, her lips lingering against his skin. "Pain, my love, is not always the enemy."

Epilogue

My Darling,

I looked through your book of letters today. It's thick and growing all the time. In these five years, we've managed to make a great many beautiful memories. I laughed when I saw the letter you wrote to me on the day you fixed me dinner for the first time and burned the entire meal. Remember it? I ate it anyway and you cried while I did.

I couldn't help but smile when I read the letter I wrote you when I told you we were going back to DC for a visit so you could see Dinah and meet her husband and son. That was the trip I first met your mother. It was a healing trip for everyone. And then when you were back with Dinah, you flitted around like a schoolgirl. I was lost to you all over again.

You wrote me a sorrowful letter when Honeysuckle died. Remember how we both cried? I miss that dog. I don't think there's another dog out there who loves the mud like she did. Remember how she'd roll in it, then come inside and shake herself off? Everything was covered in mud. She was a brave dog to do such a thing. Your eyes would flash with anger and I was sure she was going to be run out of town. But you always welcomed her back.

I wrote you on the day we attended Eliza and Hugh's wedding. I remember that day. We both felt like we were witnessing a miracle. They are a perfect match. Their union brought smiles back to Eliza's face. You've been a good friend to her.

And now today I am writing again. Today is another one of those days I want to remember forever. You told me early this morning that your back hurt, and three long, horrible hours later I heard the sound of a baby crying. My baby. Our baby. I will always remember the way you looked when I was finally admitted into the room. Your brow was sweaty and your fair skin flushed, but your eyes gleamed with happiness. "Come see our daughter," you said. And there in the crook of your arm was the tiniest itty-bitty girl I'd ever seen. Just a little bug of a girl.

She has the most beautiful cap of black hair, just like her mother. I'd never held a person so small. But I held her and I'll hold her as she grows. I'll be the father she deserves. I'll take her and show her the good things in the world. I'll pick her flowers and buy her a pony. I'll even let her name it a ridiculous name if she wishes. And then one day when she is older, I'll tell her how I met a green-eyed beauty who changed my life. I'll tell her the road to you was long and hard and riddled with sorrow, but it was a blessed road.

And you I hope will share with our little miss all the

advice and wisdom your father told you so long ago. I hope she laughs like you do. I hope she feels everything the way you do. I never knew love until I met you and now it grows and grows.

Yours truly,
Thomas

Discussion Questions

1. When Penny stumbles upon Thomas's letter, his words speak to her heart. Have you ever read something or seen something that really resonated with you? Why do you think it did?

2. Penny does not have a great relationship with her mother. Can you think of anything Penny could have done to improve the relationship? Have you ever felt like Penny's mother and struggled to accept change?

3. Penny's mother is eager to go live with Uncle Clyde, but Penny is not. If you were in a similar situation, do you think you'd choose to continue working at a busy job or live a leisurely life with little freedom?

4. Thomas struggles to feel at home in Azure Springs. He doesn't feel like he deserves to be welcomed or accepted. Have mistakes in your past ever kept you from wanting to feel joy in the future?

5. The night Thomas punches the intoxicated man, Margaret tells him that he gets to choose what he becomes.

Have you ever seen two people go through similar trials and come out of them very different from each other?

6. Dinah decides to marry a man she respects and cares about, and she believes she will come to love him eventually. Do you think this was a wise decision? Can love blossom later in a relationship? Does a couple have to feel enamored with each other to have a strong marriage?

7. Thomas writes letters to Clara despite the fact that he knows she'll never read them. Why do you think he does this? Have you ever wished you could change something in the past, only to realize you cannot undo what's been done?

8. Penny's father told her long ago that pain was not always the enemy. Can you think of a time when something painful led to something beautiful?

9. Thomas and Penny's relationship moves quickly. Does a courtship have to be long to be successful?

10. Thomas confesses he has never taken care of someone the way he takes care of Penny when she is injured. Have you ever grown closer to someone by serving them?

11. Eliza's marriage to Jeb is an unhealthy union. Her fear dictates many of the decisions she makes. How could you help someone you suspect is living in an abusive relationship?

12. Clara's father becomes bitter and enraged over her death and chooses to seek vengeance. How else could he have found peace? Why was it important for Oscar and Thomas to forgive each other?

Acknowledgments

I wrote *Yours Truly, Thomas* a couple of years after writing *The Hope of Azure Springs*. I knew I wanted to go back and revisit some of my favorite characters while also introducing new ones. The idea for this book occurred to me when my family was on vacation with my sister Stephanie's family. We were touring an old post office in the Midwest and the guide told us letters that were not claimed or addressed correctly went to the dead letter office in Washington, DC. I remember looking at my sister and saying, "I have to learn more." That night in our vacation house, I searched the internet for information on the dead letter office. What I found captivated my imagination. I decided I'd try to combine a lost letter, a guilt-ridden man, and a woman searching for a place to belong, and *ta-da!*, *Yours Truly, Thomas* was born!

Like any novel, it was not a solo project. My sisters and mom were early readers, as well as several amazing friends (you know who you are). I'm in your debt for all the hours you put into this story. And more importantly for the kindness and encourage-ment you continually offer me. My agent, Emily Sylvan Kim, and my editors, Lonnie Hull DuPont and Amy Ballor, were there for me as I trudged through edits and bouts of self-doubt. I'm truly grateful. The entire team at Revell has a place in my heart!

On the home front, I had endless support from my kids and husband. I couldn't ask for a better crew. They cheer me on, listen to my endless book talk, and always believe in my abilities. When Tyler and I had been married for a couple years, I gave him a journal. We call it our "Love Journal." It's similar to Penny and Thomas's book of letters. We write back and forth when something special happens or when we want to say "I love you." We've filled multiple journals now and they are truly some of my treasures. I don't think I could write romances without all that I've experienced with my own husband and family. I'm truly thankful for the real-life love that surrounds me.

I'm grateful God gave me a love for writing and storytelling. Often when life has been particularly trying, I've been able to find a peaceful escape in my projects. I believe God knew I needed a fulfilling hobby that challenged me. His ways are good!

I hope you've enjoyed your time with Penny and Thomas. Thank you, readers and friends, for sharing this journey with them as they struggle to overcome the past and live for the future.

Thank you to everyone who has reached out to me since I was first published. It's been a joy hearing from and connecting with you. None of this would be possible without you.

Rachel

Rachel Fordham started writing when her children began begging her for stories at night. She'd pull a book from the shelf, but they'd insist she make one up. Finally, she put her love of good stories with her love of writing and she hasn't stopped since. She lives with her husband and children on an island in the state of Washington.

Alone in a strange town, can she find healing for her new home ... *and for herself?*

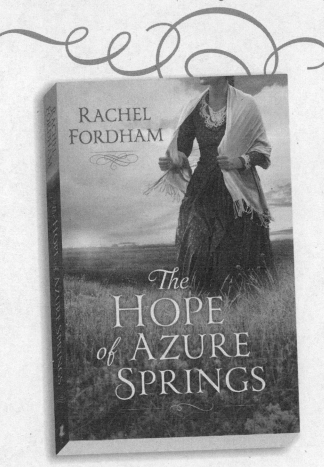

When a young woman wakes up injured and alone in the frontier town of Azure Springs in 1881, she must find a way to face her past, embrace her future, and rescue what she's lost.

Meet
Rachel Fordham

RachelFordham.com

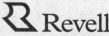